CW01626565

Take the Plunge

Susan Carew

Copyright © Susan Carew 2023

The right of Susan Carew to be identified as the author of this work has been asserted in accordance with the Copyright, Designs and Patents Act 1988.

All rights reserved. No part of this publication may be reproduced, stored in or transmitted into any retrieval system, in any form, or by any means (electronic, mechanical, photocopying, recording or otherwise) without the prior written permission of the publisher. Any person who does any unauthorised act in relation to this publication may be liable to criminal prosecution and civil claims for damages.

This is a work of fiction. Any resemblance to actual persons, living or dead or events locales is entirely coincidental or used in a fictitious manner.

Ebook ISBN: 978-84-126643-0-0

Paperback ISBN: 978-84-126643-1-7

First published in 2023

Cover design by Kari Brownlie

Cover design copyright © Susan Carew

To my husband

Prologue

Andalusia, October 2022

Salt. It is everywhere, scouring Claire's skin wherever her swimsuit meets it. It leaches her eyes of moisture. Her mouth is filled with her swollen tongue and the graze on the back of her neck screams every time she turns her head to breathe. Treading water, she allows herself a brief respite while adjusting her goggles. Her left eye is burning. The sea stretches endlessly and there is no longer any sign of the boat. She is alone and afraid, terrified for the friend she has left behind. She plucks at the straps of her swimsuit in an attempt to alleviate the misery created by the friction of the sea salt and fantasises about peeling off the object of torture. She expels the thought, replaces her goggles and pushes on.

The monotony of motion is unrelenting and she strives not to let her mind drift to the last image she has of her friend. It torments her but pushes her forward. As she struggles against the current, the strength bleeds from her body. She can barely move her legs and feels them drag behind her as if paralysed.

There is a sudden burning sensation on her hand,

then her face is grazed by something and that burns too. A gelatinous wisp in her peripheral vision. Jellyfish. Darting away, she is stung once, twice more. Panic now as she twists left, then right, trying to avoid that which she cannot see. Her ankle smarts with a new sting and she kicks forward, swimming with force, her heart pounding, her body pumped with adrenaline. All vestiges of exhaustion now quelled, she flees the scene. Face down, looking for her foe and swimming as if for her life, until eventually she is forced to stop. She rips the goggles away from her eyes and looks about her. Nothing. She falls back against the water and floats, trying to breathe. The sound of her heart is all she can hear. Once she is sufficiently still, she reaches for the tow float where her water bottle rests. Then, the realisation that it is empty. She starts to weep, but dehydration means she has no tears to shed. Her ears are filled with a scream that takes a few seconds to identify as her own. She thrashes at the sea, venting her frustration.

The rage has been cathartic and she exhales, a dry sob shuddering from her body. Looking at the horizon she searches for something, anything, she can sight. There is nothing. The sun is starting to dip and she needs to swim in the direction of the setting orb. She has to keep going; stopping is not an option. She presses forward and begins the grind of stroke, stroke, stroke, breathe. Repeat. Repeat. Attempting to block out all but the physical act of swimming. She continues, and some unreadable time later, rewards herself with a rest and eases off the goggles that press painfully to her face.

More out of habit than belief that she is any nearer, she probes the horizon again. Squinting, not quite believing what she sees. Yes! A small cove is within reach. Clinging to the last scraps of strength, she swims again. But it is different now. Salvation is a distinct possibility.

Chapter One

West Sussex, May 2022

'Claire, I've got a James Garfield on the line asking for you. I know you're busy. Do you want me to put it through or take a message?'

Debating whether to defer another frustrating conversation or deal with it straight away, Claire opts for the latter.

'He's my estate agent, I'd better take it. Thanks.' She lets out a sigh.

'Good afternoon, Mrs Sadler, it's James Garfield from Crawford and Green here. I sent you an email letting you know that I have taken over the sale of your father's property. Sorry I haven't been able to speak to you before now, but I'm just getting up to speed with my new client list.'

'It's Ms Sadler.'

'What?'

'Mrs Sadler was my mother. I haven't been a Mrs for some time.'

'My apologies, Ms Sadler. As I said, I—'

'Yes, yes, you're getting up to speed. Don't mind me,

it's been a long day. I hope you have some good news for me.'

'Er ... a bit of a setback with your buyers.'

'Don't tell me they've dropped out? This would be the third time. You do know the house has been on the market for well over a year now?'

'Yes, I am aware of that. Don't worry, the buyers are still very keen, it's just that they were a bit optimistic about how much they thought they could borrow. Turns out their mortgage offer is a little under what they were expecting. Given that the property has, as you've said, been on the market for some time, I thought it might be worth considering lowering the price. That's if you want to make this sale.'

Here we go, she thinks. 'How much lower are you suggesting?'

'Nine thousand, better ten.'

'Christ, really? And if we refuse?'

'Unfortunately, without dropping the price, the buyers would have to withdraw their offer. Look, I know it's frustrating, but this may be the last one you get for some time. I'm showing a lot of similar properties at considerably less than you are asking for, and right now it's a buyers' market.'

'Um ...' Claire does some mental arithmetic. 'I'll have to speak to my brother about it as half the proceeds will go to him.' If it were up to her, she'd drop the price without quibbling, but she knows that her brother, pushed by his wife, will want to make as big a profit as possible.

'Do you think you could let me know today?'

'Not likely. He does shift work and often takes time to get back to me.'

'That's unfortunate. I'd hate for you to lose this sale. They're a young couple with a baby on the way, very keen to get moved in as quickly as possible. And there are a lot of other properties in the area they could be looking at.'

'Yes, you said. Look, I'll call you as soon as I know, that's all I can do for now.' Putting the phone down, she presses the heel of her palm to the centre of her chest and exhales. As if she didn't have enough on her plate. Damn Stuart. Why did he have to be so hard to get hold of? There was always some excuse to dodge family duty. She reels off a brief email. With any luck he'd see it was in his best interests to reply to her sooner rather than later.

One of her colleagues, overhearing the exchange, says, 'Estate agents, hey? Bloody bastards, can't stand 'em. A few of us are going out for a drink after work. Do you want to come? Might take your mind off your troubles.'

No stranger to a large glass of wine and a laugh with her colleagues, Claire would normally accept. It was a good way to unwind after a hectic day at the firm where she was an accountant. But not today. 'No can do. Thanks anyway. I've got a different sort of stress buster planned for this evening.'

A whistle blow pierces through the sounds of tinny music, shouted instructions and bodies grappling with floats, the indoor acoustics amplifying the cacophony.

Oliver, one of the swim coaches at the Aquarium, crouches down by the poolside edge where a group of swimmers gather, treading water. As he speaks, Claire strains to hear him as she is on the outer reaches of the group. 'Alison, what did he say? I didn't catch it.'

Her friend swims over to her. 'About not overusing your legs and needing to glide more. Why are you over here? Get a bit closer.'

'I'm over here because if I get any closer, I'll be sucked into the vortex created by whatshername. She's whirling her legs around like a bloody helicopter.'

'Wicked woman.' Alison laughs, coughing up water as her body momentarily dips down.

Why doesn't she hold onto the edge of the pool if she's that panicky about sinking? If she carries on like that, she's going to really get on my nerves, thinks Claire. It was bad enough dealing with estate agents; she doesn't need another irritation to put up with. This is supposed to be a time when she isn't stressed.

Meanwhile, Oliver is handing out pull buoys. 'Now, for those of you not familiar with these: place them between your thighs while you swim – they'll help keep you horizontal in the water and stop you from using your legs. You'll have to rely on your arms to move you forward. Do six lengths and then we'll finish up for tonight. Don't worry about speed, just focus on your arm action.'

It doesn't take Claire long to complete the six lengths. In fact, she throws herself into the swim with manic abandon to eradicate the crappy day she has had. These lessons have always been a source of enjoyment for her, along with the challenge of open-water events at nearby Worthing Pier and the ten-kilometre marathons to neighbouring Shoreham-by-Sea.

God, she needed that. Claire recognises that her swimming has become more of a necessity than a hobby these days. Better than pills, she reasons.

Having finished before the others, Claire expects to have the changing rooms more or less to herself. She is looking forward to a long hot shower – quiet time before she meets Alison in the cafeteria. The showers, however, are all occupied, two of them by a mother-daughter duo. Why is it so busy at this time of day? The young girl is about ten years old and has long, abundant hair. The mother is beside her, humming as she applies copious amounts of shampoo onto her daughter's head.

'You rinse that off, darling, while I shower,' the mother says. The little girl does as she is told. The woman sees Claire waiting and smiles. Glad she's been noticed, Claire assumes they will speed up their ablutions or share a shower, but the fact that they now have an audience seems to turn the hair care into a performance. Claire looks at the other places, but they are being used by two friends who are deep in conversation. Oh dear God, someone get a move on. She feels the calm from her swim slipping away. After what seems an age, the woman and her daughter finally finish.

'Come along, Charlotte. Let the lady have her shower now.' She looks indulgently at her daughter as she bustles her, wrapped in a huge towel, out into the changing area. Claire manages a tight smile as they walk past her.

She is less than pleased to find them both there when she goes back into the changing rooms. The little girl has her belongings strewn about the place, her wet swimming costume taking up space on the bench. There is water everywhere and Claire sidesteps the puddles as she attempts to put on her jeans and socks without getting them wet. Mother and child are oblivious to how much room they are taking up and are loudly discussing Charlotte's day at school. 'Give me strength,' Claire mumbles under her breath as she makes a hasty exit.

As is their custom, Claire and Alison have arranged to meet in the cafeteria after the lesson. Despite the delay in the changing rooms, Claire gets there first, and by the time Alison arrives, she has polished off a large cake and is sipping coffee. She waves at Alison in the queue, who's searching for her over the mass of heads while being jostled by a gaggle of wet-haired children. Drink in hand and arms held aloft, Alison makes her way over, past a crowd of people who are chattering excitedly on a post-water-aerobics high. The air is hot and humid, laced with the tang of fried food and coffee. Alison looks red in the face as she plops herself down in front of Claire. Looking around her, she says, 'Gosh, busy in here tonight.'

'Yes, Sophie told me the centre has decided to open the diving pit in the evenings,' Claire says, referring to the other swimming coach. 'They're running those national Learn to Swim diving lessons. I think they want to find Sussex's answer to Tom Daley.' She absentmindedly dabs her fingertips at the remaining crumbs on her plate and licks them.

'Oh yeah, I know the sort of thing you mean. The boys did diving lessons a few years back.' Leaning forward, Alison says, 'So, let's hear about your hot date. I want to know all about it.'

Claire had hoped to forget about the awful encounter and relegate it to her ever-growing list of failed dates. She really doesn't want to talk about it. Rolling her eyes, she says, 'Oh yeah, my hot date turned out to be distinctly tepid. If it wasn't for the fact that it's nigh on impossible to cancel my subscription, I'd knock all this internet dating on the head. And Perfect Partners need to change their name, more like Dating Wallies R Us. The guy turned up half an hour late, swaggered over to me with no apology, and said, "You look fatter in real life".' She winces; it hurt more than she cares to admit. 'Then he got himself a drink without offering me one and proceeded to brag about all the women he's slept with, while knocking back three rum and cokes in the twenty minutes of our date.'

'Maybe he was nervous?'

'Does that give him the excuse to insult me? Nah, more like he was an arrogant prat.' Claire doesn't tell Alison about the overwhelming urge she'd had to tell him just that, to throw a drink in his face and walk away in a dignified manner. Instead, she had sat there like an idiot, listening to him and she hated herself for it. 'I swear, many more dates like that and I'm giving up and getting a cat.'

'Hey there,' Alison says. 'Nothing wrong with owning a cat.'

Claire says nothing and watches Sophie coming through the swing doors of the cafeteria, flanked by two women. Reaching for her cup, she sees it's empty and tuts. She'd love another but can't face joining the unruly queue. She begins to peel away at the top of her paper cup, gritting her teeth while she does so. Aware of Alison's eyes on her, she looks up. 'What?' she questions.

'Nothing,' Alison says.

'You're looking at me in a funny way.'

'You seem fed up about something.' She reaches across the table and lays her hand on top of Claire's. 'You know, if you need to talk—'

'I'm going to get another coffee. Want one?' Shaking off Alison's hand, she stands. She is tempted to confide in someone but can't bring herself to talk about her own grief. How can she burden Alison with how she's feeling when her friend has had to cope with the loss of her husband? Losing a parent isn't the same, is it?

'Why not? Better make it a decaf though,' Alison says.

From her position in the queue, Claire sees Sophie leave the women and join Alison. Ahead of her, she is dismayed to see the same woman and child from the changing rooms. Have they only just got here? she wonders. What have they been doing?

'What would you like, darling?' the mother says to her daughter.

'A chocolate doughnut.'

'No, remember I said you could have a piece of fruit. You can choose which.'

'I want a doughnut. The bananas look funny. I don't like them.'

Claire rolls her eyes.

'Don't be silly, darling. Bananas are your favourite.'

'No. I don't like them.'

Oh, for crying out loud, hurry up! Claire moves from one foot to another and sighs loudly. The woman glances at her but says nothing. In the queue behind Claire children are pushing each other and bumping into her. She clenches her hands and shouts, 'Oh, for God's sake. Are you going to be all night or what? Some of us would like to place our order. You're not the only people here, you know.'

The mother whips her head around. 'I beg your pardon?'

'Granted,' Claire says, pushing past her to stand in front of the smirking cashier. 'Two flat whites, please, one decaffeinated, and this.' She reaches for a chocolate bar, putting it on the counter.'

The young man at the till does as she commands. 'That's eight ninety, please.'

'There you go,' Claire says, slapping a ten-pound note

onto the counter. 'Put the change in the charity box.' She marches back to Alison and Sophie.

'What was that all about?' Alison says, nodding in the general direction of the woman, now sitting with her friends and pointing at Claire.

'Oh, just some people and their kids. They act as if they're the only ones on the planet.'

Despite her flippant remark, she is unnerved by what has just happened. Claire sees that Alison and Sophie are looking at her and she knows she's overstepped the mark. Time to put on her happy face. 'Sorry, too much of this stuff,' she says, waving the coffee in front of her.

Alison and Sophie fall into easy conversation, while Claire pretends to listen. The heat of anger bubbles in her chest and tears smart her eyes. It is taking all her concentration to keep it together. She sits there until it is safe for her to speak. 'Ladies, I'm going to love you and leave you, I'm afraid. Early start tomorrow.'

'Er, okay,' Alison says. 'You don't want to stay and hear about the holiday?'

Claire has no idea what Alison is talking about. 'What?'

'The swimming holiday that Sophie and Oliver are arranging.'

Not wanting to admit she had zoned out during the conversation, Claire says, 'Oh yeah, sure. No, er, not now. I've just remembered I need to do something … a work thing. At home.' She all but runs away. Outside she shoves her trembling hands into her jacket pockets, frightened by her emotions. That was a close one.

Chapter Two

Walking through the doors of the Aquarium the next day, Claire goes up to reception. In her delicate state that morning, she had forgotten to include a towel as part of her swim kit and needed to request a loan of one.

She sees Sophie reaching over the counter to retrieve a clipboard, checking it and frowning, then saying something to the receptionist.

Claire steps forward, taps Sophie on the shoulder and smiles. 'Hiya, how's it going? Everything all right?'

'Not really. I was due to finish my shift early today' – she returns the clipboard – 'but I've just found out that Oliver has volunteered my services and I'm covering someone off sick. I take it you're here for a swim?'

'Yes, I come here most days, work permitting. I just need to hire a towel, forgot mine.' She pushes a one-pound coin across the counter and the receptionist pulls a towel from a stack behind her. 'Sounds like you're going to be busy this evening.'

'Thanks to my wonderful boyfriend. Still, I suppose a little overtime doesn't hurt the bank account. Oh well, I'd better get off, don't want to keep the little devils waiting.' Picking up her bag, she trudges to the pool.

Finishing her second length, Claire pauses briefly to catch her breath. She watches Sophie file out from the family changing rooms with a troop of children. Claire gives a little wave, glad that she's not heading up a diving lesson. Rather you than me, Sophie; looks like you've got your work cut out there, she thinks as Sophie does her best to control the bunch. A boy at the back of the group is nudging the child next to him, pointing up at the ten-metre-high platform and Claire wonders exactly what a diving lesson for this age group will entail. Pushing off, she continues with her swim, the thought forgotten.

Claire puts in length after length. For a lesser being it would be a punishing workout, but for her it soothes and calms. She enjoys the sensation of strength that a vigorous swim gives her. As each length is completed, she begins to relax. In the water, all her problems recede. Taking a moment to drink from her water bottle, she looks over to the diving lesson and can hear some of the children squabbling. Two of the boys tussle together and she sees Sophie go over to them to break it up, shouting at them.

'Hey! You two. What are you doing?'

'He pulled my ear!' complains the boy who had been at the back of the group earlier on.

Claire continues with her swim, the bickering boys left behind. By the time she has finished, Sophie and the children are nowhere to be seen. Drying her face with a towel, she slings it around her neck and is walking past the diving pit to the changing rooms when she sees one of the boys who had been in the diving lesson. He is at the five-metre level of the diving platform and is making his way up. And I suppose you think you're going to dive from up there? she jokes inwardly, then realises that's exactly what he intends to do.

'Hey, you! Get down from there!' she shouts up at the boy. He hesitates, but continues regardless, hurrying to reach the top before someone stops him. He walks to the end of the ten-metre platform and peers over the edge. He puts his arms into position as he has been taught and tumbles into the abyss.

'No!' screams Claire. But it is too late, and he hits the water with a huge splat. Claire is frozen for the few seconds it takes for his body to resurface. As it does so, she sees there is no movement from him. Shaken into action, she dives into the pool, swimming as fast as she can. Reaching him, she senses someone else is in the water too, moving toward them. Claire turns the boy's face up. 'I don't think he's breathing,' she chokes and sees that it is Sophie who is coming towards them. 'Thank God you're here. He dived from the top. I couldn't stop him.'

'Let me.' Sophie cradles his head with her hand and sidestrokes to the edge of the pool. Claire swims ahead and is ready to help lift him out. As they lay him in the recovery position, they both see that his wrist is at an impossible angle. Claire shudders, recoiling slightly, while Sophie leans into him, checking for signs of life.

A woman has just come out from the changing rooms. 'Vihan!' She races over to them. Kneeling over the unconscious boy, she moves closer to his face, then looks up at Sophie and Claire. 'Call an ambulance now! Tell them it's urgent.'

Sophie is immobile, rooted to the spot.

'Go. *Now*!'

Sophie dashes off, slipping in her bare feet on the wet tiles, leaving Claire with the woman. The boy, Vihan, isn't moving.

Beams of pulsating blue light are reflected in the glass doors of reception. An ambulance has pulled into the space directly in front of the entrance. Two paramedics prepare to make their way inside while the receptionist responds to a group of customers who are asking why the pool is temporarily closed, doing her best to pacify them.

By the pool, Vihan – still unconscious and covered with a blanket – is flanked by Claire, Sophie and the woman who had joined them. Periodically, the woman, who has identified herself as Vihan's mother, Nisha Sharma, checks his breathing and pulse. For now, there is nothing more she or the others can do. It is not a long wait but feels interminable. Vihan's mother asks Sophie what happened.

'He dived from the top platform. Luckily Claire saw what happened and jumped into the pool.'

Claire says nothing, and once again she's glad she isn't in Sophie's shoes.

'Why was he up there in the first place? He's meant to be doing the first-stage diving, isn't he? Not the bloody Olympics! And where were you when all this was happening?'

'I was called away; someone had collapsed in reception and I was the only first aider about. I'm so sorry, Mrs Sharma. I told all the children to go and get changed. I thought they had all gone. I would *never* have left them alone. I came back as soon as I could.'

'Hmm, we'll talk about this later.'

'I don't think Sophie is at fault here.' Claire hesitates as she takes in the look on Nisha's face. 'What I mean is, I think your son might have come back from the changing rooms. All the other children had gone … he was alone.'

Nisha purses her lips, not speaking.

Claire hopes she hasn't made things worse for Sophie as she tries to read Nisha's expression. She sees the paramedics approaching with a member of staff.

'Hello, I'm Vihan's mother,' Nisha says. 'I'm so glad to see you. He's been unconscious for about ten to fifteen minutes. During that time, I've been checking his breathing and pulse – they are shallow and weak. Looks like he has a badly broken wrist as well. He jumped from the top diving platform.'

'He hit the water pretty hard,' Claire says. 'I saw him.'

'Right, let's take a look.' The paramedic places a collar around Vihan's neck. 'Vihan. Vihan, can you hear me?'

Vihan's eyes flutter open and he tries to move. Still lying on his side, he vomits. Claire and Sophie jerk back, but the paramedic remains kneeling and repeats, 'Vihan, can you hear me?'

It takes a moment for Vihan to fully come round, and as he does so, the pain of his twisted wrist hits him. He howls, and tears stream down his red, contorted face.

'Oh, thank God!' Claire sinks onto her knees, shaking uncontrollably. The smell of sick and the sight of Vihan's wrist make her feel nauseous. She wants to go but doesn't think it would be right to do so just yet. The paramedics confirm Nisha's assessment of her son's condition.

The paramedic puts a splint around Vihan's wrist and straps him to a spinal board. 'This is a precaution; looks a bit scary, I know. He'll have a CT scan to check he hasn't injured his spine and he'll be kept in for observation in case he's suffered a concussion.'

'Yes, yes. I know – I'm a nurse. It just feels different when it's your own child,' Nisha explains.

'Come on, young man, let's get you into the ambulance. Mrs Sharma, are you coming with us or do you want to follow on?'

'I'll follow behind. I have two other children with me and I know there won't be room for all of us.'

'Okey-dokey. So just you and me then, Vihan.'

Nisha's shoulders drop and she dabs at the slight sheen of sweat on her upper lip. She turns to Claire, swathed in a blanket. 'Thank you, my dear. Claire, isn't it? This could have been a whole lot worse if you hadn't acted so quickly.'

Claire attempts a smile. 'I just did what anyone would have. Sophie was great, she knew exactly what to do. I was floundering a bit.'

'Nonsense. Not everyone would have jumped in like you did, very quick acting. Often people just call for help; or worse, get their phone and start filming,' Nisha says, tutting then turning to Sophie. 'As for you …'

'Yes?' Sophie says.

Claire sees the young woman swallow and feels sorry for her.

'How has this sort of thing been allowed to happen? Why was no one else available to help? It is unacceptable that there was only one person with first aid knowledge in a place like this and I shall be telling the management so.'

'Well, normally there would be, but we've got a few people off sick and on annual leave.'

'Be that as it may, they should have made provision. There are health and safety regulations to keep to, after all. Anyway, you're not the person to say all this to. You two should get dressed. I expect you'll be wanting a nice cup of tea.'

Claire, shivering despite the blanket, says to Sophie, 'I'm going to have a hot shower. I take it they won't be reopening the pool this evening? It hardly seems worth it now,' she says looking up at the time.

'Oh, I hadn't thought of that – God, it is late, isn't it? I'm going to check out what's happening. I could really do with getting out of here.'

Claire couldn't agree more, but the thought of going back to an empty house is not an appealing one. She is still trembling. 'Um, Sophie, how about a drink when you're finished?'

'Okay, I'll meet you at reception and perhaps we can have that tea.'

'Fuck tea,' Claire says.

Claire dumps her handbag on the bar, the bag containing her swim kit thrown unceremoniously onto the floor at her feet. She hoists herself onto the bar stool and slumps. Boy, does she need a drink. She waves at the barman.

'A large dry white wine, please' – she looks at Sophie – 'and …?'

'Vodka and cranberry juice, please.'

They sit in silence and when their drinks arrive, reach for them, still not uttering a word. Each of the women is reflecting on the earlier events. Twilight moves to darkness and the bartender starts lighting candles on the surrounding tables. The soft light is soothing, as is the effect of the alcohol, and they begin to relax.

Claire finishes her second drink and lifts a finger, catching the barman's eye. 'Same again for me, please. Sophie?'

'Er, no thanks, I'm good,' Sophie replies, eyeing Claire's empty glass. 'I'm driving.'

Fresh drink deposited, Claire swallows a third of it before setting it down. 'Not quite the relaxing evening

I'd had planned and I promised myself I would have a booze-free day too.' So much for good intentions.

'I'm sorry you had to get involved like that, Claire, but thank goodness you were there. I'm concerned that this isn't the end of it, though. What if Mrs Sharma decides she is really pissed off at me and complains to the Aquarium?'

'Honestly, I really don't think you have anything to worry about. All things considered, she was pretty cool about everything. I think her being a nurse and all that helps. Imagine if she was one of those stuck-up yummy mummy types.' She thinks back to the woman she had encountered in the changing rooms. 'Trust me, Mrs Sharma is not the type to complain about you. She probably sees too many of the wrong people being blamed for stuff at the hospital.'

'Well, I hope you're right.' Sophie drains her glass. 'I'd better go. Do you want a lift anywhere?'

'No, I drove here. I'm going to stay for another, maybe get something to eat. Don't worry, I'll get a cab home. I can pick up my car tomorrow.'

'I'd stay, but …'

'I'll be fine. I'll have the barman for company. Off you go.'

Chapter Three

Thursday evenings see Claire at the Aquarium for her objective openwater class. The centre is so named because of the free-standing fish tank that graces reception. It is floor-to-ceiling in height and a metre thick, providing an aquatic paradise for the tropical fish inside. Its magnetic beauty draws people, mesmerised by the gentle propulsion of its residents. Small children press their noses to the glass as if hoping to be drawn into its magical world of intense colours. This evening is no exception, Claire notes as she walks past a group of small children, their tiny hands and noses leaving imprints on the glass.

Despite the aesthetic appeal of the building, the real draw for Claire is the Olympic-sized, fifty-metre pool. It is deep throughout and only for serious swimmers. When Claire first started coming it was a revelation to her. After years of doing battle in narrow swimming lanes, she actually has the space to swim. No longer does she have to negotiate the neck-craning breaststrokers who insist on hogging the middle of the fast lane, their leg kick lethal should you dare to pass. For those less serious about their swimming there are a myriad of features: Jacuzzis and steam rooms, relaxation zones and a Turkish bath, not for the faint-hearted nor those modest about bearing all. A whole wing, thoughtfully provided out of earshot from the main pool, is devoted to children: a wading pool, wave-making machines and numerous water slides.

The changing rooms are all empty, save for the helicopter-legs woman who had so irritated Claire last week in the pool. The woman, already changed, spots her and calls out. 'Hiya. You do the objective open water lessons, don't you?'

'Yeah, that's right. You came back then?'

'Well yes, I wasn't overly sure. I'm not the strongest swimmer in the world, but Alan, my husband, comes and I thought it might be nice to have a hobby in common. He does a lot of triathlons and all the training that involves. There are times I barely see him, what with the training and his work. He does a lot of commuting and works late nights. You know how it is.' She laughs.

Claire knows Alan from the swim club and is surprised that this chatterbox is his wife. The woman continues: 'So, I said to Alan that I could do some training with him. You know, for moral support. I tried cycling, bought a bicycle and everything. Pretty expensive it was too. In the end, it was all a waste of money. I could never keep up with Alan and he would have to keep waiting for me to catch up.' She laughs again and fiddles with the strap of her costume. 'Then when I fell off on a busy road and gave myself a nasty fright, I thought it would be for the best if I stopped. Of course Alan was very disappointed, but he said my welfare was the most important thing and it would be best if he cycled alone. So considerate, don't you think?'

Claire wonders when the woman is going to take a breath.

'Anyway, I can't run to save my life so I thought I'd come with Alan to these classes, see if I can improve on swimming. I was quite good as a child, got all my life-saving medals; well, the bronze and silver. Never made it to the gold. Wasn't expecting these lessons to be so intense. I expect I'll get used to them, though. Alan said he'd quite understand if I didn't want to continue, but I'm going to try and stick it out.'

Great, thinks Claire.

'I'm Debbie, by the way.'

'Claire.'

'I noticed you swimming last week, Claire, you're very good. You'll have to tell me your secret!' Turning to the mirror she starts to put on her swimming cap, stretching it back and forth over her head, then stuffing her hair into it without much care. Long strands of it escape and coat the back of her neck. Then she picks up a pair of goggles, still in their packaging. 'I was having such trouble with my old pair I thought I'd treat myself,' she says as she tears at the plastic and cardboard. Adjusting the straps so they are very short, she pulls them on and pushes them against her eyes with her fingertips.

'There. No water getting in here.'

'Er, actually, you've got them way too tight. That's

going to hurt like hell after an hour's swimming. You need to check the fit around the eye socket first. Take them off and just place them on your eyes. If they're a good fit, the suction will hold them onto your face without straps,' Claire says.

'Righto.' Debbie does as instructed, and immediately the goggles fall straight to the floor.

'Yep. Way too big. You need something smaller.'

'Oh, but these cost such a lot. Plus the colour matches my costume. See? I think I'll persevere and see how they are in the water.'

Sighing, Claire pushes her rucksack into the locker. Closing the door, she fidgets with the combination, screwing up her eyes as she does so, silently cursing the blurry numbers.

'You go ahead, Debbie. Don't let me hold you up.'

'Not a bother, not a bother. I'll wait for you.'

Claire doesn't reply but vows to arrive earlier the following week.

Unfortunately, Debbie does nothing to alter Claire's initial opinion of her, and throughout the lesson she lags behind, chatting and asking inane questions. *Does she ever stop talking?* thinks Claire. *I can barely hear Oliver with her prattling on non-stop.*

'I'm sorry, Oliver,' Debbie is now saying, 'could you just go over the bilateral breathing again? I'm finding it really tricky.'

Oliver complies and goes over the technique again.

'He's very patient,' Alison whispers.

'Too patient. Shit, this is embarrassing,' Alan says.

Debbie attempts to breathe bilaterally as Oliver has demonstrated, but ends up spluttering. 'Can't I just breathe to one side like I've always done?'

'Well, Debbie, you could if you were just swimming in a pool, but out there in open water it's imperative you are aware of what's all around you. All the time you're breathing to your left something major could be happening on your right that you wouldn't be aware of. Give it another go.'

Debbie tries again and this time makes a semi-reasonable stab at it. Rejoicing, she babbles on. 'Oh, I think I might be getting the hang of this. What do you think, Alan? Alan? Where's he gone?'

'Bloody hell, Debbie. I'm right behind you.'

The lesson continues at a halting rate and Claire can't wait for it to be over with, which annoys her. Even Alison is looking fed up. After what seems an age Oliver rounds things up and scurries away just as Debbie is about to ask him another question.

Claire and Alison meet in the cafeteria afterwards. As usual, Claire has got there first. She waves Alison over.

'Oh, I barely saw you there. What are you doing hiding in the corner?' Alison says.

'I'm here just in case that new woman Debbie decides to make an entrance. I've already been ambushed by her tonight.'

‘Gosh, I know. She’s a bit much, isn’t she? Poor Alan, he seems so normal and she’s, well, a bit needy.’

‘That’s a polite way of putting it.’

Spotting a pile of leaflets on the table Alison leans over and takes one. ‘Oh, this is the holiday that Sophie was telling us about, remember? The one she’s heading up with Oliver. They are looking for anyone who might be interested.’

Claire has a vague recollection of it. She reaches over for the leaflet. ‘Where are they going?’

‘Spain. Oh, that would be great. Imagine not having to wear a wetsuit or freeze your toes to death. You could actually put in some kilometres without getting hypothermia. I wonder why Oliver didn’t mention it after class?’

‘Why do you think? Couldn’t wait to get out of there fast enough.’ Claire takes a sip of her coffee. ‘Mmm, El Cabo de Gata, Almería. Bit more exotic than swimming round Worthing Pier, lovely though that is.’

She puts the leaflet back on the table. ‘Quite a few companies are doing similar holidays, but it would be nice to go with instructors we already know. What do you think?’

‘I’ve been thinking about doing one of these holidays for ages, but they are so expensive. This is really cheap in comparison.’

‘You have to ask yourself why that is,’ Claire says. ‘I mean, have either Sophie or Oliver ever done anything like this before? There’s a lot to consider, a lot of planning.’

'Oh, I think it would be okay. We know Oliver is a good coach and Sophie seems sensible enough. They wouldn't have put her in charge of a group of children here if they didn't trust her.'

'Um.' Claire doesn't bring up the diving accident. While she wouldn't say Sophie was to blame for that, she can't help but think she won't have the skill set or experience to organise a swimming holiday. However, it would be nice to have something to look forward to, a break away from the madness – if she can swing the time away from work; it's always busy at that time of year.

'I don't think I could leave the boys, though,' Alison says.

'Course you could. Look, it's mid-October. Callum will be installed at university by then, and wouldn't that be half-term? You'd be off work. It's perfect.'

'What about Jamie?'

'Surely your parents or Gavin's could have him for the week? He's fifteen, he won't exactly need babysitting, just someone to feed him and make sure he doesn't spend all night gaming.'

'It's very tempting,' Alison says, taking back the leaflet and rereading it. 'I know it's a good price, but with the flights and meals, it will all mount up. Don't know whether I can justify spending that much on myself for a week's holiday.'

'Tell you what, I'll pay for the flights.'

'Oh no. I couldn't let you do that.'

'Why ever not? It won't cost the earth. There'll be some bargains about.' Though at half-term she doubts it. This could be just what she needs to get her back on track, but she doesn't want to go alone. She has the money and she thinks Alison deserves it.

'Well …' Alison says.

Claire can see Alison is starting to waver. 'If you don't go, I won't want to. Come on, what's the worst that can happen? Go on. Say yes.'

'I'll have to clear it with my mum, see if she's okay about taking Jamie.'

'Is that a yes then?'

'Yes. Yes, it is!' She beams. 'I'm sure I can talk Mum round. Oh gosh, it would be great to get away and have some guaranteed sun. Seems like years since I went abroad.'

'It has been. For all of us,' Claire replies.

'Oh look, there's Sophie.' Alison beckons her over. 'We were just talking about the holiday.'

'Great! What do you think? It's pretty small-scale, at least for this first trip – we're looking at six, maybe eight people max, to cover costs and break even. I'm really excited about this, it could be the beginning of our swimming holiday business. God knows Ollie and I need to start making some cash if we are ever going to get a place of our own. Not to mention paying back our student loans …'

'Well, I'm definitely keen and I think I've talked Alison into it. Although I would still like to find out some more of the details. You're lucky you planned it for half-term, otherwise it would have been a non-starter.'

'Claire has been very persuasive,' Alison adds.

Sophie looks confused. 'Didn't Oliver go through it after the lesson?'

'Nope,' Claire says.

'Oh. I wonder why. He was supposed to lay the groundwork for me, then I'd swoop in and make a sale.' Sophie attempts to smile, as if joking, but it's clear she's unhappy.

Claire can see Oliver making his way toward them. This will be interesting, she thinks. He sits down, enveloping them in a lemon-scented cloud.

'Why didn't you say anything about the holiday after the class today, like you were supposed to?' Sophie says through gritted teeth.

'What? Oh yes. Sorry, it slipped my mind.'

Alison laughs. 'More like you wanted to make a quick getaway from someone who shall remain nameless.'

Claire can sympathise with Oliver wanting to escape Debbie's clutches, but she doesn't approve of him leaving Sophie to broach the subject of the holiday, particularly when he'd had a captive audience at the end of the lesson, an ideal opportunity to pitch it. She wonders how many other duties he's going to shirk.

Oliver switches on the charm. 'If you have any doubts, I want you to think about swimming in the cold, murky Channel water, then instead imagine the Mediterranean. Clear and warm, with the sun shining. After a swim, you can top up the old suntan and reward yourself with a cocktail or two on the beach. Maybe even find yourself *un señor*,' he says, winking at Alison, who goes red and starts to examine the leaflet again.

Unimpressed with Oliver's patter, Claire shakes her head, thinking he has a lot to learn about customer relations. He continues: 'Yeah and let's not forget about where you'd be staying. Villa Hermosa: luxury accommodation with a swimming pool, barbecue area, the works, only a few minutes from town. Sophie's brother, Josh, found it for us. He knows the locals and has been able to hire a boat at a very reasonable rate. That's why we've been able to offer you such a great deal.'

'Oh, does he live out there then?' Claire asks.

'He travels back and forth. Not one to stay in a single place for too long is Josh. Isn't that right, babe?' He is leaning back, his right arm stretched out along the back of Sophie's chair. Occasionally he strokes the nape of her neck. She is sitting very still, hunched over the table, leaning forward toward Claire and Alison.

'Yes, he's a bit of a nomad,' Sophie agrees.

'Lockdown must have driven him mad.' This from Alison.

Still reclining, Oliver grins. 'Joshie boy had his ways and means of bypassing lockdown.' He chuckles.

Alison is a stickler for the rules and Claire knows that she won't be impressed with this piece of information.

'Could you tell us a bit about the actual swimming involved? How much would we be doing each day?' Alison asks.

'Around three to five kilometres, although with swimmers like Claire we could extend that if need be. Mainly we'd swim by the coast, dropping anchor in small bays or coves where we can have lunch and relax.

Might see if we can wangle a crossing from one of the small islands to the mainland,' Oliver says.

'Five kilometres a day? Um, that's quite a lot. Maybe this isn't for me after all,' Alison says. This information, however, has piqued Claire's interest, but she knows she will have to convince Alison.

'If you get tired you can just hop back on board. You only need to swim as much as you like. That's right, isn't it, Sophie?' Claire says.

'Yes, the boat will be nearby and it's your holiday. You don't even have to swim every day if you don't want to.'

'Plus,' Oliver says, 'I'm going to offer extra classes to those who sign up for the holiday.'

Turning to Claire, Sophie says, 'I have your details already from your Shoreham swims. I'll forward you the itinerary and, in the meantime, if you have any questions, you can email or message me. And of course I'll be here' – she pulls a face – 'next week, giving the kids' class if you want to have a chat with me in person.'

'Thanks, Sophie, I'll look out for your email.'

'Right, I'd better get going and see if anyone else here has read the leaflet and is interested,' Sophie says. 'Oliver, perhaps you can come with me?' It's more of an order than a suggestion.

'Er, I was going to … sure. Come on, then,' he says, pulling out a raft of leaflets from his sports bag. 'Bye, ladies, see you next week.'

As the two make their way out, Claire and Alison look at each other.

'Wouldn't fancy being in Oliver's shoes right now.

Reckon he's going to get it in the neck for not announcing the trip to everyone at the club,' Claire says.

'He's a bit full of himself, don't you think? Doesn't come across that way when we're in the pool, thank the Lord. I don't know if I'd be that comfortable having him arrange a holiday for me if I hadn't seen how professional he is when instructing us. There he's so, well, sensible and mature.'

'Maybe he was just showing off in front of Sophie, trying to impress her. She gets a lot of attention from the lads in reception. He's probably a little insecure, truth be known, despite his pretty-boy looks. As far as the holiday's concerned, though, I do wonder if he's up to the job.'

Chapter Four

A heatwave hits the South Coast and 'Sunny Worthing' is living up to its more hopeful than accurate tourist slogan. Tabloid newspapers are full of headlines such as 'Phew, What a Scorcher!' and front pages are emblazoned with images of a packed Brighton beach. Claire has just arrived home after a hot and uncomfortable journey from London. The train was packed with perspiring, irate commuters, anxious to get to their back gardens.

Kicking off her sandals and opening the fridge door, she grabs a bottle of mineral water. Holding it to her forehead, she revels in its chill. Her phone rings. It's her ex, Geoff.

'Hi Claire, good time to call?' The standard preface for an unscheduled phone call these days.

'Good as any,' she says as she stands by the sink and looks out at some children loitering on the street.

'I have some news, really good news – I'm going to be a dad!'

'Wow … Geoff, that's wonderful! Congratulations. I'm very happy for you,' she says, surprised at the genuine joy she has for him. Yet there's a lurch deep within her that she cannot fathom. When they had been married, there had been years and years of trying for a baby – obsessively on his part, half-heartedly on hers. His patience finally gave out when she flatly refused to even entertain the notion of IVF. For Geoff, this had been the final straw for their marriage. Somehow, though, they had managed to avoid a toxic divorce and remained on friendly terms.

'Thanks, Claire, that means a lot. I didn't want you to hear the news from someone else. I know you've had a lot to cope with lately with having to sort out your dad's estate, and Stuart being no help.'

'Yeah, you're not wrong there.' She doesn't need reminding of how much work she still needs to do, but at least her brother has agreed to dropping the price of the house, so they haven't lost their buyers. It looked like the exchange of contracts was imminent. She makes a mental note to call the estate agent and make him earn his two per cent; now that the sale was in the bag, communication from him has been non-existent. So much still to do. She feels a familiar pressure in her chest and knows she needs to end the call. Watching the children outside, they become blurry as her eyes fill.

Saturday morning, and for those going on the swimming holiday there is the promised open water lesson. Their rendezvous is the Dome Cinema, it being conveniently placed opposite Worthing Pier. For safety reasons, it has been decided it is best if there are two swimming coaches: Oliver in the sea and Sophie in a kayak with supplies of water and isotonic drinks.

Claire arrives, her face pink and blotchy. She mutters 'Hello' to Alison and sits next to her on the wall. There is no shade and soon Claire is hot and impatient to get into the water. She sits there, brooding. Geoff's news the previous day has unsettled her.

'You okay, Claire? You're very quiet.'

'Yeah. No.' She considers whether or not to share what's bothering her, and decides she will. 'I found out yesterday that my ex is having a baby with his child bride.'

'Oh. I see. That's gotta be tough, but you must have known this was going to happen. Neither of them made any secret of the fact that they were desperate for a child.'

'Of course, but it's just … the reality of it. Geoff and I had talked about being parents for so long. Well, he had. So it's kind of hard to imagine that he's doing it with someone else.'

'But you were never that keen, were you?'

'I know, that's what's so daft. I don't know why I'm feeling odd. When he told me, I was genuinely happy for him. It just highlights how much my life has stagnated.'

'Oh, come now. You've just been promoted. I mean, senior accountant with a major firm, that's not exactly going nowhere, is it?' Alison nudges her with her elbow. 'Plus you have great friends like me.'

Claire recognises again that sensation of guilt. How can she wallow, given all Alison has been through? 'I know, I know. I'm just feeling sorry for myself. I'll be better once I've had a swim.'

A woman rounds the corner. Nisha Sharma, Vihan's mother. Not long after the accident she joined the swim club and is so taken with it that she's already signed up for the holiday.

'Hello, ladies. How are you?'

'Very well, thanks,' Alison says. 'How's your son doing?'

'Quite well. The cast should be coming off soon and there's no lasting damage as far as we can tell.' Nisha turns to Claire. 'I will always be so grateful to you, my dear. It is nice to get to know you under different circumstances, I must say. This will be my first open water swim. I've always gone to swimming pools, apart from a paddle in the sea when it's hot. Silly, really. I don't know why it's never occurred to me before.'

'If you're anything like me, you'll be addicted,' Claire says. 'Nothing can beat it. I feel good after any swim, but the sea, well, that's something quite apart.' Looking at her watch, she tuts. 'It's getting late. What are we waiting for? Oliver's here and Sophie got in the water fifteen minutes ago.' She shouts across to Oliver. 'Any chance of getting in the water sometime today?'

'Just waiting for Alan and Debbie to arrive. They've messaged me to say they've had car trouble and are taking the bus. Shouldn't be too long.'

'I might have known,' Claire says. 'I hope this isn't indicative of how the holiday is going to be, them holding us up all the time. Well, her holding us up with her million and one questions.' She'd been less than impressed when she heard Debbie was coming on the holiday. Alan, though, now that was another matter. He was a most welcome addition to the party.

'Now I've told you a thousand times not to exaggerate,' Alison says, attempting to lighten the mood.

'Who's this we're talking about?' Nisha asks.

'Oh, just one of the other swimmers. She tends to lack confidence and so will ask a lot of questions to reassure herself. She's all right in small doses,' Alison says.

'Yeah, just we'll be getting one big dose of her on board a small boat for a week. I don't know whether I'll drown her or myself!' Even as she says it, Claire recognises a streak of nastiness which is not normally in her nature. Attempting to soften her tone, she goes on. 'Though I suppose I'm so much faster than her in the water I won't see much of her there, and I can always go to the other side of the boat if she starts to get on my nerves.'

'Exactly, just make sure you're nowhere near her.' Alison smiles. 'If you carry on moaning, you will be the person I'll be avoiding!'

'Yeah, yeah. Point taken. I'm just dying for a swim. Where the bloody hell are they? Oh, talk of the devil. Here they come.'

Alan and Debbie can be seen getting off the bus across the road, by the sea. They wait there for the group to join them. Debbie is smiling broadly and waving.

'Hello, everyone! Oh my, I didn't think we were going

to make it on time.'

'You didn't,' Claire mutters.

'Claire, shush,' Alison warns.

Claire holds up her hands and mouths the words, 'Okay, okay.'

Heaving a large bag onto his shoulder, Oliver says, 'Right, let's get to the beach.'

'Sorry, everyone. The blooming car had a flat battery. Silly me left the parking lights on last night. Here now, though, and raring to go. Alan and I went swimming in the sea at the weekend. It was glorious, wasn't it, Alan? So hot you could almost fool yourself you were already in the Mediterranean. Didn't I say that, Alan?' Debbie gushes.

Anxious to get in the sea, nobody is really bothering to listen to Debbie as she extols the delights of their swim. She seems not to notice and carries on regardless.

Once on the pebble beach, Oliver drops his bag to the ground and unzips it, extracting a fluorescent orange PVC bag. 'Now I know a lot of you are familiar with tow floats and I can see some of you have your own, but I just wanted to run through what these are for the newer members. In previous years, we haven't insisted on their use, but it's been decided that for added safety they will now be compulsory when swimming in the sea. The one I have here doubles as a dry bag, useful for popping your things into if you don't want to leave them on the beach, or you want to get out of the water at a different point than you entered. Once you've put your stuff inside you can seal and then inflate it. Debbie, I'll lend you this one today, so if you can give me your flip-flops and clothes and things, I'll put them in.'

'What about my purse? I don't want my bank cards and money to get wet.'

Alan assures her it'll be fine. Once Debbie is convinced, Oliver then demonstrates how the tow floats are attached via webbing which clips around the waist.

'What a nifty idea,' Nisha says, turning to Claire. 'But yours looks different.'

'Yes. Mine just has space for me to place my water bottle on top. Alison has my kit in her float.'

'The bottle doesn't just fall out into the sea?'

'No, well not so far, and it's useful if you have a special drink mix you want to use, or you don't have a friendly kayaker throwing you bottles.' Claire laughs, her mood lightened.

Rigged out with floats, the group pick their way over the pebbles in their bare feet and swim out amid exuberant shouts as the cool water hits their hot bodies.

In the sea, Oliver heads up the group with Claire at his side. Following them are Alison and Nisha. Alan is lagging behind because Debbie is struggling as her stamina levels are not up to those in the rest of the group. Bringing up the rear in a kayak is Sophie.

Oliver stops swimming. 'Claire, let's wait for the rest to catch up.'

'Fine by me,' she says as she floats on her back and gently sculls in the water, her upturned face to the sun, eyes closed. It's not long before they are joined by Alison and Nisha.

'Oh, isn't this the best!' Alison exclaims.

Claire bobs back up from her supine position and grins. 'I know. What a great way to spend a Saturday.'

Nisha says, 'It's certainly different to swimming in a pool, that's for sure. The buoyancy of the sea means you don't have to think so much about your body position, which is nice. Although the salty taste takes some getting used to. Mind you, if I had known the summer here was going to be like this, I wouldn't have been bothered about going to Spain.'

'But the holiday will be so much better than this. You'll have a week to really work on your technique and as nice as this is, the sea there will be crystal clear,' Alison says. 'You'll actually be able to see fish! It'll be a different experience altogether.'

'It will be nice to have a little me time too,' Nisha says.

Sophie paddles past in the kayak and Alan and Debbie join them at the buoy marker. Debbie is a bit nervous being so far from the shore and won't go anywhere near it. Claire sees her lagging back and says, 'You have to pat the buoy. I always say "hello" to one when I reach it. Gives me a sense of achievement. Come on, I'm here, nothing bad will happen.' She can see Debbie still looks wary so gives what she hopes is an encouraging smile.

Debbie swims and touches the marker. It bounces around as she does so and she lets out a delighted giggle. 'You're right! That was fun.'

'Hi guys, great going,' Sophie says. 'All good with you, Oliver?'

Oliver forms a circle with his arm and touches his head with his hand, the signage for 'I'm okay' in the water. 'Great, thanks, but thirsty. Throw me an isotonic drink, would you? I want to get rid of the taste of salt.'

Sophie hurls a bottle over to him which he deftly catches. She throws out more bottles, which bob up and down in the water. The bottles are colour-coded according to their contents. Most of the group are opting for isotonic drinks; after so long in the water they are all feeling the effects of the salt.

'Oh, that's better,' Debbie says. 'My tongue feels as if it has doubled in size, and the taste of the salt water is really foul. How do Channel swimmers cope with it? I mean, they're in the water all day.'

'They have regular feeds during the swim, which helps,' Sophie says. 'Next time I'll dish out some jelly babies for you all. They're easy to eat and the sugar is a nice way of getting rid of the salty taste in your mouth.'

'Been years since I had a jelly baby.' Alan laughs, then says to his wife, 'You did really well today, Debs.'

Looking pleased, she replies, 'Do you really think so, love?'

Claire has to concede that she's impressed with the way Debbie has coped with the swim. 'Yeah, Debbie, you've made good progress over the past few weeks. We'll make an openwater swimmer of you yet.'

Once everyone is rested and has had something to drink, Sophie collects the bottles. There is much hilarity as people try hurling them into the kayak. At one point a bottle hits Sophie on the head.

'Oi! Watch it! Who was that?' she says in mock indignation.

Debbie is horrified. How can she have been so stupid? And just as she had gained some ground with Claire, who she is half in awe of, half afraid. 'I'm so sorry. Are you all right, Sophie?'

'I'm fine. I was only joking, Debbie.'

Oliver asks everyone to come closer. 'Final stretch now and the easiest bit of sighting. See that great big pier? That's what you're sighting for now. Hard to miss, but remember to glance up just above the level of the water every three to four strokes to make sure you're aiming toward it. Think back to what I said about imitating an alligator with your eyes just above the waterline. You don't want to lift your head right out, it'll slow you down.'

'Er yes, Nisha,' Sophie says. 'No swimming to France like you were trying to earlier on.'

Debbie takes a deep breath. She's really going to focus and get this last part of the swim right. She says to Alan, 'Could you slow down a little for this bit so I can follow your lead? I think it would be easier for me – I can focus on my stroke and try to speed up.'

'Sure, not a problem. If you swim behind me, you'll get the benefit of my slipstream. There'll be less drag, you see, and you'll be able to go a bit faster.'

'I'd forgotten about that. Great.' Debbie feels a little more confident now.

Half an hour later, the small crowd of swimmers is getting out of the water. The tide has started to go out so they end up having to wade back to shore. Nisha sees her husband arriving on the beach. He is lugging a huge cool box and she goes over to him to help unpack the contents. Pulling off goggles and swim caps, the group joins Nisha and her husband while Oliver helps Sophie carry the kayak out of the water.

'Everyone, this is my husband, Devan,' Nisha says.

He smiles. 'So nice to meet you and put faces to names. Nisha has talked about you all so much. Good to see who she'll be running off with in October.' He has a rich, baritone voice and speaks with the quiet authority of the paediatric consultant he is.

They all laugh politely, though Claire can't help but read into the comment and notes the possessive way he is holding his wife.

He sees Sophie and says, 'Ah, Sophie. I hope you will take better care of my wife than you did my son in his diving lesson.' Sophie blushes and looks down at the ground. Oliver visibly bristles. Claire imagines he wants to defend his girlfriend. Let it go, Oliver, she silently beseeches him. Oliver's shoulders drop and he doesn't utter a word, but looks across at Sophie, who motions with her head for him to say nothing.

Devan breaks the silence. 'I'm only teasing, Sophie. And you'll have Claire here to help out again should anything go awry.' The barbed comment leaves everyone feeling awkward, and Nisha twists away from her husband's arm.

The detritus of the picnic lunch lay around them as the group lounges in the hot sun. The tranquillity is interrupted by squawking coming from Debbie. She is running around, flapping her hands about wildly and looking agitated.

'What's wrong with Debbie?' Alison asks Alan, who is waving his hands over the picnic.

'Wasps,' he replies distractedly.

Oh, for pity's sake, Claire thinks. 'You mean she's scared of wasps?'

'She's allergic to them, had a couple of frightening episodes. It might look as if she's overreacting, but trust me, she's not.'

Nisha joins in with trying to clear the food of wasps and says, 'Oh yes, it's no joke. Does she carry an EpiPen with her, Alan?'

'Two of them. Everywhere she goes. She's quite paranoid about it.'

'Very sensible, better safe than sorry. Allergies like that can be fatal.' Nisha stands. 'There, they're all gone. All fine now, Debbie.'

Debbie creeps back. 'Are you sure?'

'Yes, love.' Alan squeezes her hand.

'Do you have my EpiPen handy? Just in case.'

'Right here, don't worry, you can relax,' he says, patting the dry bag they have with them.

Debbie sits back down and spends the next few minutes furtively looking about her, clearly uncomfortable. Nisha makes a suggestion. 'How about a game of paddle? I brought some bats and balls.'

'Great!' Debbie says. Happy to escape, Claire guesses.

The tide is now out, revealing soft, wet sand. Soon the pair are playing and there is much laughter from them both.

Alan is looking on from his prone position on a towel and smiling. Claire is next to him. 'Now this is the life,' he says, smacking his lips with satisfaction as he drinks from a bottle of beer. 'I'm so glad I came. I wasn't going to bother, couldn't face the thought of getting on a bus in this heat. I've had enough of that on my commute this week on crowded trains.'

'Tell me about it. Do you work in London then?' Claire asks.

'Nah. Three Bridges. Couldn't do the whole London thing.'

'You're lucky. Though at least I don't have to do it every day now like I used to. After the lockdown ended my firm decided it worked in their favour to lease less office space and just have people work half their time at home. I'm not a fan of hot-desking, but it's a sacrifice I'm willing to make, although I'm still just as rushed off my feet. Everyone thinks that if you work from home you're somehow doing less.' Looking at Debbie playing paddle, she says, 'She's got a lot of energy, just the sort of adult kids love to have around, up for mucking about when the rest of us just want to be lazy. You don't have children, do you?'

'Not yet, but we're hoping to. Actually, we're trying, but it's taking longer to happen than we thought. You spend so long avoiding getting pregnant, you just assume when you want to it will happen immediately.'

Claire is tempted to share her own experiences but decides against it, instead saying, 'The important thing is to not stress or obsess about it. That'll only make things worse.'

'I've said as much to Debbie, but we have a bit of an age gap and she's worried we might have already left things too late. It's almost as if she feels guilty about being older than me and not being able to provide me with a son and heir – something daft like that. Our age difference has never bothered me. If I was older than her, no one would comment, but we do get remarks from people,' Alan says, giving Debbie a thumbs up as she waves over at him.

'Yes. People can be so thoughtless,' Claire agrees.

Alan looks at her. 'It sounds like you're speaking from experience.'

'Something like that.' She turns her head away.

Nisha and Debbie stop playing and rejoin the group. 'Phew! I'm exhausted,' Debbie puffs. 'I need to work on my stamina.'

'My God, your back,' Alan says, looking at Debbie's crimson shoulders. 'Didn't you put any sunscreen on?'

'Yes, before the swim.' She cranes her neck to look

at her shoulders, annoyed at herself for not being more careful.

'But that was hours ago! Come on, get dressed. We'd better get you home, put some ice on it and slather you with aloe vera,' Alan says, looking concerned.

'Sounds fun,' Claire says.

Why does Claire have to be like that? thinks Debbie. Making a joke out of this. Making fun of me. Again. She tries to think of a witty retort, but before she can, Nisha speaks.

'Good idea. And take some aspirin or ibuprofen too. Make sure you drink plenty of water – no alcohol.'

'Will do,' Alan says, helping Debbie who is gingerly putting on a T-shirt. 'What are we going to do with you, eh?'

'So silly of me. Sorry.'

'Nothing to apologise for, love. We'll get you home and do as Nisha suggests.' He kisses her on the cheek.

Feeling better, Debbie notices Claire watching them leave, her lips set in a rigid, straight line.

Chapter Five

'Cancel the whole thing? Are you serious?' Sophie shouts at Oliver, who is holding his head in his hands.

'I don't think we have any other option, babe. It's less than two months until we're due to leave and we still don't have a sixth person interested, let alone ready to hand over the cash in full.'

'Can't we just go ahead with five people and not make a profit? We could treat the whole thing as work experience and make a better go of it next time.'

'We won't make money with six people. In order to make any kind of profit we needed at least eight, better nine. And we can't do anything without a boat,' Oliver says, looking up at her.

'What do you mean? The boat is all paid for. We did that last month.'

'Er, no. Last month we paid for the villa in full. The owner was giving me grief because Josh had done repairs on the place, but none of the maintenance. Apparently, some tenants complained and had to be given a part refund. The owner was furious and the only way we could go ahead with the rental was if we stomped up pronto with the full payment, without the discount he'd previously offered. I had to max out my credit card to do it too. So, I made an executive decision to pay for the boat this month once we'd got the final swimmers to pay.'

'Without telling me? Thanks a lot. So, we have no working capital and you're up to your eyes in debt?' Sophie says.

'Yes, that's about the gist of it, I'm afraid. Part of the problem is that we didn't allow for the cost of us going to Spain to check things out. We might have been able to swing it but for that.'

'Hey, that needed to be done. There's no way we could have just turned up in Spain with six customers never having seen the villa, the boat or how the swim trips panned out. That would have been totally unprofessional.'

'Well you don't get more unprofessional than cancelling a holiday and giving nobody a refund.'

'Fuck. How are we going to tell them that? They're going to complain to the centre. We'll both get the sack.'

'Sophie, it won't come to that. It has nothing to do with the Aquarium.'

'Oh, you think so, do you? You don't think Nisha's husband, Doctor Snotty, will stir up trouble? You heard him that day on the beach, having a go about what happened with his son. Even if Nisha is okay about it, do you really think he will let this slide? No way. We are in the shit. Big time.'

'I just don't understand how it's come to this. I thought

we'd be beating people back with a stick wanting to sign up. I mean, we have twenty members in the swim club. I was sure at least half of them would want to come,' Oliver says.

'Maybe you're not as popular as you think you are.'

'What the bloody hell is that supposed to mean?'

'You figure it out. Look, I need this job. I don't have a rich mummy and daddy I can run to if I fuck up, nor expensive habits to maintain.'

'Not that again. I haven't got a "habit". Stop being such a bitch. And for your information my parents have told me I'm on my own with this, they're not going to help.'

'Oh, so you've already gone begging then? Did you think you could paper over this and I wouldn't find out? Unbelievable!'

Sophie gets up from their kitchen table and grabs her phone and purse.

'Where are you going?' Oliver says.

'I'm going to make a few phone calls and see if I can salvage anything from this mess. One of us needs to pull our finger out and actually do something. I'll see you later. You'd better get a move on if you want to make sure you're not late for your shift. Keep your job while you still can.'

The objective open water session has come to a close, and as swimmers get out of the pool and start towelling off, Oliver says he'd like a quick word before they leave.

'You did really well, guys. I'm sure you have all enjoyed the great summer we've had and the chance it's given us to spend a lot of time in the sea, something we wouldn't usually be so lucky to do. Unfortunately, the forecast for the next few weeks is not that great. So, we will probably be moving all the sessions into the pool.' With this proclamation there are groans from the group. 'Yeah, I know, there's nothing like the freedom swimming in the sea gives you. I feel your pain, honestly. However, all is not lost, because we still have space left on our swimming holiday next month. It would be a really nice way of getting extra sea swimming in and enjoying some sunshine before those dark nights draw in and winter arrives here in England. Have a think about it. Don't forget that there are also free weekly sessions available if you sign up. I'm sure that those who have already been taking them will tell you how enjoyable these sessions are and how much more practice they've been able to put in.'

There are murmurs among the group, but no one shows any active signs of committing to the holiday. Oliver looks downcast as he motions to those who have already signed up. 'Do you have time for a quick coffee in the cafeteria? I'd like to talk about the holiday.'

Once settled at a table with an assortment of beverages, Claire with her obligatory cake, Oliver begins. 'Um, this is a bit hard for me to say, but I wanted to be straight with you all and let you know that we've hit a bit of a glitch with the holiday.' No one says anything so he continues. 'The thing is. The thing is … well.'

‘The thing is … what, Oliver?’ Claire says, losing patience.

‘Well, I’m afraid it’s looking as though we may have to cancel the holiday. We just don’t have the numbers to make it viable.’

‘Really, and why is that?’ Claire says, feeling calm but knowing that Alison will be distraught; she’d had to do a lot of grovelling to persuade her mum to look after her youngest son. She’d also put a lot of effort into her training, which now might have all been for nothing.

Alison sighs. ‘Well, I suppose the refund will come in handy. It was all going to cost me more than I could really afford. When will we be getting that?’

Oliver looks uncomfortable. ‘That’s the thing. We used all your money to pay for everything: the villa, the deposit on the boat … we can’t get that back at this stage.’

Alan leans forward. ‘So, no holiday and no refund. Is that what you’re telling us?’

‘Yes, I’m afraid so.’ Oliver at least has the decency to look embarrassed. ‘Well not at the moment. We’ll try and sort something out, but it may take a few months. I’m really sorry.’

‘It’s not just the money we’ve paid you. Debbie and I have booked our flights. What about that? Are you going to compensate us for those?’

‘Yes, Oliver. Alison and I have our flights booked too,’ Claire says. ‘The airline may change them, at a cost, but they won’t refund them. Christ, what a mess.’

‘Isn’t the Aquarium covered for eventualities like

this? A big company like them?' Nisha asks.

'This has nothing to do with the Aquarium.'

'But I assumed as it was advertised here and being run by two members of staff, that it must do.'

'No, that's not the case. I'm sorry if you thought it was. We did tell those people who'd booked up with us at the beginning. I'm sure I mentioned it to you. Look, I know this is rubbish, but all is not entirely lost. There's still a chance of someone else signing up. We just need one more person and it can all go ahead, so if you can think of anyone, please try and encourage them. In the meantime, Sophie and I are doing some more advertising further afield which may result in some positive news to tell you next time.' He glances at his watch. 'I have to go, I've got a private swim class to give, but I'll be in touch via the WhatsApp group if I have any news. Obviously if any of you hear of someone who wants to come, please let me know ASAP.' Looking at the somewhat stunned group, he repeats, 'I'm really sorry. See you next week.'

'Yeah, see you next week. Thanks a bunch, Oliver,' Alan says.

There's a collective sigh of exasperation as Oliver leaves. Alison says, 'Talk about a great way to ruin your day.'

'Not good news, is it?' Alan says. 'Well, Debbie, what do you want to do about this? We have our flights booked. Do you want to see if we can book a hotel or Airbnb?'

'It would be one way of doing it, I suppose. We'd

get a holiday and we'd still be able to swim, nothing to stop us doing that. Won't be the same, but better than nothing.'

'I can't blinking afford any extra,' Alison says. 'What a cock-up. And no refund, all that rubbish about paying us back in a few months. We'll never see any of our money again, I can tell you that for nothing. It might not seem a lot to you, but to me it represented more …'

Claire can see Alison welling up. Bloody hell! She knows how much this holiday has meant to her friend. 'It's not just the money though, is it?' she says as she fidgets with her coffee cup.

Nisha agrees. 'Yes, I trusted them because of who they are and where they work. I feel such a fool. Devan is going to be so angry when I tell him. God, I'll have to listen to him going on about how he knew there was something dodgy about the whole thing. That will be almost worse than it being cancelled.'

'Hey, I think we are perhaps all jumping the gun a bit here,' Debbie says. 'Oliver said that the holiday may have to be cancelled – it's not a done deal yet.'

Alison says, 'I dunno. He didn't sound that optimistic to me.'

'Tell you what, I'll phone Sophie a bit later and get her take on it. If the whole thing is really cancelled, I would have thought she'd be here too, as a matter of courtesy,' Claire says. 'I'll get back to you all either way.'

'I almost feel sorry for her,' Debbie says. 'Did you see the way Oliver delivered the bad news and made a run for it before we had time to properly react? What a coward. Who do you imagine will be picking up the pieces?'

'Yeah, I know what you mean. I've always thought he was a bit fly-by-night. Sophie is definitely the more reliable of the two,' Claire says, glancing at Alison. She pushes a tissue towards her.

Alison takes it. 'I feel a bit silly getting so upset.' She dabs at her eyes. 'It was so much more than just a holiday for me.'

'Don't beat yourself up about it,' Alan says. 'And Debbie's right. This could all end up going ahead. I suppose it was decent enough of Oliver to give us a heads-up now, rather than right before we're supposed to leave. Let's keep in touch and hopefully Sophie can give us some better news. Ready to leave, love?'

'Anyone fancy a drink at the Red Lion?' Claire says. 'They have a nice beer garden we can sit in, maybe order a bite to eat? I'm sure we could do with something to take our minds off this.'

Alison is at least now smiling again. 'Really, Claire, after that massive piece of cake? You must have hollow legs!'

'Oh, I'll only have a sandwich or something, it'll save me doing anything for dinner. Well, what do you think? Are you up for it?'

'Sure, why not. What about you, Nisha?'

'Might as well. My mother-in-law has taken the children to the cinema – last treat before they all go back to school – and Devan is at some work meeting. Yes, it could be just the ticket after this news. A bit of mummy me time,' she says, chuckling.

'Atta girl! Tell you what, ladies, I'll treat us to a bottle of Prosecco and we'll put the world to rights.'

'Sounds like a plan,' Alison says, managing a watery smile. Claire is pleased she seems to be feeling a little better.

It's late in the evening, a few days later. Sophie and Oliver are in the garden of their houseshare. Their housemates, sensing the tension between the two, have wisely left them to it and are holed up in their rooms. 'I still can't believe that Ben is coming on this trip. I mean, Ben bloody Dankworth! Can he even swim a length of a pool? He's going to be a right liability on this holiday. God knows what the others will think,' Oliver says, shaking his head.

'The others will be glad that there is going to be a holiday and they won't have lost all their money. That's what they're going to think. And, if we're talking about disbelief, I can't believe you went and told everyone that the holiday was going to be cancelled.'

'I only said it might be cancelled. I wanted to be upfront with them, thought it would be the best policy.'

'Oh really? I don't see *you* having to deal with the fallout of your little meeting – the one you never bothered mentioning to me!' It has been a hellish few days fielding messages and phone calls, and she's not going to let him off the hook lightly. 'I thought we were supposed to be a team, you know, in this together. It seems to me that I'm doing most of the work here.'

'I think you are exaggerating a bit there, babe.'

'Don't "babe" me. I am so angry with you right now. I told you I had a few people to contact who might be interested in coming and to hold back on giving out bad news. Now we're going to have to do some damage control.'

'Chill, no one's going to back out now. They know they'd lose their money. They're invested.'

'That's not the point, Oliver. I'm already on thin ice with Nisha, after that accident with her son. What if she complains to the centre about how two of their employees misled her about the holiday being endorsed by the Aquarium?' Despite what Oliver had said to Nisha, Sophie knows that's exactly what he had done. 'If that happens, our jobs could well be in jeopardy. Being sacked for something like this isn't going to do wonders for our CVs, is it? And the way things are going, it's unlikely our swimming holiday business is going to be enough to support us both. Getting a new job with no references won't be easy either. I don't think you realise the problems you've created by opening your big mouth.'

Oliver looks sheepish. 'You are totally right, I've been an utter prat. I admit it. But I will try and make amends. In the future, I will run everything by you first, I promise.'

'You'd better,' Sophie says, calming a little but wary of a charm offensive; she's fallen for that one too many times in the past. 'In the meantime, what can we do to rebuild bridges with our clients?'

'How about we take them all out for a meal, a few drinks, get a bit of a rapport going. What do you think?'

'Too expensive. A meal out for eight with drinks' – she thinks back to the evening at the bar with Claire and imagines her wine bill alone – 'is more than we can afford. No, we'll have to think of something else.'

'A party?'

'What, just the eight of us, or do you plan to invite a load of your mates? Don't think they'll appreciate that, do you? It would hardly show us as mature professionals, more like a bunch of students in a houseshare who still haven't grown up.' Really, Oliver could be a right idiot at times. 'Not exactly the image we want to portray. Anyway, you keep thinking and I'll message the group, tell them about Ben and that we're still on for the trip.'

Chapter Six

The following day Claire calls Alison. All of them have had good news. Sophie and Oliver have managed to find someone to make up the numbers and the holiday is now definitely on. Everyone has been invited to a barbecue at their place next weekend. It's their way of apologising and they want to introduce the group to the person who'll be joining them, Ben.

'Be nice to meet him before we go. Hope he's not some dickhead friend of Oliver's,' Claire says. 'What do you think? Are you up for it?'

'Yeah, why not.'

'Okay, I'll let Sophie know. In fact, it will probably be when I next see you. I have a lot on at work at the moment and I have to be in the office rather than work from home. Don't think I'll be able to make this week's swim session.' Claire thinks back to the meeting she'd had with one of the partners earlier that day. It had not gone well. She'd dropped the ball a couple of times recently and got a real dressing-down. She's finding her responsibilities in her new role difficult to adjust to.

Claire ends the call, relieved that one problem has

been overcome. At least now she has something to look forward to. What she is not looking forward to is going to her dad's house and starting the heartbreaking task of sorting through his possessions. Contracts have been exchanged and the buyers are keen to get moved in. Fortunately, they have expressed an interest in purchasing some of the contents, so at least that's something she doesn't have to concern herself with. However, the personal effects, those which haven't already been picked over and taken by her brother, still have to be sorted. She is dreading that. Her throat feels dry and as she fills a glass with water, her hand trembles. She steadies it and drinks. Get a grip, Claire, she admonishes herself.

The weekend comes around and Sophie has employed their housemates, Evan and Nathan, to spruce up the garden and arrange tables and chairs for everyone. Normally the domain of Oliver, Sophie has promised Evan that if he cleans the barbecue, he can be chief meat incinerator. Oliver has been sent out to the supermarket with strict instructions not to go above budget, nor stray from the shopping list he has been given. In the kitchen, Sophie is haphazardly throwing together pasta and potato salad. Cooking is not her thing; neither, for that matter, are barbecues. As a vegetarian she finds the smell of meat – and the copious amounts being cooked – rather stomach-churning, so she gives the cooking area a wide berth. She looks up at the clock,

11 a.m., then at the lads in the garden, and wonders if things are going to be ready in time. She is anxious that this goes well. Ever since Oliver put his big foot in it, she has had a knot in her stomach that won't go away and she can't exactly pinpoint which she is more worried about: the holiday or the potential threat that someone will complain to the Aquarium.

An hour later there's still no sign of Oliver. Exasperated, she picks up her phone to message him, when the doorbell rings. 'Don't tell me you forgot your key,' she says as she opens the door. 'Oh, Ben. You're early. I did say from one p.m.' She would have been cross, but Ben is standing there with flowers and a heavy-looking bag, its contents clinking together. He has a childlike smile on his face.

'I know, I know. I'm really early, but I misjudged the train times and how long it would take to find your place. You know how I hate to turn up late for things, so I end up being super early. Anyway, I'm here and offering my services. I am rather the expert barbecuer, even if I do say so myself, plus I've brought my special marinade sauce – guaranteed to please.' He smiles broadly, walks over the threshold uninvited and plants a noisy kiss on Sophie's cheek. Disarmed, she steps back and directs him to the kitchen. By the time Oliver arrives twenty minutes later, Ben has helped Evan light the barbecue and the two are chatting and drinking bottles of beer.

'What's he doing here already?' hisses Oliver to Sophie.

'He came to help.'

Spotting the long-stemmed, expensive-looking pink roses in a vase on the windowsill, Oliver says, 'And I suppose they're from him?'

'Yes, they are. Got a problem with that?'

Oliver mumbles something she cannot hear as Ben makes an appearance at the back door. 'Ollie, mate. Thought we were going to have to send out a search party for you.'

Without asking, Ben starts unloading the shopping bags, unwrapping the meat and putting it onto plates already out on the table. He begins brushing sauce on them and then takes them out to Evan.

'Evan, meat's here!' He deposits the meat next to Evan and heads back inside.

'Right, that's done. Evan says the barbecue needs a bit longer to fire up. In the meantime, anything you want me to help with, Sophie?'

'Yes, could you empty the ice into the buckets outside and put the wine and beer in?'

'Your wish is my command, milady,' Ben says, lugging out bags of ice.

'Your wish is my command,' mimics Oliver once Ben is out of earshot.

'Don't start, Oliver!'

'Well, he's taken over.'

'So what? It's nice to have someone volunteer to help rather than have to be nagged to do something.'

'I volunteer. Tell me what you want me to do and I'll do it.'

'Hmm, there is something.'

'Name it.'

'The downstairs loo is looking disgusting, and as it is the one our guests will be using, it needs a right going over. I suggest you stick on your rubber gloves and get to it.'

Oliver opens his mouth to protest but says nothing. Sophie allows herself a chuckle as he slouches off.

By 2 p.m. all the guests are assembled in the garden, drinks in hand. The heatwave of the summer has abated, though it is still fairly hot in the sunshine. A slight breeze provides relief from the heat for those not lucky enough to be sheltering under the one sun umbrella. Ben has gallantly given his seat in the shade to Sophie, whose fair colouring means she has to be careful. Debbie is there too, wary of getting sunburnt again.

As seems to be the case at most barbecues, the men have gathered around the grill and are vying with each other to give advice. Evan is bent over the flame, looking intent, his face shiny. Ben says something to Alan, who laughs and slaps him on the back, while Oliver looks on, scowling.

Nisha and Claire are sitting together near the partial shade of the garden fence.

'What do you think it is about men wanting to do all the cooking at a barbecue? Devan is the same, but I can't get him to boil an egg for himself in the kitchen,' Nisha says, slurring her words ever so slightly. She's had two glasses of wine on an empty stomach and it is starting to affect her.

'Oh, it'll be their caveman instincts coming out. You know, "me man, me make fire, ugh",' Claire says. She eyes both men, her gaze lingering on Alan.

Nisha bursts out laughing. 'Oh Claire, you are funny! How do you come up with things like that?'

'Years of practice. Hey, do you think Ben's good-looking? The bloke who's coming with us to Spain. More attractive than Oliver?'

Nisha squints across the lawn, giving the question some thought. 'Um. No. I mean, he is a nice-looking boy, but Oliver is very striking, kind of exotic, dark with those amazing green eyes. Why do you ask? Are you going to pounce on one of them?' At this, she giggles.

'No, I prefer my men a little older,' she says, glancing at Alan, then catching herself. What is she doing? A married man – seriously? She looks at Nisha to see if she's picked up on the comment, but Nisha hasn't noticed, too busy slurping her wine. 'I sense the tension between Oliver and Ben, well certainly from Oliver. I wonder if Ben and Sophie were once a couple?'

Ben breaks away from the group and ambles over to them. 'Can I get you ladies a top-up?'

'Oh, yes please,' Claire says smiling up at him from her seated position. 'I think Nisha could do with some water though, she seems a bit dehydrated.' She doesn't want Nisha to get in trouble with that awful husband of hers.

'Yes, I think I should slow down a bit.' She hiccups, covering her mouth.

Returning with their drinks he refills Claire's glass and hands Nisha the water. He's about to walk away, but Claire stops him.

'Come and sit with us for a bit, Ben. You've been on the go since we arrived. Let Oliver do some of the work; he is one of the hosts, after all.'

Smiling, Ben pulls up a chair.

'So, Ben, what made you sign up for the holiday? How did you come to hear about it? Do you live locally?' fires Claire. She's curious to find out what Ben's story is.

'No, I'm not local, well not any more. I live in London, but I used to live in the same street as Sophie. We went to school together.'

'Oh, childhood sweethearts?' Claire enquires. She knew it!

'I wish.' Checking himself, he quickly adds, 'No, just friends. Sophie was always really nice to me. She was so popular but she always had time for me, well, for everyone. That's why everybody liked her so much. Teachers too. I hadn't heard from her for ages, kinda lost touch when I moved to London, so it was great to get a message from her asking if I'd be interested in the holiday.'

'Are you able to do much open water swimming if you live in London?' Nisha asks.

Ben looks a bit embarrassed. 'Actually, I've never done any of that type of swimming. I've swum in the sea when I've been abroad with the lads, but nothing serious like you lot.'

Nisha persists. 'Do you train in a swimming pool? We've

been doing that as well as sea swims. It can be an easier way of assessing how many kilometres you're putting in per session so you can estimate how fast you swim. How long does it take you to swim a kilometre, Ben?'

Ben looks stumped and admits, 'I have no idea. To be honest, it's been a while since I've swum.' Seeing the surprised looks on Nisha and Claire's faces, he adds, 'But I was really good at school, used to go every week to the local pool with my mates.'

'I see, you were a member of a swimming club? Did you compete?' Claire asks. If he was a competitive swimmer when he was at school with Sophie, that would explain his presence.

'No, no. Nothing like that, just mucking about really, racing each other, that sort of thing,' Ben says. Eager to redeem his lack of swimming prowess, he is quick to continue. 'Look, I know I don't go swimming like you lot do, but it's like riding a bicycle, isn't it? You never forget, and it's not as if I'm unfit. I do football training twice a week and a match at weekends, plus the gym. I reckon I can hold my own on this holiday if that's what you're worried about.'

'No need to get defensive,' Claire says, waving her wine glass about. 'We're just being inquisitive, that's all.' Oh dear, she thinks, he doesn't sound as if he's going to be very good. This could be a mistake, having him along.

'Yes, take no notice of us old nosey parkers,' Nisha says.

'Think I'll go and see if Sophie needs any help in the kitchen with the salads.' Ben gets up and leaves, clearly looking to escape the interrogation.

'Christ alive. The poor bloke doesn't know what he's in for. Do you think he has ever swum more than a couple of lengths in a pool?' Claire says.

'No, doesn't sound like it.'

'I know they said you can get out of the water at any time, but is he even going to manage to swim a kilometre, let alone the three to five a day planned? He'll spend more time on the boat than in the water.' Poor bloke. Is he hoping to impress Sophie on this trip? Good luck with that! she thinks.

'How on earth did Sophie persuade him to come? Do you think she told him about the sort of time we'd be spending in the water?'

'It's obvious, isn't it?'

'What do you mean?'

'He's got the hots for Sophie. Sounds like he had a crush on her at school, and then years later she contacts him asking if he wants to come on holiday with her, so of course he jumps at the chance.'

'But she must have explained what the holiday was about. I mean, he wasn't surprised to meet all of us here today, was he?' Nisha says.

'Maybe she glossed over a few facts to get him to come. They were pretty desperate to get the final member of the group signed up. She could have stretched the truth. Hmm, I wonder … once we've all eaten, I might try and get her alone and see if she's aware of just how little swimming experience Ben has.'

Though, of course, if Ben drops out, the holiday is doomed.

Chapter Seven

It's Thursday evening and Alison has got to the pool early to do a few gentle laps before the session begins and to give herself some headspace. To say that the past week has been hectic is an understatement in the extreme. She's still getting used to her new pupils and the head has called three early morning meetings, so the days have been long and arduous. She spots Alan and Debbie coming from the changing rooms so swims over to the side of the pool and gets out to say hi.

'Cor, you're an eager beaver, aren't you?' Debbie exclaims. 'We thought we'd be here ages before anyone else, didn't we, love?'

'You did say that, Debbie.'

Alison smiles. 'Yeah, it's just been such a frantic week, I wanted to take my mind off things. I've been hunched over books so I needed the exercise too, plus with the holiday in sight I want to keep up with my training so I'm not struggling with those four- and five-kilometre swims.' As well as work there are a lot of things going on at home. Normally she would have already chatted to Claire – her go-to person in times of trouble – but she's noticed recently that her friend has been distracted and edgy. She's put it down to her promotion and the extra work involved.

Debbie says, 'To be honest, I'm a bit worried about how I'll cope with those too, but if need be, I can always go back to the boat. Those long swims will really be good practice for Alan with his triathlons, so he'll probably do them all, won't you, Alan?'

'Here's hoping,' Alan says. 'I'm not one to give up on things though. Once I set my mind to something I tend to follow it through.'

They continue chatting, and one by one other members of the swim club join them and sit on the poolside benches. Claire makes an appearance – always happiest by water, she has a big smile on her face. 'Hi guys. How's it going? Alan, you're looking well, all suntanned, and … have you been working out?' She touches his bicep.

Alan looks pleased. 'Actually, I have stepped up my regime a bit these past couple of weeks.'

'Been on the old suntan bed too?' quips Claire.

'Naw, as if. I've been in the garden, putting out new decking.'

'Is there no end to his talents, hey Debbie?'

'Er yes, I mean no,' Debbie stutters.

'Well, you hold onto him. It's slim pickings out there, I can tell you.'

Alison feels embarrassed on Claire's behalf and notes Debbie's discomfort.

Claire says, 'Oliver's late.'

'Only by five minutes.' Nisha has joined them. 'Give him a chance.'

'Oh blow this, I'm getting in. The water is too tempting.' Claire, her cap already on, adjusts her goggles and dives into the pool, barely leaving a ripple on its surface. As she does so, Oliver arrives, apologising for his tardiness.

The group are put through their paces and work hard. The difficult week and the pre-lesson swim have taken their toll on Alison, though. After what seems an age, the session is over and she drags her body up the steps of the pool, too tired to lift herself over the edge. Claire is hovering, waiting for her.

'Wow, what a great session. Just what I needed after the day I've had. I really feel like my training is coming along. I had my doubts about this holiday but I'm looking forward to it now. I'm really glad we're going.'

'Yeah, right. Look, I'm wiped out. Think I'll go to the spa for a bit and relax before heading home.' Alison wishes the swim had had the same regenerative effect on her.

'Oh. Okay, fine, I'll see you in the cafeteria. I'm starved.'

'Mind if I join you, Claire?' says Alan.

'Be my guest. I'm supposed to be meeting Alison here, but I think she must have melted away in the sauna.' Claire looks at her phone to check the time and to see if she's missed any messages. Alison seemed out of sorts earlier on and she wants to check she's all right.

'Debbie was talking about using the jacuzzi for a bit, maybe she's met up with Alison and they've got chatting.'

'Oh Lord, then I might as well go now if Debbie's—' She catches herself, remembering it's Alan she's talking to. 'What I mean is—'

It's all right, Claire.' Alan laughs. 'As her husband, I know that Debbie could talk the hind legs off a donkey.'

The potential awkwardness avoided, the two of them get to talking about the evening's swim session.

'I have to hand it to him: whatever lack of holiday-arranging skills Oliver might have, he is a very good swim coach,' Alan says. 'My timings have really improved since I've been coming here and, as for my stamina—'

'Okay, Alan, a little bit too much information.' She sniggers while playfully pushing his arm.

'That's not what I meant and you know it,' Alan says, laughing along. 'What a filthy mind you have.'

'I'm sure I don't know what you mean.' She flutters her eyelashes at him in a comic fashion. God, what is she doing? This is Alan, not some bloke from the dating website.

He laughs, not offended. 'Yeah, right. Anyway, I'm going to get a coffee, looks like I could be in for a bit of a wait.' Then seeing her almost empty cup, he asks, 'Do you want another one?'

'No thanks.' She decides it's probably best if she doesn't spend any more time alone with Alan. 'Think I'm going to head off. If you see Alison, can you tell her I had to go?' She drains her coffee. 'See you next week,' she says and hurries away.

Debbie enters the cafeteria and makes her way over to Alan. 'Was that Claire I saw leaving?'

'What? Oh yes. She was waiting for Alison but had to go.'

'Oh, I was chatting to Alison in the Jacuzzi. She seems really stressed out, poor thing. Did you know that her son is leaving this weekend to go to university in Bristol?'

'No, I didn't realise she even had kids. Doesn't look old enough to have a son going to university.'

'Um … she's very attractive, don't you think?'

'I suppose. Not my type, all those freckles.'

'Your type is more like Claire, is it?' Debbie fishes.

'I'm married to my type. That's all you need to be concerned with, love.'

Debbie can't resist pushing it. 'I think she likes you. You know what I mean. I think Claire fancies you.'

'Whatever gives you that idea?'

'She's always touching you and making googly eyes at you.'

'Googly eyes? What on earth does that mean? Whether she fancies me or not is beside the point. I do not fancy her, so let's drop it, shall we?'

'I was just saying.'

Changing the subject, Alan says, 'How did your appointment with Doctor Everett go today?'

'Oh, the usual prodding and poking. At least she

didn't tell me to be patient. She understands that at thirty-eight I am right to be concerned about not getting pregnant after two years of trying.'

'Did she mention IVF?'

'Yes, but she said that's something we'd need to discuss as a couple with her. She gave me some leaflets about what to expect. The hormone injections sound a bit dire. She said a lot of women experience mood swings and depression because of the high levels of oestrogen being taken.'

'Like PMS?' Alan suggests.

'Probably worse. I feel so useless not being able to get pregnant. Bet you wished you'd married someone younger now.' She's aware she's sounding whiny but can't help herself.

'Let's not go over this again, love. I've told you a hundred times that our age difference means nothing to me, and let's face it, we're only talking about six years.'

Sensing that Alan is getting irritated, Debbie drops the subject. 'So, what did you think of the session this evening?'

'Good. I was just saying to Claire how much my timings have improved. If I carry on like this, it'll make a real difference to my triathlon ratings. You know that swimming has always been my weak point, so I'm dead chuffed at how it's going. The holiday will be a great opportunity to push myself and really go for it over a sustained period of time. Plus I really like coming to the sessions here. They're a good crowd.'

Debbie's not sure if she'd agree with him there but is

willing to reserve judgement – for the moment. 'It's nice we can do something together too, isn't it?'

'Yes, it is. I wasn't too sure how you were faring, but you seem to have really taken to it.'

Claire is in the car park when her phone pings with a message. Expecting it to be from Alison, she waits until she's in her car before checking it. She is surprised to see it is from the man she met for drinks the night before. It turned out to be another disastrous mismatch, certainly from her point of view, but he wants to meet again. Oh God. Really? Was he on the same date as me? She groans inwardly; she'd only been able to get through it by drinking more wine than she should have. How desperate must he be if he's willing to put himself through that torture again? She quickly sends a 'Thanks, but no thanks. I just don't think the chemistry was there' message, and promptly forgets about him. She's pulling out of the car park when she sees Alan and Debbie leaving the centre. How did she land him? she asks herself for the umpteenth time. Why can't I be that lucky? The swim and the gentle flirting she'd done with Alan had put her in a good mood. Now, though, she plummets into gloom. She decides she'll crack open a bottle of wine at home to cheer herself up.

Later that evening, the promised wine is all but consumed. The rest of it beckons but she manages to stop herself; it's late and she still has a day of work to get through before the weekend. She's fed up and lonely.

She'd been hoping for a proper catch-up with Alison, but when she'd tried her earlier on, her call had gone straight to voicemail. She wonders if she's done something to upset her. Normally they were in regular touch, but for the past few weeks she's hardly heard from her. Casting the thought aside, she logs onto the Perfect Partners website and trawls through the profiles with the hope of finding a date to break up the weekend.

Chapter Eight

The fine weather breaks and the much-anticipated rain begins with a vengeance. It's a swim-club night and the swimmers are waiting to start their lesson. Outside it is pelting down and the windows surrounding the pool are streaked with water and clouded with steamed condensation. The nights are drawing in and it has started to get dark. Tonight there's a chill in the air. At the Aquarium there is none of the harsh glare normally associated with public swimming pools; instead, a luminosity which calms and makes use of the natural daylight available. When it darkens outside, spotlights within the pool and along the flooring are illuminated, offering discreet lighting. Despite the awful weather, or perhaps because of it, there is a feeling of welcoming comfort and shelter. A refuge from the storm. The swimmers nestle together, almost excitedly, as thunder reverberates around the building. Someone shrieks, childlike.

Debbie looks embarrassed and says, 'Sorry.' The others laugh good-naturedly. 'It took me by surprise, that's all,' she explains. 'I was miles away, thinking how nice the water looked.'

Nisha agrees. 'Yes, it's almost hypnotic in this light, isn't it?'

'Oh, flipping heck.'

Claire looks across to Alison. 'What's up?'

'I got soaked coming in from the car park and my hair's so wet I'm having trouble getting my cap on without ripping it out by the roots.'

'You should get your hair cut short like mine,' Claire suggests. 'It's so much more practical if you're a swimmer.'

Oliver waves from the other side of the pool. He's wearing a T-shirt and shorts, along with flip-flops. He must have been caught in the rain too as he is wet through. Shaking his hair like a dog, he offers them a toothy smile. 'Think I would have been less wet if I'd have jumped in the pool.' He proceeds to peel off his sodden top, much to the appreciation of the women and some of the men in the group.

There is a murmur of circumspect approval and someone jokingly says, 'Is there still space on that holiday? Maybe I will go after all,' to which there are muted giggles.

Far from being embarrassed Oliver just smiles. 'Always room for a small one,' he says, and everyone bursts out laughing. 'No, seriously, anyone interested in going, we have two more places available.'

Recognising the start of another sales pitch, people start fiddling with their caps and goggles, avoiding eye contact. Not one to be offended easily, Oliver dismisses the rejection and outlines what they will be doing in the training session that evening.

'Right, guys, today we'll be looking at making the most efficient use of your stroke. First, I want you to do six lengths of the pool and as you swim, count how many strokes you do per length. This is not about speed, so take it at a regular pace. This evening we've got the use of four lanes. I'll put you with people of more or less the same ability.'

'Who's Sophie talking to?' Claire enquires.

'It's Ben,' Alan says. 'Don't you recognise him without his clothes on?'

Debbie digs Alan in the ribs and shushes him. 'What?' he says, rubbing his side. 'Just a little joke.'

'It's okay, Debbie, it would take more than that to make me blush.' Claire thinks that Debbie's being a bit prudish. She winks at Alan.

Sophie and Ben come over and join them. Claire sizes Ben up with approval. Not overly muscular, but toned and pretty fit-looking, she notes to herself. Oliver might have competition.

Sophie is smiling and she looks relaxed with Ben by her side. 'Hi guys, you remember Ben? He's down on the South Coast for a few days, and I suggested it might be nice for him to join us for a session and we can see which of you he'd be best paired with. He hasn't done any open-water training so this will be a bit of a crash course for him. Ben, we'll give you a few of the basics today so you can go away and practise when you get back to London. Okay?'

'Sounds good to me. Looking forward to it.'

Ben smiles.

Oliver, who up to this point has been quiet, says, 'Let's get started with a gentle warm-up. Shall we say ten lengths? While you swim, try to put everything you've been learning the past few weeks into practice. Ben, if you join Claire and Alan in lane four.' He puts the rest of the group into twos and threes and assigns them a lane. Despite being told it's only a warm-up, swimmers dash off in a flurry of arms and legs. Ben is still adjusting his goggles as Claire and Alan swim away.

Sophie hisses at Oliver, 'What's the deal putting Ben with the two fastest swimmers in the group? Are you deliberately trying to show him up?'

Oliver replies, 'Of course I'm not. Claire and Alan's techniques are good and I thought it would be useful for Ben to observe them at close quarters, that's all.' He has a small smile on his face.

Sophie tuts and shakes her head. She looks over at Ben, who is only halfway through his first length. Meanwhile, Claire is drawing up close behind him doing her third. Alan is swimming on the other side of the lane, so Claire can't overtake and has to tread water behind Ben while she waits. As Alan passes, she zips around Ben towards the end of the lane, tumble turns and is halfway before he has even completed his first length. Once there, Ben clings onto the edge of the pool, panting. Alan is directly behind him.

'Do you want to go first?' Alan asks.

'No mate, you go,' puffs Ben, before meekly following him. Claire gains ground behind him and the pantomime is repeated once more. Oliver has a smug look on his face and comments, 'Oh dear, Ben is a bit out of his depth, isn't he? No pun intended.'

'That's not funny,' Sophie says. You've made him look a right wally.'

'If the shoe fits …'

Ignoring him, Sophie strides over to the end of the lane nearest to them. Ben is still making his way there. She thinks back to the barbecue where Claire had asked her if she was aware of how little swimming experience Ben had. At the time, she had brushed aside the comments, reasoning that he couldn't be all that bad. It is with a feeling of despair that she now observes him. In an attempt to move faster, he is rotating his arms around in the water with abandon and kicking his legs so hard it's difficult to see him for all the splash. She cringes and wonders when he last swam and if he's even had any formal swimming lessons. Finally, he gets to the end of the lane, gulping for air.

'Are you okay, Ben?'

Catching his breath, he replies, 'Just gotta get used to swimming in a fifty-metre pool. The lane feels really long.'

Sophie knows that the length of the pool is not the problem but lets it slide. 'You could do with some coaching on your technique. In the meantime, I think it would be best if we put you in another lane.'

'You're the boss,' Ben says.

'Why don't you join Debbie in lane one? Let's see how you get along there.'

Ben ducks under the lane dividers into lane one. Debbie is at the other end, which gives him plenty of space to take his time. Unfortunately, even with Debbie's much slower pace, he struggles to complete lengths and stay out of her way. The group finishes their ten laps while Ben is yet to complete half of that. Waiting for him, people are getting antsy.

'Oh my God, he's crap,' whispers Claire to Alison.

Even Alison, normally so forgiving, agrees. 'He really is. How embarrassing for him. How on earth is he going to cope with the holiday?'

'Quite. I tell you what, it's going to put a real dampener on things if we're all waiting around for him like this.'

Looking on, Sophie says to Oliver, 'You go on with the next task. I'll get Ben in a lane on his own and try and work on some of the basics with him. I don't think he'll last the whole hour if he tries to carry on like this.'

Crouching down near Ben in the water, Sophie smiles. 'Are you finding this a bit tough?'

Good-naturedly he says, 'Is it that obvious? I thought my drowning-man stroke would impress you.'

Sophie giggles. Ben's self-deprecating humour has always been one of the things she liked about him. 'Well, you're certainly putting a lot of enthusiasm into it. You've just got to learn how to channel it so you can swim longer without exhausting yourself. It's all about technique. You've been swimming for twenty minutes instead of doing the whole hour. Why don't you just do another twenty and we'll call it a day?'

'If you think that's a good idea.'

'First off, let's think about your stroke. You've got to forget about using your legs.'

'Really? I thought it was all about using them to push forward.'

'No, in open water swimming you kick very little; it's your arms that do most of the work, although not in the way you are doing. I'm going to give you a pull buoy – that should help your body stay level in the water. In the sea, you're naturally more buoyant, so it's not as big an issue there.'

She hands him a pull buoy and they work on Ben's stroke. He's an attentive student and does what she says. 'Okay, you've done really well. I can already see an improvement. If you want, I'll meet you in the cafeteria afterwards and we can go over a training programme for you.'

'That would be great. Any chance I could have a couple of private lessons with you over the weekend while I'm down here?'

'I don't see why not …'

Cosied up together in the cafeteria, Sophie outlines a training programme for Ben to do once he gets back to London.

'This is really good of you, giving up your free time to coach me.'

'It's a pleasure. What are friends for? Actually, it's

me who should be thanking you. You really saved our bacon by agreeing to come on the holiday, especially as swimming is not your thing.'

'Oh, I dunno, I think I could get into it. I'm really looking forward to swimming in the Med. When I went there on holiday, I loved going snorkelling, so I think swimming with a group should be fun.'

'Do you think you can finish the programme I've given you? It is rather a lot.'

'Yeah. I should be able to work it into my regular routine. The gym I go to has a nice pool, so instead of all the cardio stuff I usually do, I'll swim. Reckon I'll be able to go up to four times a week.'

'That would be good. It's a shame I didn't think of this before, rather than leaving it to the last minute. I mean, we only have just over two weeks to go. It's all a bit of a rush. I feel guilty for talking you into this.'

Ben reaches across and places his hand on top of Sophie's. 'Hey, I'm a big boy. I decided to go, despite my lack of swimming abilities. Whatever happens it will be great spending time with you again. Plus there's nothing too shabby about being on a boat in the Med. Remember, I am quite the sailor.'

'Of course. Do your parents still have their boat? We all used to have such fun going out together, the two families.'

'Yep, Dad got a mooring in Chichester Harbour, so now they don't have to travel far when they want to use it.'

'Fantastic. I bet he spends all his time down there,

now he's retired.'

'Yes, Mum never sees him. Why don't you come down on Sunday, after our lesson, and we can go out in the boat for a few hours in the afternoon? They'd love to see you.'

Sophie considers the idea. 'I haven't seen Mum and Dad for ages. They've been nagging me to visit. Yes, please, that would be lovely.'

'Tell you what, invite your parents along. It'll be like old times.'

Reliving happy, carefree days of her childhood sounds appealing, Sophie can think of nothing she'd rather be doing at the weekend. 'That's a great idea. Yes, I'll call them and arrange it now.'

'Do you want to run it by Oliver first?'

Shaking her head, she says, 'I don't need permission from Oliver. I'm my own woman.'

Chapter Nine

'Ladies and gentlemen, the captain has switched off the seatbelt sign and you are free to move about the cabin. However, we recommend for your safety that you keep your seatbelt fastened while seated.'

Claire gets the onboard menu out of the seat pocket in front of her and peruses it. 'Oh, they do little bottles of cava, I might treat myself.'

'On top of the two glasses of wine you had at the airport?' Alison says. 'Go easy there. Remember, we've got a four-hour bus journey once we arrive in Murcia. You'll be legless by the time we get to the villa.'

'Yeah, perhaps you're right. Fizzy water it is then, best to keep hydrated anyway on a flight.' She turns the card over. 'Think I'll have a Danish pastry to go with my sandwich. What about you?'

'Just a sandwich for me. You sure you want another cake? You had a doughnut at the airport.'

'What, are you my mother now?' Claire snaps. 'I'm on holiday and I reckon the way the past few weeks have been at work I deserve to treat myself. And don't even get me started about all that I've had to do to get Dad's house ready. Plus, we're going to be swimming loads. I'll burn off the calories.' She certainly hopes so; already the top button of her jeans is undone. She hadn't worn them all summer and got a nasty shock when she put them on that morning to wear for the journey. Realising she's been a bit short with Alison, she says, 'I'm just relieved to be away from it all, if only for a week.' She thinks how nice it would be to never have to go back, to run away forever, but that's hardly an option.

'You're right, you deserve to let your hair down for a bit.'

'Do you know, it occurred to me the other day that I haven't been abroad for four years. And what a crap four years they've been. In fact, it feels like forever since I was really happy.'

'It'll get better. Time helps.' Alison gives Claire's arm a little squeeze.

'God. Listen to me wallowing in self-pity when you've had to deal with losing Gavin. I don't know how you've done it. Coping with Dad being gone is bad enough.'

'Somehow you manage. What's the alternative? I still don't know how I got through those first couple of years. I suppose I had to keep going for the boys … I don't think I could have survived without them. And work helped.'

'Yeah, work. About the only constant in my life, and that's gone to pot recently.'

'It'll only be a glitch, you'll see.'

'I certainly hope so. I can't go on like this,' she murmurs.

'What was that?'

'Nothing,' Claire says, turning to look out of the window as tears smart her eyes.

The others have settled in at Villa Hermosa and the six of them are sitting at a large round table. In its centre is an enormous paella dish with half the contents eaten.

'Ben, you outdid yourself. That was great,' Sophie says, smiling across at him. 'When did you learn to cook?'

'I started at uni. I was determined not to be one of those students living off junk food. Plus I didn't have the money to buy pre-made stuff, so I used to cook up batches of food and freeze it to eat during the week.'

'Very sensible,' Oliver sneers.

'I lived on pasta and tomato sauce for three years,' Alan says, laughing.

'So, Ben, where do you live in London?' Nisha asks.

'Barking, East London.'

'Is it expensive to rent there?'

Sophie interrupts. 'Ben is buying his flat, lucky devil.'

'How can you afford to do that?' asks a surprised Alan. 'Did you get help from your parents?'

Shaking his head, Ben responds. 'No. I had some savings and my gran left me money. I work for a bank so I was able to get a good mortgage deal.'

'Good for you,' Debbie says. 'What's your place like?'

'Small!' Ben chuckles. 'But it's a step on the property ladder, and Barking has good transport links for getting into the City.'

With a touch of pride, Sophie adds, 'Ben is on the graduate management programme at his bank, he's really clever. He'll have a big house in no time. Think I chose the wrong career. At the rate I'm going, I'll be renting forever.'

'You're only twenty-five, Sophie. Plenty of time to change things if you want to,' Ben says.

'Do you really think so?'

'Sure, you can do anything you set your mind to. You have a great skill set. Don't let yourself get held back from doing what you want to do.'

Oliver pushes his chair abruptly away from the table. 'Think I'll go into town and see Josh, talk about the schedule for tomorrow's orientation. You'll be all right clearing up, won't you, Ben?'

Alison looks up at the bus departure board and curses. 'Oh no! We missed the bus to Almería by five minutes, and the next one isn't until seven thirty. By the time we get to San José, it will be gone midnight. I hope there will still be taxis at that hour.'

'Oh great,' Claire says, looking up at the board. 'An hour and a half waiting around and bus stations are always such pleasant places to be.' She eyes a vagrant lounging on a bench, his worldly possessions packed into a shopping trolley next to him. 'Let's get our tickets, then put our cases in the left luggage. We'll find a bar to spend the time in. I'm a bit peckish too.'

'Might as well. Give me your case and I'll see to the

luggage. You get the tickets,' Alison says.

It turns out there aren't any nice bars close to the bus station so they resort to going to a hotel opposite. They install themselves in the lounge area and order a couple of glasses of wine and some tapas. Stuffing a piece of bread and tortilla into her mouth, Claire says, 'This isn't so bad, is it? I'm starting to chill now, finally here. How about you?'

'Oh, a bit fed up about missing the bus, but it's hardly the end of the world, is it? Just as well we don't have a full-on swim tomorrow though. What time did Sophie say the orientation was?'

'Ten o'clock. It shouldn't take long. They'll go over safety and the hand signs we need to use in the water, then they'll tell us who we'll be pairing up with. I imagine they've already got that sorted. They've seen us swim plenty so they're well aware of our abilities.' She giggles. 'I wonder who Ben will be swimming with?'

'Oh gosh, don't. I just hope it isn't me.'

'Look at it this way. If you're paired with Ben, you'll get an awful lot of swimming done.'

'How so?' Alison looks at her quizzically.

'Well, you'll get so far ahead of him, you'll have to keep swimming back to him. You'll swim twice as much!'

'Easy for you to say. You're bound to get paired up with Alan.'

'Oh, I do hope so,' Claire says. She sees Alison's expression change.

'About Alan,' Alison says, 'I can't help but notice how you've been acting around him.'

'What do you mean?'

'You're really flirty with him. It's obvious you find him attractive.'

'No law against that, is there? We have a laugh together, that's all. It's just banter. It's harmless.' She feels embarrassed that Alison has noticed. Has she been that obvious?

'Is it? How do you think Debbie feels when you're all over her husband?'

'Oh, for crying out loud! I'm not "all over" Alan, as you put it.' She knows she's being defensive. 'Has anyone else said something? Has Debbie been complaining to you?'

'No, not exactly.'

'There you go then. If I was married and I felt another woman was being out of line with my husband, I'd say something, trust me.'

'Well, that's you. Debbie's …'

'A wimp?' Claire suggests.

'No. That's not what I mean. She's just not as confident as you; plus she's got a lot on her mind. Look, I shouldn't say anything, but she told me last week that she's started having hormone injections. She and Alan are going for IVF. They're trying for a baby. So why not be a bit more thoughtful, hey? It can't be easy for her.'

Claire feels bad about her comments. 'Oh, I see. I didn't know. Alan did tell me they wanted kids.' Looking up at Alison and blinking rapidly, she says, 'I guess I'm envious. Not about having a baby, God no. Just having a partner, someone to come home to.'

Alison touches Claire's arm. 'Of course I know. Don't you think I wish I still had Gavin with me? That I don't feel crushingly lonely, despite having the boys about?'

Claire sniffs. 'And Muffin the cat. Don't forget about her. I'm sorry. It's just, the last few years, well … you know I'm not a bad person. I would never try and steal someone's husband. It's just we get on so well, and you've got to admit, he is pretty fit.'

'Granted. But back off, right?'

Claire's phone pings with a message. 'Er, Alison.'

'Yeah?'

'Don't get pissed off, but I messaged Alan earlier on and asked if he would pick us up from the bus station in San José. He's just replied and says fine, no problem.'

Chapter Ten

The group are seated on the lush patio of Villa Hermosa. There is a sprawling fig tree and the scent of honeysuckle is carried to them by a gentle breeze. During lulls in conversation, all that can be heard is the sound of bees, busy at work. It is the first morning and the remains of breakfast are scattered on the table in front of them.

'You can't swim on empty,' Oliver explains to Alison when she tells him she doesn't usually eat anything before her morning swim. 'I know that today we are just doing orientation and won't be swimming much. Even so, eating breakfast is a habit I want you all to get into, even if it's not what you do at home.'

'You'll have no complaints from me about having to eat more, Oliver!' Claire laughs. 'So, what's on the agenda for today then?'

'We'll go to San José beach and from there we'll do a kilometre or so swim. We're going to put you into pairs and see how you get on. We've also got a GoPro camera to record your swimming, and this afternoon we'll have a look at the videos to assess your stroke and your leg kick. If there's a problem with technique, it's better if we can address it at the start of the week, then you can work on improving it. At the end of the holiday, if you want, we can record you again to gauge if you've made progress.'

There's all-round approval that they will be filmed swimming; all, that is, apart from Debbie, who looks appalled at the idea.

'Let's get going, shall we?' Sophie says. 'Before we leave make sure you apply plenty of sunscreen, especially to your back. Get someone to slap on loads of it for you. The last thing you need is to get sunburnt on your first day. We'll see you outside in fifteen minutes. Okay?'

On the walk into town they chatter, excited at the prospect of getting into the water. It is warm even though it is early in the morning and by the time they arrive they are all feeling hot.

At the beach, they gather around Oliver, who goes over the hand gestures and signals they need to use in the water. They have been practising them on their sea swims during the summer, but it is welcomed by Ben, who hasn't actually been on a group swim.

'I feel a bit nervous,' he confesses to Nisha.

'Don't be, we're all in it together. You just stick close and follow what everyone else is doing.'

'Easier said than done,' Ben says. 'I've been putting a lot of work into my swimming, but there's no way I'm going to be able to keep up with you lot.'

Oliver is speaking. 'Luckily we've been able to acquire

the use of a Zodiac, which I'll drive, and that gives us an added layer of safety in that I can get to any one of you quickly should you need me. Plus we'll have a lot more flexibility about where we lunch as we'll be able to get to beaches not accessible to bigger boats.'

'I didn't realise there was going to be another boat,' Alan says.

Sophie speaks now. 'Yes, bit of a last-minute addition. My brother, Josh, who'll be piloting the main boat, was able to borrow one from a contact he made in the summer. Owed him a favour for some work he did.'

There's a murmur of approval with regard to the addition of the Zodiac. Ben, in particular, looks pleased. 'Hey, Oliver, any time you want to trade the boat for the water, let me know. When I lived in Chichester, I used to take one out a lot with my mates during the summer. Great fun.'

'Yeah, maybe. We'll see, eh?'

Sophie is standing beside Oliver and whispers, 'That may not be a bad idea, you know, if Ben isn't able to keep up with all the swimming. Surely you'd like to get into the water for a couple of the sessions? I mean, look at it.' She casts her eyes toward the clear blue water. 'I know where I'd rather be.'

'I said maybe, didn't I? Let's see how things pan out, shall we?'

Not pushing it, Sophie moves on and looks at notes she has brought with her. 'Now, I know you will want to find out who your swimming buddy is going to be. This is what Oliver and I came up with, based on what we've seen you are capable of. As there is such a small number of you, we weren't able to match you exactly in terms of ability. If need be, we can change things around during the week. Okay, so Alan, you're paired with Claire.'

'Yes!' shouts Claire.

Ignoring her, Sophie continues. 'Alison and Nisha, Debbie and Ben. Now, Debbie, I know Ben won't mind me saying this, but he has voiced a few concerns about his swimming. If you get too far ahead of Ben, you'll be asked to wait or you can swim back to him. You can take things at your own pace, it's up to you. I hope that's okay?'

'Fine, not a problem at all.' Debbie says. 'I intend to swim very slowly anyway; my stamina is not as good as the others. Don't you worry about holding me back, Ben.' She touches Ben's arm and smiles. He smiles back and mouths, 'Thank you.'

Sophie has taken a GoPro camera out of her bag. 'Before we go for our swim, we're going to do some filming. I want you to swim out to the buoy, one at a time. Don't race, just a nice steady pace. I will place myself halfway between the beach and the buoy, and film you coming toward and away from me. Any questions?'

There are none, so Sophie gets into the water. She turns back to the group, beaming. 'The water is fantastic!' Then she swims further out. 'Alan, you first.'

Alan, looking serious, gets in and swims to the buoy. One by one they file in and swim to and from the buoy while Sophie films them. When they finish they congregate by the shoreline. As Sophie swims back, Oliver produces three deflated tow floats. 'There's one float per pair and each one can hold two bottles. The blue will have water, the grey, an isotonic drink. Usually, we would throw the bottles out from the boat, but as we are solo today you are carrying your own. There's more than enough to last a short swim like this. However, I do need to stress that it is important to keep hydrated. Just because you are in the water does not mean you are not sweating or losing minerals.'

The floats are handed out and inflated, then secured around the swimmers' waists. Sophie, now back on the beach putting the camera away, says, 'Looks like we're ready to go. Oliver is going to lead out and I will be at the back of the group. Try to keep together as much as possible. If you hear a whistle from me, it will be to let Oliver know he is to stop so we can all regroup. Today he will be sighting. All you have to do is keep the person in front or beside you in your line of vision.'

Claire is eager to swim. 'Come on, I'm dying to get in the water.' She nudges Alan. 'What are you waiting for?' She indicates with her head that Oliver is already in the sea, so the two set off, followed by the rest of the group.

Treading water, Oliver lets Claire and Alan catch up to him. He asks them if they are okay non-verbally by placing his hand on top of his head and forming an O. They respond in kind. He swims at an even pace, effortlessly gliding forward with each stroke. The water is so flat he barely has to turn his head to breathe. Claire catches up to him and swims at his side, while Alan follows in their slipstream. Behind them are Alison and

Nisha, who initially start swimming at the same speed. However, as Nisha's technique is not as accomplished, Alison is soon swimming directly behind Alan. At the back of the group is Sophie. In an attempt not to outswim Ben and Debbie, she is swimming sidestroke. They swim for fifteen minutes and Sophie can barely make out Alison's orange tow float. All three are falling too far behind so she stops and blows her whistle. On hearing it, Oliver stops.

'Why have we stopped?' Claire asks, beside him.

'Sophie blew her whistle. The group is spacing out too far.'

'I didn't hear her. I was in the zone. Great conditions, aren't they?'

'They sure are. I think I'll be taking up Ben's offer of driving the Zodiac. This is too good to pass up. Alan, mate, how's it going?' he says as Alan swims up to them.

'Perfect! This is gorgeous. All the marine life. I even saw a starfish. Worthing it ain't.' Reaching for the attached tow float he grabs a bottle and waves it. 'Do you want some water, Claire?'

'Please.'

Next to reach them is Alison. She lifts her goggles away from her eyes. 'Do you mind if I have a drink? Nisha has ours.'

'Sure. Catch.' Claire lobs over a bottle. Alison is handing it back as Nisha arrives. The four of them float or tread water while they wait for the others, enjoying the warm sunshine and the sensation of the sea gently lifting them up and down.

After about ten minutes Oliver says, 'Well, they're certainly taking their time.' He stretches his neck out of the water to get a better view of the swimmers in the second group. 'I don't think they are moving. Let's get back to them. We're about halfway through anyway.'

Rejoining Sophie and the others, Oliver asks, 'Everything okay?'

'My fault, I'm afraid. Sorry,' Ben says. 'I thought I'd be quicker than this. Swimming in the sea feels a lot different to the pool, but I'm sure I'll get the hang of it in no time.'

Alan has swum up to Debbie. 'Are you all right, Debs?'

'Sure, all fine.' In a quiet voice she says to him, 'Didn't think anyone could swim slower than me. Ben is all over the place.'

Chapter Eleven

It's the next day and the swimmers are congregated in the hallway of the villa. They are in the midst of sunscreen application and backs are being smothered with gloop in those hard-to-reach places.

Sophie and Oliver appear. They are loaded down with floats, drinks and food supplies for the day. Sophie looks on approvingly as the last of them finishes putting on sunscreen. 'Good job, everyone, doing that before we head out. No use putting on a load of cream then jumping straight into the water. I hope no one has gone below factor 50?'

Claire has but reasons that as she is naturally olive-skinned and has a tan, she can get away with less. She'll make sure she reapplies, maybe get Alan to do her back?

'As you can see, we've got quite a lot of stuff to take down to the boat so we'd be grateful if you could all help,' Oliver requests.

Everyone takes something from either him or Sophie. Leaving the villa, they chat and joke as they walk to the marina. The sky is blue and cloudless. A waft of salty air hits them as they make their way down the windy, narrow street into town. The arid, desert landscape of Cabo de Gata means there is less of the bougainvillaea than would normally be associated with Spain. However, the surrounding land, with its ochre hues interspersed with the greens of impressive cacti, and wild, vast beaches, offers spectacular scenery. Not to mention the draw of the translucent sea.

Debbie takes Alan's hand. 'Isn't it lovely? Hard to believe that just a couple of hours away on a plane this is all here. Talk about a world of difference.'

'Yes, to think we had to wear coats to the airport. I reckon we should consider coming to Spain in October again. It would make the oncoming winter in Britain seem less depressing.'

'I'd be up for that. What a nice treat to look forward to every year.' Debbie smiles and gives his hand a squeeze. 'You never know, this time next year we might have a little baby to take away with us.'

Alan leans down and kisses Debbie gently on the lips. Behind them, Claire is watching. As they kiss, she abruptly looks away and says to Alison, 'I'm so looking forward to doing a proper swim today. It's going to be great.' She all but pushes past Debbie and Alan.

The group approaches the marina. Debbie says, 'I wonder which boat is ours?'

Nisha points. 'I'd say that one.'

Looking over they spy a very tall man in his late twenties. He has sun-bleached blond hair and a strong jaw, and aside from being very brown, he looks exactly like his sister. Sophie waves, and he waves back and steps off the boat.

Claire comments, 'I wasn't expecting it to look like that. It's a bit small. Do you think we'll all fit in it?'

Hearing her, Sophie's brother grins. 'Don't you worry. She's deceptive, like the Tardis, bigger on the inside. I'm Josh, your captain.' He flashes a smile and his white teeth contrast sharply with his bronzed face. Claire is instantly won over and smiles back.

Josh turns to the rest of them. 'This is the *Alba*. She's just under twelve metres long, so not that small. Come aboard and I'll give you the guided tour.' He nimbly gets back onto the boat and the group files on. Alison wobbles a little as she places her foot on the deck, and Josh catches her hand to steady her.

'What's your name?' he asks, still holding her hand.

'Alison,' she stammers, pulling away as soon as she can.

Claire has no such shyness, grabbing Josh's hand as soon as it's proffered. 'Hi there, I'm Claire and this is Nisha.' She indicates behind her.

'Welcome, welcome,' Josh says, helping both of them.

Oliver is the last aboard. He and Josh bump fists then hug, clapping each other on the back.

'Good to see you, mate.'

'You too,' Oliver says as he places a large cool box on the deck. 'If you could take this, I'm going to get into the Zodiac. As we said, I'll be trailing behind you and the swimmers, keeping an eye on things. I'll whizz up to you from time to time to check in. Okay?'

'Fine with me, mate. We'll have a beer later, catch up.'

'Great! See you then.'

Ben and Alan are helping with bags and boxes. Alan looks at the exchange between Oliver and Josh. 'Those two are very pally, aren't they? I notice Josh didn't bother asking us our names. I went to introduce myself and he ignored me.'

'Yeah, bit of a ladies' man is Josh.' Ben leans forward, 'Bit of a wanker too, but don't tell Sophie I said that; she worships him. I had to put up with him when we were kids, always lording it over me cos I was younger. He's so different to Sophie, she's just lovely.' He looks over at her.

'Going a bit misty-eyed there, Ben,' Alan says, raising his eyebrows. 'Got a bit of a crush, have you?'

'That obvious?'

'Don't worry, your secret is safe with me. Mind you, you've got competition with Oliver.'

'Maybe, but Sophie's not as smitten with him as he thinks she is.'

Alan, now curious, says, 'Oh yeah, has she said anything to you?'

'Not exactly, but a couple of weeks ago we spent a Saturday together. We went sailing with our parents and had a great time. Our families used to see each other a lot. Sophie and I have always got on well, but back then I was definitely confined to the "friend zone", if you know what I mean. But her parents have always really liked me. I get the feeling they don't overly approve of

Oliver. Anyway, from things she said, I reckon she's fed up with the fact that as a couple they are still living like students, in a shared house. She wants more than that, but Oliver is happy with the status quo, and I think it's driving a wedge between them. She needs a partner with more maturity – she pretty much said so.'

'And that person is you, right?'

'Could be. I'll be waiting in the wings when things go pear-shaped between her and Oliver. I'm biding my time.'

As the boat makes its way out of the harbour, Sophie leaves her brother and goes down into the saloon, to the small table surrounded by cushioned seats. She calls to the others, who are all out on deck. 'If you could come inside for a few minutes, please. I want to go over the swim we'll be doing today.' She unfolds a chart of the coastline. The others come in and they pore over it as their swim route is outlined. 'So, heading out from the harbour, we're going to sail to Punta de Cala Higuera, here.' Sophie indicates the route on the chart. 'Hugging the coastline, we'll swim back to the marina and then cross the harbour. It shouldn't be too busy with boat traffic now it's low season. Nonetheless, everyone will need to be very aware of their surroundings and sight frequently. Above all you will need to listen to our instructions and follow them. Once we've crossed the harbour, we'll be aiming for Castillo de San José. Thought we'd give you something nice and big to sight'

– she smiles – 'then we'll have lunch on the boat and a couple of hours to chill before the second swim of the day.'

Peering at the chart, Ben asks, 'How long is this swim?'

'The first part is two and a half kilometres,' Sophie says.

'And the second part?' Ben looks a little concerned.

'That's to Morrón de los Genoveses. It's only a kilometre and a half.'

'So, a total of four kilometres then?' Claire says. 'Hmm, that's a nice number for the first day. I like the way you've broken it down into two parts.'

'Yes, there's no need to wear yourselves out on the first day. And if you want to ease gently into things, you don't need to do the afternoon swim.'

Sophie is conscious of the discussion she had with Oliver about Ben after the orientation swim. Both of them are aware that the amount of swimming involved on the holiday is wholly unsuitable for a novice like him, and they don't want to disrupt the others' enjoyment with the need to constantly slow down. As a contingency, they have agreed that it would be best to gently discourage Ben from swimming in the afternoons and get him to drive the Zodiac as he'd suggested before.

Fortunately, it looks as if Ben is already thinking along these lines. 'I reckon I'll definitely be taking that option, Sophie,' he says. 'It'll be more than enough for me. Nothing wrong with relaxing onboard and watching the world go by.'

'I might join you,' Debbie says. 'After all, it's not a competition, is it? I'll have to see how I get along.'

'Not me. If anything, I'd like to swim more,' Claire says. 'What about you, Alison?'

'Well, I don't know about that, but certainly I'll be doing both swims.'

Sophie adds, 'One last thing before I let you go out on deck and enjoy the ride: while swimming we would like you to keep as close to each other as possible. From yesterday's orientation swim it's obvious that we have mixed abilities within the group. So, in order to mitigate this a little, we're going to ask the fastest swimmers to wait and give the slower ones a head start at the beginning of the swim. Is that okay with everyone?'

Everyone agrees that it is a sensible idea. Sophie continues. 'I'll come out shortly before we get to our jump-off point so you can get ready.' She leaves and sits with Josh at the wheel.

The rest of them go back out on deck. It's hot but as the boat moves forward, a pleasant breeze is created. Claire sits next to Ben. He raises his head to the sky, closes his eyes and says, 'Ah, wonderful! When I'm onboard a boat it always makes me question whether I want to spend the rest of my working life in a bank. Maybe I should just become a diving instructor like Josh and live this kind of life.'

'Oh, is he PADI qualified?' Alan asks, interested.

'Yes, been doing it for a few years now, according

to what my parents say.' Then, speaking for Alan's ears only, he adds, 'About the only qualification he has got. Dropped out of A levels, even though he was brilliant and earmarked for Oxbridge. Broke his parents' hearts. They had high hopes for him, but he's been bumming around doing a bit of this and that for years. Diving is the only thing he has stuck at.'

'What are you two gossiping about?' Claire says, shading her eyes with her hand.

'Oh, nothing,' Ben says.

Ten minutes into the journey, Sophie reappears. She is wearing latex gloves and is holding a large plastic tub. 'We're nearly there so time to put on your caps and get out your goggles. If you haven't already done so, you need to inflate your tow floats, then I'll hand out the drinks. Now you may be wondering what this is.' She holds up the tub.

'Looks like petroleum jelly,' Nisha says.

'Correct. Before you get into the water, I'll grease you up with it on some of the spots where your costume meets your skin. Seawater is very abrasive and with the action of swimming, the friction created can cause some nasty chafing. Putting on petroleum jelly can help to eliminate this. You may also find the back of your cap rubs against your neck. Sometimes men also complain that the stubble on their face scrapes against their arms as they raise them to swim.'

'Can't we just apply the stuff ourselves?' Nisha asks.

Claire says, 'Oh no, the last thing you want to do is transfer petroleum jelly from your fingers to your goggles. I did it one time on a ten-kilometre swim and spent the whole time looking through greasy smear marks on the lenses. It was quite disorientating trying to sight.'

The boat stops and they hear the splash of the anchor being dropped. Josh joins them at the stern, where there is a platform. He is carrying a small ladder which he attaches to it. The swimmers put their goggles in place and Sophie says, 'You can either use the ladder to get into the water or just jump from the platform.'

Standing on the platform, Claire looks into the transparent water. She can see a shoal of small, brightly coloured fish darting away from her shadow. The anticipation of the swim makes her feel extraordinarily happy, then she remembers the significance of this week and her stomach lurches. She grips the handrail of the platform. Shaking, she exhales and takes the plunge.

Chapter Twelve

Claire and Alan are behind Sophie in the water. She has asked them to swim parallel with each other and keep the flexible torpedo buoy, which is attached to her waist via webbing, in their line of vision. She is sighting for them. Claire has a tow float, which Nisha and Alison are using to sight. Every so often Claire stops and checks those behind. At the start of the swim they are able to keep relatively close to one another, but despite the substantial lead Ben and Debbie were given, those faster quickly overtake them.

Further back are Debbie and Ben, with Oliver keeping watch over them. Debbie is being very understanding, her patience is commendable. She often stops to wait for Ben, who is making painfully slow progress. Oliver picks up the radio.

'Hi, Josh, can you stop for a few minutes? We're going to have a hydration break here. Over.'

Josh, ahead of Sophie's group, replies, 'Roger that. I'll let Sophie know. Over.'

Drawing even with Debbie and Ben, Oliver signals them to stop. 'How are we doing, guys?'

'Good,' Ben says, pulling back his goggles onto the top of his head. 'The buoyancy of the sea certainly helps, although it's a bit tough not having the end of the pool to hang onto for a break once you've finished a lap. I'm trying to do everything I learned in the classes, but it's difficult to remember it all.'

'Actually, your stroke is a lot better than the last time I saw you swim,' Oliver says.

Debbie swivels the tow float toward her and says to Ben, 'Water or isotonic?'

'Water, please.'

'Oh, this is just so great, isn't it? I feel as if I could swim for ages. It's so much more interesting than just swimming up and down in a pool. All that work is paying off.' Debbie drinks, then pops her bottle back onto the tow float.

Oliver smiles. 'Okay, before we do the crossing at the harbour, just a few things to remember. We're going as one group. The others are waiting for us now and will have been told to slow down their pace so we can do it together. I want us all to stay as close to one another as possible. Josh will be keeping a lookout for boats, and of course I will be behind you doing the same as well as keeping an eye on all of you. I have to keep a safe distance, so it's important that you sight frequently – every fourth stroke or so. Don't stick your head out of the water when you do so, otherwise it will slow you down. As you breathe bilaterally, be aware of who or what is either side of you. Any questions? No? Okay, let's get going.'

All the swimmers come together. Oliver moves forward to Sophie. 'Everything okay with all of you?'

Sophie signals the affirmative, then turns to the swimmers. 'Right then, let's do this crossing. As I said, all you have to do is to follow me, but it wouldn't be a bad idea to practise sighting. You should keep the castle dead ahead of you in your line of vision. Now, we won't be stopping for hydration for this part of the swim, but if you get into any difficulties and need to stop, let Oliver know, using the appropriate hand signal.'

They move forward as one. The sea is as still as glass and there is no current to speak of. The conditions are great for swimming. Normally eager to plough ahead, Claire contents herself with looking at the sea beneath her. It is deep but so clear she can see all the way down to the bottom. She loves the sensation of this and the sense of freedom it gives her. She becomes engrossed in observing the sea life, as entranced as the children peering at the fish in the huge tank at the Aquarium. Without warning, she bumps into something. Looking up, she realises it is Sophie, who has stopped.

'Oops. Sorry, Sophie. I got distracted by the sea and the fish.'

'I'll let you off for today.' Sophie laughs. 'Actually, I'm finding it hard to focus on sighting myself. It's all so beautiful – very distracting.'

'Good job you're here paying attention, Sophie. It's been hard remembering to sight. It's very absorbing. I feel like I've gone into a kind of trance,' Alan admits.

'We're just waiting for the others. We'll need to slow

down a bit more if we want to keep together,' Sophie says, spotting Oliver zipping toward them in the Zodiac.

He pulls up beside them. 'I think Ben is finding it quite hard to keep up. If he gets too far behind again, I'll ask him to get into the boat with me. I don't want us to spread out too far apart while we cross the harbour entrance. I can see a couple of boats heading out from the marina and I'm keeping an eye out for them. Josh says they're not coming in our direction, but I want to be cautious.'

As the others reach them, Sophie says, 'No stopping, I'm afraid. We need to get this stretch done, then we can have a little break.'

Ben puts in a huge effort, thus allowing them to complete this section of the swim without the need for him to stop again. I bet he's glad to be finished, thinks Claire as Sophie calls a halt and Ben swims to the main boat. This can't have been easy for him.

'Well done,' Sophie says. 'You swam as a team and followed instructions. And you've got the first two and a half kilometres under your belt. Now it's time for lunch and a break.'

As Ben swims to the rear of the boat, Claire is standing on the platform, her hand outstretched. He reaches for it.

'How are you feeling?' Claire says.

'I have never been so glad to get out of the water! Keeping up with all of you has been really difficult. That's it for me today as far as swimming goes.'

'Hey. You made it though, didn't you? Well done!'

Back at Villa Hermosa later that evening, Claire is scooping up the remains of dessert with relish, layers of puff pastry filled with condensed milk. 'Oh my God, that was delicious! What did you say it was called again, Sophie?'

'*Milhojas*. Josh recommended it, so I bought one from the local bakery when I got the bread.'

'Bit too sweet for me,' Nisha says, pushing her plate away. 'I'm not a big one for desserts.' She yawns, louder than she intended. 'Sorry about that. Must be all the fresh air and exercise.'

'Don't fall asleep before the main event,' Sophie jokes. Mystified, Nisha frowns. 'You know, the video of your swimming. Oliver is in the living room setting it up now. Come on, everyone, grab your drinks and we'll go in.'

'I'd forgotten about that,' Claire says, topping up her wine and getting up from the table. They all go into the living room and make themselves comfortable. Oliver is by the television and a still of a man in the water is on the screen.

'Who's that?' Nisha says while flopping into an armchair.

'Alan: he's up first. Is everyone sitting comfortably?' Oliver presses play and people cheer good-naturedly as they watch Alan swim.

Alan looks a bit embarrassed and says with a smile, 'Hush now, you rabble, I want to watch and learn.'

They quieten and listen to Oliver. 'Now as you can see, Alan is a strong swimmer and he has a good position in the water, nice and level. But he uses his legs too much. Alan, the next time you swim, I want you to kick less. You just want to do enough to keep your body horizontal. Remember too, kicking uses eighty per cent of your energy, but only contributes twenty per cent in terms of propulsion.' Alan concentrates as he watches the rest of the clip. At the end of it, Oliver says, 'Next up is Claire. Well, Claire, I don't know what to say about this.'

Claire is alarmed. 'Why? What am I doing wrong?'

Shaking his head, Oliver continues. 'Nothing. Everyone, take note. Technique-wise this is about as perfect as it gets. Well done, Claire.'

Claire feels pleased and embarrassed at the same time. Oliver's comment has been worth the price of the holiday alone. To cover her pride she asks, 'Who's up next?'

'That would be Ben.' Oliver turns to the screen and Ben appears.

Ben is standing behind the sofa and gripping the top of it, an uncomfortable look on his face. On-screen the group is greeted by an image of whirling water. Ben's body cannot be seen.

'So, looking at this, what would you say is Ben's main issue?'

Alan says, 'I'd say he's trying too hard.'

'Exactly. It may sound strange, but in order to speed up, Ben needs to slow down,' Sophie says.

Claire can sense Ben squirming. He probably hates having to watch this in front of Sophie. Wanting to ease his disquiet she offers her advice. 'Yes, you've got all your arms and legs moving about far too much. There's no glide. You should forget about your legs, stop kicking them.'

'I have told him that,' Oliver says.

'To be fair, he has,' confesses Ben. 'It all goes out of my head once I'm in the water. I'll really try tomorrow.'

Nisha and Alison's clips are watched and assessed. Advice is given from Oliver and Sophie, and both swimmers agree to focus on different aspects of their stroke.

Oliver stands up. 'Okay, folks, that's it. I hope it's been helpful. The rest of the evening is yours to spend how you wish.'

'What about Debbie's clip?' Nisha asks.

Debbie has gone pink. 'I-I-I didn't get videoed. Sorry. I asked Sophie not to. I'm not that bothered about getting much better. Alan is the swimmer in our family.' She finishes her wine in one go and says, 'Think I'll head off, have an early night. Want to build up my energy levels for tomorrow. Alan, are you coming?'

Looking at his watch, he says, 'Nah, not just yet, love. Think I'll go and sit by the pool and finish my wine.'

'What a good idea. I'll join you,' Claire says. It would be nice to chill out on the patio. She's certainly not ready for bed.

Alison says, 'Sounds good. I'll just go and refresh my glass and see you out there. Sleep well, Debbie.'

Claire feels a bit cross that she isn't going to be with Alan alone, then chastises herself. She's here to spend time with her best friend. 'Might as well bring the bottle out with you,' she says to Alison.

Sophie has just finished clearing up in the kitchen, Oliver having made himself scarce. She notices Ben by a bookcase in the hallway. He has a book in his hand and is reading the back cover. 'Looking for something in particular, Ben?'

'Oh, hi Sophie. Not really, just something to keep me occupied if I don't swim in the afternoon. After today I don't know if I'll be able to manage both swims without drowning.'

'You're not that bad. I could see real improvement today,' Sophie says, touching his arm. She knows he is embarrassed by the group discussion of his swimming technique.

'That's nice of you to say, even if it's stretching the truth a little. You'll have to see me on the football pitch. That's where I can impress you.'

'I'm already impressed,' she says quietly, 'coming on the holiday like this. Plus all the help you offer. You're a really nice bloke.'

'Ah, but girls like a bad boy, don't they?' Ben looks Sophie in the eye. She doesn't break contact.

'Not this girl. Well, not any more.'

'There you are, Sophie! I've been looking for you all over the place.' Oliver appears from nowhere and Sophie wonders if he heard the exchange between her and Ben. 'Look, I'm off out for a beer with Josh. I won't be long.' Without waiting for a reply, he leaves via the front door, and judging by the force of it being slammed shut, Sophie guesses he had heard everything. She's surprised to discover she doesn't care.

Chapter Thirteen

'Come on, lazybones! Out of bed.' Alison is up and dressed in shorts and a T-shirt.

Claire picks up her phone and looks at the screen. 'God, Alison, it's only seven o'clock. Do we really need to be up so early?'

'Not necessarily, but I want to get a good breakfast inside me and give it a couple of hours before we swim.'

The mention of food prompts Claire to swing her legs out of bed. 'You're right. Mmm, I fancy eggs.'

Alison throws back her head and chortles. 'It's like being with my boys. Obsessed with food.'

'I just have a healthy appetite, that's all.' Claire smiles, flinging on the clothes she wore yesterday.

They are not the only ones up. Oliver and Sophie are in the kitchen getting breakfast together and Alan is at the table tucking into an enormous bowl of cereal. Debbie is nibbling at a slice of toast.

'Morning,' Alan says with his mouth full. 'Woke up ravenous and couldn't wait for the cooked breakfast. Sophie said to go through and let them know what you'd like. How did you sleep?'

As she heads to the kitchen, Claire replies, 'Like a baby. Best sleep I've had in weeks. It feels so good to leave the stress of work behind.' She can't remember the last time she's slept this well. Once back in the UK, she knows she'll have to think about addressing some issues, but not today.

'Me too. Think I'll have some of that cereal,' Alison says, reaching for a bowl from a nearby pile. 'How are you feeling after yesterday's swim, Debbie?'

'Pretty good. My shoulders are a bit stiff, but apart from that I'm fine. I'm glad we only have one swim today.'

'But you do know it's fairly long, don't you? I think Sophie said it's nearly four kilometres.' Alison sits next to Debbie.

'That far? I'll give it a go, but without a break in between I don't know if I'll be able to manage it.'

'I don't imagine Ben will be able to do the whole thing, so I wouldn't worry about having to ask to get back into the boat.'

'Oh, I'm not worried. I'm just glad I'm not the slowest swimmer here.'

By eight o'clock breakfast has finished, with Ben being the last one to eat. He is cheerful, unlike Oliver, who is nursing a mild hangover. His quick beer with Josh turned into a bit of a session and he had stumbled back to the villa at one a.m. Popping two painkillers from a blister pack and washing them down with some orange juice, he grumbles to Sophie, 'Why do I never learn that I can't keep up with Josh when it comes to drinking?'

'Um, I don't know, it's a mystery. Are you okay to drive the Zodiac?'

'Oh yeah, I'm not that bad. Bit of fresh air will do me good. In fact, I think I'll go for a quick swim before we head off, that'll do the trick. Will you be all right taking all the stuff with you?' He doesn't bother waiting for a reply.

The kitchen looks like a bomb has hit it and Sophie noisily starts stacking plates in the sink. She is fuming that Oliver has gone off, leaving her not only with the cleaning but also the transportation of all the equipment to the marina.

All onboard the boat, with Josh at the helm, Sophie goes over the day's swim. 'Bit different from yesterday. Instead of two swims, you're going to do just one, which will be four kilometres. We want you to get a sense of what that feels like because tomorrow you'll be doing a crossing of about the same length.' Ben and Debbie look a bit doubtful. 'However, unlike the crossing, where it's not as easy to stop because of the boat traffic, we can easily do so today as we'll be hugging the coastline. The added advantage is you don't have to sight as much, so you'll be able to take in and enjoy your surroundings. Usually around the rocks, there are lots of fish and it makes for a more interesting swim.' She points to a spot on the chart. 'We're going to swim from here, Los Escullos, to here, Punta del Negro. Instead of lunching on the boat, we'll go to the nearby beach, Playa del Peñon Blanco. We'll use the Zodiac to get there and back.'

Nisha glances up from the chart. 'That will be nice. I love swimming with all the little fish. It's like being in an aquarium – feels so exotic.'

'Doesn't it just?' Debbie agrees. 'I can hardly believe how much life there is in the sea. I mean, you expect it somewhere like the Maldives or Seychelles, but to think that Spain's waters have all this variety is amazing. So much nearer too.'

'And cheaper. We can certainly make this a regular holiday, love,' Alan says.

'I'm glad you're enjoying it. I knew you'd all like the swimming, but it's nice to know Oliver and I chose a destination that's going to be popular.' Sophie looks pleased as she takes the chart and starts to fold it.

'Do you intend to make this an annual event?' Nisha says.

'That's the plan. Our intention is to build on this and possibly do a few trips a year, maybe add another destination, but it's early days yet. Let's see how this one goes. Now, it'll take a while to get there, so just relax and enjoy the views. I'll let you know in advance when to get your caps and goggles on, and I'll be coming round with the petroleum jelly.'

People settle into seats and there is companionable silence as the swimmers look out to sea, each lost in their own thoughts. The only sounds are the rhythmic put-put of the boat and Sophie and Josh chatting. Oliver is at the wheel of the Zodiac, following them.

Claire shifts her body and faces Debbie and Alan. Debbie is resting her head on Alan's shoulder, a small smile on her face. She has her hand placed on his thigh and he is stroking her hand with his thumb. Claire sees the exchange and tears smart her eyes. She turns abruptly and looks out to sea, wondering how she can feel so wretchedly alone in circumstances as idyllic as this.

Sophie walks across the deck, latex gloves donned.

'Okay, everyone, it's time to grease up! Has anyone been having problems with chafing?'

Alan is smirking. Nisha notices and frowns slightly. 'Oh yes, under my arm, where the costume meets the skin. By the end of yesterday's swim it got really uncomfortable.'

'Um, it does look a bit red. I'll put extra petroleum jelly there.' Sophie dabs Nisha's armpit with her finger. Anyone else having a problem?'

Ben raises his hand. 'Yeah, my inner bicep, both arms.'

Sophie steps forward and takes a look. 'That'll be the stubble on your face rubbing against your arm as you raise it. You should shave before you swim, that will help.'

'But I did.'

'It's cos you're so manly, mate. All that testosterone,' quips Alan.

'Yeah, that'll be it,' Ben fires back, before turning his attention to Sophie, who has greased his arms and is now applying petroleum jelly to his face. She catches him looking at her as she does this and holds his gaze for a few seconds. She steps back. 'That should help.'

Josh appears once the boat comes to a halt. 'Lovely day for swimming. Take advantage of it. Tomorrow will be windy, so it might be a bit choppy.'

Sophie strips off her T-shirt and shorts to reveal the bathing suit underneath. She deftly puts on her cap and goggles and attaches the torpedo buoy to her waist. 'Last one in buys the ice creams!' She giggles in an uncustomary display of silliness before jumping into the water.

There are whoops of delight from the others, and like giddy children they launch themselves from the platform at the back of the boat. Josh, standing at the stern, laughs. 'Reckon the ice creams are on Nisha.' By his side, he has a stack of water bottles, which he throws out to those with tow floats.

Ben and Debbie swim off first with Sophie. Alison and Nisha go next, and after a good while Alan and Claire follow. Sophie leads them to the coast, which is bordered by a sheer face of rock, and they hug this for the duration of the swim. Josh has moved the boat some way ahead, the engine out of earshot. There are outcrops of rock, which they skirt around, and as promised, the group are treated to visual delights of dozens of fish moving hither and thither in a flourish of fish entertainment, as if showing off especially for the swimmers. The fish nibble at the rocks and then bolt as hands move toward them; the temptation to touch is irresistible.

Sophie stops, waiting for her swimmers, who have pulled away from Ben and Debbie, to draw level with her. They tread water while drinking from the bottles. 'How is everyone doing? We're about halfway now. Not finding it too difficult?'

Claire shakes her head. 'Not at all. I'm loving it. I think I could do this every day of my life.'

'Same here,' Alan agrees. 'Swimming in a pool is never going to be the same again. At least living in Brighton we can get to the sea.'

'Yeah, but it's going to be far too cold to swim, even with a wetsuit,' Nisha says. She shivers as if imagining it.

Oliver comes over to them in the Zodiac. 'Sophie, Ben is struggling a bit so he's asked to get in with me. I think Debbie would be fine keeping up with the rest of you, she's been holding back for Ben. Can you wait here for her and let her drink and have a break before going on?'

'Sure, no problem.'

Oliver gives her a thumbs up.

The party makes gentle progress for the rest of the swim, stopping frequently to rest and hydrate. The tempo is relaxed and there is no pressure to pick up the pace. As a group, there is mutual support and if one of them begins to lag behind, the others naturally slow down until they are one again.

The main boat can be seen in the near distance. Sophie, aware that Claire and Alan have slowed down considerably for the others, decides to give them the opportunity of swimming the last leg at their own pace. 'Claire and Alan, if you want to you can swim ahead, just the two of you. I'll stay with the others.'

Claire is thrilled. She has been dying to swim faster and has found holding back for the others rather frustrating. She looks at Alan. 'I'll race you there.'

'You're on!' Alan says, and the two of them speed away.

Alan has strength on his side and quickly pulls away, but Claire's superior technique means she soon draws level with him and the two of them are evenly matched. The race is a close-run thing; however, Alan pips Claire to the post. Panting and clinging to the platform of the boat, they both laugh, dizzy with the exhilaration of the swim.

'Ha ha! I won!' Alan heaves himself onto the platform without the use of the ladder, and holds his hand out to Claire.

'Don't get used to that feeling.' Claire takes his hand and gracefully exits the water. Still with her hand in his, she moves closer. 'I could take you any time.' She's aware she's flirting but the joy of the swim has emboldened her.

Looking down at her and relinquishing his hand, he says, 'Is that a challenge?'

'It most certainly is.'

'Well then, Claire, I accept,' he says, and springs onto the boat, leaving Claire fizzing with excitement – from the race or Alan's touch, she is not sure.

Chapter Fourteen

As Josh had predicted, the following day sees gloomy skies. Despite only being in Spain for a few days, the group has grown accustomed to waking up to brilliant sunshine, and they are disappointed to see the heavens reminiscent of England. The murky light dulls the excitement they have felt on previous mornings. Claire and Alison are already at the breakfast table when Nisha joins them.

'Oh dear, this is a bit depressing, isn't it?' she says.

Claire is in the middle of a stretch. 'Yeah and it's not helped by the fact we had to get up so early.'

'You can have a doze on the boat. Sophie said the journey is about an hour and a half,' Alison says, buttering some toast.

Sophie comes out of the kitchen with a platter piled high with scrambled eggs and bacon. 'More toast anyone?' Debbie and Alan appear. 'Good timing. Grab a plate and help yourselves.'

Claire looks at the loaded plate and considers whether she should eat some more. The amount of food being foisted on them certainly meets with her approval. It's great not feeling guilty for having a healthy appetite, although she admits to herself that she has been over-eating a bit too often these days.

'Would you like coffee or tea?' Sophie offers.

'Think I need a coffee to jump-start me today,' Alan says, looking a bit bleary-eyed.

'Coming right up. Anyone seen Ben? It's getting a bit late if he wants to have breakfast.'

'I saw him going into the bathroom as I came out of my bedroom,' Nisha says, 'so he's up and about. Oh, here he is.'

Unlike the rest of them, who are rather subdued, Ben bounds out onto the patio. 'Morning!' he hollers.

Claire looks up at him over her cup with narrowed eyes. 'Jeez, no coffee for Ben, he's already full of beans.' Though it is good to see a cheery face at the breakfast table.

Laughing, Ben sits down. 'Sorry, I'm a morning person. I know it can get a bit annoying. I slept so well, and actually I am looking forward to the swim this morning. Plus, I get to drive the Zodiac later.'

'Ah, that's what's put a spring in your step. Boys and their toys,' Alison says, smiling and shaking her head.

'Oh, not just that. I know I'm a pretty crap swimmer, but there's plenty about the holiday to enjoy.' Claire sees him cast a discreet look at Sophie.

Oliver comes out onto the patio. 'We'll need to make a move soon.' Then looking up at the sky, he says, 'Please remember to put on sunscreen. I know it doesn't look like it, but you still need to be cautious and the cloud cover is not expected to last all day. You don't want to be caught out and get sunburnt. Sophie told you we'd be heading north, past Las Negras, right?' The party nod. 'Okay then, see you in ten out front.'

As the journey is a long one, the Zodiac is towed by the main boat and Oliver joins them onboard. He is regaling them with anecdotes and dishing out coffee. Sophie is at her usual post, sitting next to Josh, Alan and Ben behind them inside. The rest of the women are out on deck, laughing at something Oliver has just said.

Nisha has got a fit of the giggles and wipes away a tear. 'Oh, he really is very funny, isn't he? And when he wants to, he can really turn on the charm. I can see what Sophie finds attractive in him now.'

'Yeah, his wit and charm,' Claire says, eyeing Oliver's taut bum as he walks past her. They all snigger.

'What are you lot laughing about?' enquires Oliver.

'Oh nothing, just happy, you know,' Debbie says, and they all laugh again.

An hour or so later Sophie calls them inside, where she has positioned the chart on the table. 'So today will probably be the longest swim for you, up to seven kilometres, but don't worry if you don't feel up to that. We've built in a few shortcuts for those of you who are slower or just don't want to swim that much.' She draws their attention to a point on the chart. 'Our starting point is Punta Javana, and from there we do a mini crossing to Islote de Pedro. Then we head to Cala de San Pedro. We'll split into two groups; those who want to go further can come with me and we'll swim into the *cala*.'

'Is *cala* Spanish for cove?' Nisha asks.

'That's right,' Sophie says and continues. 'The others can just cross straight to Cala Hernandez. The beach there is pretty rocky, so today we'll drop anchor and have lunch on the boat.'

'How far is that in total?' Alan asks.

'About five or six K, depending on which route you take.'

Inspecting the chart, Claire says, 'And the afternoon swim?'

'A lot shorter. To Playa de Las Negras, a little under two kilometres.'

'Quite the challenging day then. That's good,' Alan says, looking pleased.

At Punta Javana, Sophie gets in the water with Debbie and Ben. She asks Alison and Nisha to wait ten minutes before they start to swim, wanting to ensure that Debbie and Ben have a good head start. Both of them have already told her they want to take the shorter route across the mouth of the *cala*. Those remaining on the boat watch the small group head off.

'You know, Ben has really made a lot of progress in the time we've been here,' Claire says, watching him in the water.

Agreeing with her, Alison says, 'Yeah, when you consider what his technique was like that first day. He's done well.'

Josh is there with the drinks bottles and hands them

to her. He looks at his watch. 'I make that ten minutes, ladies. You can get in now. Alan and Claire, give them five minutes then you can go. Okay?'

Alan is adjusting the strap of his goggles. 'Sure thing, Josh.'

All of them reunite at the small island, five hundred metres from Punta Javana and the boat. As the crossing is short and with no boat traffic, Oliver has not followed them, instead waiting on the other side of the tiny island. The swimmers drink before dividing. Alison has elected to swim with Sophie, Claire and Alan. Oliver will accompany the rest of them to the other side of the *cala*.

Not until they are out in more open water do they become aware of just how rough the sea is. The waves are choppy and they have to employ all of their skills to sight and avoid getting mouthfuls of salt water. Even Sophie is finding it challenging. She stops to allow them to rest and drink. They are about a third of the way through the four kilometres of the second stretch of the swim.

'Bloody hell, this is tough going,' Alan says to Sophie. 'Do you think we should carry on, now that it's started raining?'

'It's pretty bad, I admit. The forecast said nothing about the wind coming up like this. I think we need to push ahead as Oliver is not within signalling distance at this point. Although I suppose we could swim up to him.'

Alison says, 'Do you think we should call it a day? I think I've had enough.'

Claire shouts, 'No! I want to keep swimming. We've only just started. I don't want to give up so soon. We can do it, come on.'

Sophie looks at Alison and Alan. 'What do you want to do, guys?'

'Look, I know it's not ideal, but I think it would be good to meet the challenge of today's conditions,' Alan says. 'This would be a useful experience to apply to a triathlon swim. I'd like to give it a go.'

Outnumbered, Alison gives in. 'All right then. But I have to say I'm not finding this pleasurable.'

'Attagirl!' Claire says, who is already replacing her goggles, eager to go.

'Right, let's not hang about then. Without the sun we'll get cold if we don't keep moving,' Sophie says.

The slower group are not faring much better. A steady rain is now falling and there's a chill in the air. Ben is in the Zodiac. He is shivering despite the towel wrapped around him. Debbie is doing her best to keep up, but the current is against them and coupled with the sea swell they are making little progress. They battle on but eventually Debbie calls a halt.

'I've had enough,' she says to Nisha. 'This is too much for me.' Even the thought of struggling to get into the Zodiac doesn't deter her. She's seen how difficult people have found this and would not usually suffer the humiliation; however, at this point she doesn't care. At least Claire isn't around to see her making a fool of herself.

Nisha says, 'Thank goodness for that. I've been desperate to get out for a while now, but didn't want to leave you to swim on your own.'

'Oliver!' Debbie shouts. 'We're done. It's too rough to keep swimming. Can you help us get in?'

'Sure thing,' Oliver says, leaning down and grabbing Debbie's hands. Despite his best efforts, he cannot manage and Debbie wrestles to hook her leg over the side of the inflatable. She is beyond embarrassed. Ben helps and grabs her ankle, and with their joint efforts they haul her in, like a catch of fish in a laden net, and she slithers to the floor of the Zodiac.

Laying there winded, she laughs. 'I'm glad nobody got the GoPro out for that!' She's glad to be out of the water and pleased for being able to laugh off the exhibition she's just made of herself.

Next in is Nisha, who doesn't go through quite the same palaver. They are huddled together for warmth. Nisha has brought along a fleece and it's zipped up to her chin.

'I'm going over to Sophie to let her know what's happening,' Oliver says, manoeuvring the Zodiac towards land. 'I want to check out how they're doing too.' Before proceeding, he holds a pair of binoculars to his eyes. 'Looks like they are swimming toward us.'

Claire is sitting on deck and Oliver is kneeling in front of her, attending to a bloody gash on her leg. Getting back onto the main boat via the ladder, her foot had slipped on a rung and she smacked her shin onto it. To add insult to injury, she is also nursing a jellyfish sting on her hand.

Scrutinising the wound, Oliver dabs at it with cotton wool and iodine. 'Not too deep. The blood made it look worse than it is. I'll pop a plaster on it, just while it clots, then it's probably best to leave it open to the air to dry out as much as possible before the next swim. How's the sting?'

Claire's gaze is far away. 'What?'

'The jellyfish sting. How is it?'

'Oh, it's nothing, I was able to scrape off most of the tentacles.' How she is physically feeling is the last thing on her mind. 'How's Sophie?'

'It got her pretty bad, all down the side of her face. Unfortunately, she touched her face automatically when it happened and spread the venom. Of course, that also means her fingers are affected. Nisha is taking care of her. I think Alison got stung a couple of times too, but not as badly.' Leaning back on his haunches, Oliver gives Claire's leg a last look, then stands up. 'Check the plaster in a bit and see if it's stopped bleeding. Are you coming inside?'

Claire shakes her head. 'No, I'll stay here.' She needs to be alone for the task ahead.

Oliver shrugs his shoulders and leaves her.

She picks up her dry bag and looks inside. She reaches for something then hesitates. No. She can't do it. Tears spill down her face and she's grateful no one is there to see her.

Chapter Fifteen

Fortunately, the weather improves by the afternoon and the sun makes an appearance. The mood of the group lifts; all, that is, apart from Claire, who is unusually quiet. During lunch, she separates herself from the others and eats at the bow of the boat. Even an entreaty from Alan to join them won't entice her.

Debbie has decided to sit out the afternoon swim. She has been rather put off by the thought of jellyfish in the water. Ben is not swimming either and is going to pilot the Zodiac.

Before they set out again, Oliver approaches Ben. 'Okay, let's both get into the Zodiac. I want to point out a few things to you before we go.'

'I do have my Level 2 Powerboat licence, you know,' Ben says, clearly a bit miffed.

'Yeah, I know that, but this baby has a few little quirks you should know about. First, you need to keep an eye on the outboard motor. It tends to stutter if you leave it in neutral and you have to keep moving so it doesn't conk out.'

'Really? I haven't come across that before.'

'Yeah, I know. It's a nuisance trying to go as slowly as the swimmers. I move forward and double back if the group is very slow.'

'You must have had to do that a lot with me in the water,' Ben says sardonically.

'Yes, well … of course, you have your VHF radio for communicating with Josh on the main boat, which gets recharged every night. As you know you're supposed to keep it around your neck at all times, but that can get a bit uncomfortable, particularly when it's hot, as the strap rubs against the back of your neck. Most of the time I sling it on the floor, but the bag has to be properly sealed. If it gets wet, it won't work.'

'Gotcha,' Ben says, picking up the radio and looking at it.

'I'll stay with you for a bit, just to make sure you've got the hang of it, then I'll get into the water and swim with Alison and Nisha. Remember to keep sufficient distance from the swimmers, and always keep them in front of you. Whatever you do, *do not* let them swim up behind you or get close when the engine is running. As I'll be with them, it shouldn't be an issue, but just be aware. Right, I think that's about it. Any questions?'

'No, I think I'm good, thanks.'

While Oliver is giving his tutorial, Sophie and the swimmers are getting ready to enter the water. The side of Sophie's face is an angry pink. It is burning and she is struggling not to keep touching it. Debbie looks at it, slightly horrified, and is glad she's elected to stay on the boat.

Alison touches Claire's arm. 'Are you okay? Why did you have lunch on your own? What was that all about?'

Claire looks about her and sighs. 'I can't go into it now. We'll talk later. I just want to get a good swim done, that will sort me out.' She dons her goggles and jumps into the water, leaving Alison behind.

Now, as twilight hits Villa Hermosa, people are gathered outside on the terrace, lounging by the pool or seated on squishy outdoor chairs. Those who are not reading are chatting, at ease with one another, the swimming they have done together a unifying force. The afternoon swim had been a success and more than made up for the disappointing morning. Claire attacked it as though her life depended on it and outswam Alan to such an extent that he had to ask her to slow down. Ben relished his time on the Zodiac and enjoyed not being under pressure to try and constantly keep up with his fellow swimmers. While Debbie, left alone on the boat with Josh, was treated to a charm offensive, which she took delight in, her self-confidence definitely getting a boost as Josh plied her with compliments and flirted.

Alan is lying on a sunbed, a half-finished beer by his side. 'Where's Claire? Missing again?'

Looking up from her book, Alison says, 'She's having a shower and getting ready for our big night out.'

Josh has managed to reserve them a table at one of the few restaurants that are still open this late in the season. Promises of flamenco entertainment and dancing have been made, and the group are looking forward to letting their hair down.

'Well, I for one shall be very glad to get dolled up and put on a pretty dress. Be nice to do something different in the evening, though I don't know how late I will be able to stay up,' Nisha says, stifling a yawn.

Debbie is flicking through a small notebook she has balanced on her lap. 'What's the date today, Alan?'

He picks up a discarded newspaper under his lounger. 'The twenty-fifth.'

'Twenty-sixth,' Nisha corrects. 'It's the twenty-sixth today. That must be an old newspaper.'

Debbie leans over to Alan and whispers in his ear. 'It's that special time of the month. Play your cards right and you might get lucky again tonight.'

Hearing the talk of dates, Alison sits up with a start. The twenty-sixth of October. Suddenly she knows why Claire has been acting strangely.

Putting the finishing touches to her make-up, Claire looks at her reflection. The fluorescent light of the bathroom is bright and unflattering. She had been looking forward to going out, but now she feels flat. She sits on the edge of the bath and through the open door can see her dry bag, propped up against the bed. Sorry, Dad, let you down again. Tears fall and drip onto her lap. She wipes at her eyes, grabbing at the toilet paper and yanking with such force that the flimsy mounting comes away from the wall and the paper rolls out of reach. The tears, now unleashed, rain down. Her attempts to curb the deluge are useless and a howl rises from deep within her. She hears Alison come into the room, so she shuts the bathroom door and leans against it. Panicking, she seizes a towel and rams it into her mouth, the effort of trying to be quiet making it difficult to breathe.

'Claire! Claire, open the door.' Claire says nothing. 'Please, Claire, open the door.'

'Go away!'

'No. I'm not going anywhere. You might as well open up.'

Quaking, Claire holds the towel against her face, inhaling, trying to calm herself. She cracks open the door. 'I know, Claire. I know what date it is. Your dad's anniversary.'

Sobbing into Alison's shoulder, Claire is unable to speak.

'Come on,' Alison says, leading Claire to the bed. 'I'll get you some water.' Claire sits there, shuddering as her breathing returns to normal.

It is a while before she can speak. 'Thank you. You know, I haven't cried since the day I first visited Dad's grave. I was terrified by what I felt then. Ever since I've pushed it down, locked it away. Until now. Now it seems out of control.'

'I know how you feel. I still get upset about Gavin,' Alison says, her eyes bright.

Claire's seen Alison break down a number of times, helped her cope with the grief of losing her husband. She gives a lopsided smile. 'God, what a pair we are.'

Sniffing, Alison says, 'Yeah, don't let the others know; they'll be so jealous of all the fun we're having. Tell me this: when your dad got Covid and was hospitalised, when he passed away, I never saw you this upset. To be honest I've been really worried that you weren't dealing with his death at all well. I mean, I never saw you cry or anything, you always seemed, well, so calm and together. Lately, though, something's been off. For starters, you are really bad-tempered a lot of the time and get cross at the drop of a hat. It's not like you at all. I think perhaps this is because you've kept everything bottled up for so long – it was bound to come out in some way.'

'You're probably right. When I think back to that time, it all seemed so unbelievable, like I was on autopilot. I thought I would fall apart when Dad died and then – nothing. I couldn't feel anything. It was like it hadn't really happened. I've been trying to get my head around why it's been affecting me so much lately. I know I've been behaving badly, I just can't seem to stop myself. I feel angry all the time.' She gets out her dry bag and reaches inside it. 'I think this must be the reason why I am so upset now.' She pulls out an urn. 'Dad's ashes. I was going to scatter them today from the boat. Years ago, Dad joked that he'd always fancied being buried at sea, said it seemed very noble. Well, that wasn't an option, so I thought the next best thing would be to scatter his ashes in the sea. Turns out I couldn't even do that for him.' Her head drops to her chest.

'Why do you think that was?'

'I don't know. I couldn't bear to part with all that

I have left of him, I suppose. It was bad enough not saying goodbye to him while he was dying. When I think of him, abandoned in hospital, with no one to hold his hand … he must have been so scared. He'd always been very afraid of being alone at the end, I knew that. And I'd promised him that while I was around it would never happen, and then I broke my promise. But the worst of it is,' she says, wringing her hands, 'it's my fault he got sick. I knew he was vulnerable, but still I insisted we celebrate his birthday, told him he'd be fine if we ate outside. Said I wanted to spoil him! He wasn't happy going, but I pestered him until he said yes – to please me.'

She buries her head in her hands. 'I miss him so much, still. What am I going to do? I can't bear feeling like this, but nothing I do seems to make me feel better.'

'You're going to take one day at a time. That's all you can do. And, you're going to get some help. When you get back to England, the first thing you need to do is to face this. You can see that you can't bury these feelings, that it's making you ill. I don't suppose you feel up to going out tonight, do you? We can stay here while the others go. Chill out on our own.'

'No, I'm all right, honestly. Actually, I feel better, think that cry did me a lot of good. I'd prefer to be out and about, rather than wallow. I know what will help.' She leaves the room for a few minutes and comes back carrying a bottle of wine and two glasses. 'Here, some of this and we'll be good to go.'

'Claire, you know alcohol isn't the answer, don't you?'

‘It’ll do for now. I’ve gone this long. I don’t want to collapse in the middle of a holiday with a bunch of people around.’ She can’t bear the thought of that. ‘Don’t worry, I’ll be fine.’

‘Well, if you’re sure.’

Passing her a glass of wine, Claire says, ‘Yes, I am. Come on, drink up. We have a dinner to go to.’

It is close to midnight and they have only just finished eating. Service has been slow, and they waited an age for the food. Bottles of wine, though, have been quick to appear on the table without being ordered, and Alison suspects that the staff are deliberately bumping up the bill, making the most of the last tourists of the year. No doubt when the bill finally arrives there will be a few extras on it and everyone will be too inebriated to notice or care. Josh has joined them and is sitting at the end of the table with Oliver, the two of them downing tequila shots in a display of macho one-upmanship. If it is bothering Sophie, she isn’t letting it show, and she is absorbed in conversation with Ben.

The flamenco show turns out to be an impromptu display from some of the locals. Not that this detracts from the table’s enjoyment of it, nor Claire’s attempts to emulate them. She tries to lure Alan onto the floor and join them, but he vehemently declines, laughingly rejecting her entreaties.

On her way back from the ladies, Debbie looks on disapprovingly. Sitting down next to Alan, she says, ‘I think I'd like to go now, love, I'm pretty tired.'

Alan looks at her, a little cross-eyed. 'Already?'

Debbie doesn't want to make a big deal of this so she decides to joke. 'Must have been our "siesta" this afternoon.'

Alan giggles. 'Yes, it was pretty energetic. Still, it's not late, is it?' He looks at his watch and is none the wiser as to what time it is.

Seeing she is getting nowhere, she addresses Nisha opposite. 'I'm going to make a move. Do you want to go? I don't fancy walking back on my own.'

Nisha, who is looking bored, readily agrees. 'What about you, Alison?'

'What?' Alison says, trying to hear over the raucous singing.

'Debbie and I are going to go. Do you want to come with us?'

Alison looks over at Claire, who is being propped up by one of the singers and waving a glass of wine around, its contents slopping onto the floor. 'Give me a minute, I'll see what Claire is doing.'

'Claire, some of us are leaving now. I think you should too.'

'Oh, do you?' Claire says, gazing at her with a glassy-eyed expression.

'Yes, I do. Come on now. Don't you think you've had enough to drink? We've got a swim tomorrow, remember? We'll need to be up fairly early for that.'

'Oh, don't be such a spoilsport. You go. I'm having fun. For once!'

Clearly Claire has no intention of leaving, so on their way out Alison has a word with Sophie and Ben. 'Debbie, Nisha and I are going back to the villa. We've given Alan our share of the bill. Do me a favour, will you? Make sure Claire leaves with you?'

Ben looks across at Claire. 'She seems in a better mood. Yeah, don't worry. We'll look after her.'

Once the bill has finally been paid, Oliver and Josh decide to continue partying with some of Josh's friends. Sophie waves them away and walks on ahead with Ben. Alan, trying to corral a very drunk Claire, gets left further and further behind. The night air and the responsibility of looking after her has sobered him up. Claire's drunken exuberance turns to maudlin, and by the time they get back to the villa she is hanging onto him and crying copiously.

'Alan, Alan. You're such a good person. We get along, don't we? We have a laugh, right?'

'Yes, of course we do,' Alan replies while trying to extricate himself from Claire's grasp. 'I think you should have some water.' He gets her a glass. 'Here, drink this, then you need to get to bed.'

Not taking the glass proffered, Claire staggers toward him and slurs, 'That's not what I need.' She lunges at him, ramming her tongue into his mouth while fumbling at his crotch. Horrified, Alan pulls back, pushing her away.

'What the fuck are you doing?'

'Oh, come on. This is what you want, it's obvious.

You've been flirting with me for months. And why else would you plan it so we'd be alone now?'

'Boy, have you got the wrong end of the stick! Yes, we have a bit of a laugh, but that's it. Do you hear me? I love my wife.'

'Debbie? Are you kidding? That mouse?' She sidles up to him. 'I'll show you how real swimmers do it.' Laughing at her own joke, she aims for Alan's mouth.

Shoving her back, he shouts, 'I said no! Christ, get the message, will you? I. Am. Not. Interested. Just back the hell off!'

Stunned, Claire stumbles away from him, and as she spins around, she sees Debbie standing in the doorway of the kitchen. Before it can properly register, Debbie is on her, tearing at Claire's hair, pulling it at the roots.

'You fucking bitch!' Debbie screeches and rakes her nails down Claire's face.

Screaming in pain, Claire tries to escape her, but Debbie is enraged and will not be shaken off. Claire cannot believe that this is timid Debbie. This, more than anything, shocks her. Alan stands by, frozen by his wife's reaction, before jumping in and prising them apart.

'Debbie, Debbie. Stop it. Calm down.' An exhausted Debbie falls into Alan's arms, a clump of Claire's hair in her hand.

As they leave, Claire touches her face and is shocked to find it bleeding. The realisation of what she has done, dawning on her.

Chapter Sixteen

Nisha is in the kitchen making a pot of coffee. She's had a disturbed night's sleep, woken by shouting and screaming. Only half awake, she had not investigated its source, but it had taken her hours to nod off again. As she leans against the countertop, sipping her coffee, she hears the slam of the front door. Oliver walks in.

'Good morning, Nisha. What a wonderful day! It's good to be alive, isn't it? The sun makes you feel great; that's why the Spanish are so upbeat and chilled. No wonder the Brits are a bunch of miserable bastards.' He laughs, throwing back his head as he does so. 'Not that I think you're miserable, Nisha,' he says, putting his arm around her shoulders. 'You're a little ray of sunshine, especially compared to my girlfriend.' He leans in as if to impart a secret. 'She may look all sweetness and light, but she can be a real nag. Ben's welcome to her.'

As he breathes over her, Nisha flinches. He reeks of alcohol. He stares at her earnestly, and then she notices his eyes; the pupils are fully dilated even in the bright light of the room. 'Have you been up all night, Oliver?'

Tapping the side of his nose, he says, 'Yes, but don't

tell the missus.' Swinging around violently, he spies the coffee pot. 'Ah, coffee. What a splendid idea! Just get myself a cup o' joe, as our American cousins say.' He laughs again and slops coffee into a mug.

'Are you thinking of driving the Zodiac this morning, Oliver?'

'But of course, my dear Nisha. I wouldn't dream of neglecting my duties.' He slurps a mouthful of coffee. 'Talking of which, I'd better get breakfast started.'

Coming out of their en-suite bathroom, Alison wrinkles her nose. 'Phew, it reeks of booze in here! I didn't notice when I got up.' She draws the curtains and opens the window. Claire, still lying in bed, winces as the light floods in. She doesn't think she has the energy to get out of bed, let alone do a swim this morning. Her listlessness vanishes as she is hit by a wave of nausea that sends her rushing to the bathroom.

'Claire, are you all right?'

Claire emerges and wobbles back to her bed. 'Oh, dear God, I want to die.'

'Hmm, you were rather knocking it back last night. What time did you get in?' Alison says, handing her a glass of water.

To remember that, Claire also has to recall the other events of the evening. Her face burns at the mere thought of it. 'I didn't disturb you then?' She wonders who else heard the altercation.

'Nah. I didn't want to get woken up when you

stumbled in, so I put in earplugs. I always take them with me when I'm away from home.'

'Oh, right. I'm not sure what time I got back actually.'

'I'll leave you to get yourself together. What you need is a big fry-up, get something in your stomach. See you out there.'

Continuing to sit on the bed, Claire is not sure what her next course of action should be. The last thing she wants to do is face Debbie and Alan, but she can't exactly stay in her room all day. Besides, she is gagging for some tea, lots of it. Why oh why did she have to go and make a fool of herself like that? Alcohol has played its part in many a regretful night out, but at least in the past she's been able to crawl away and pretend it never happened. Now she is going to have to confront Debbie and Alan. I hope to God there's nobody else around, she thinks. Then an even worse thought occurs to her. What if Debbie goes ballistic again, like she did last night? She brushes her teeth and looks in the mirror. 'Time to face the music, girl,' she says out loud to the reflection.

Rolling over to silence the alarm on her phone, Sophie rubs her eyes and stretches. The other side of the bed is empty. She is surprised but not alarmed that Oliver isn't there. He is not often up before her, but today is his turn to make breakfast. Shoving her feet into flip-flops, she goes to the bathroom. She has a slight headache and wonders how Oliver is feeling. She hadn't heard him return last night.

There is a gentle knocking on the bedroom door. She opens it. 'Hi, Nisha. What can I do for you?'

'I want to speak to you about Oliver.' Without being invited to do so, Nisha walks into the room.

A little taken aback, Sophie says, 'What's this about? Is there a problem?'

'Yes. A big one. I've been speaking to Oliver in the kitchen. He's only just come in from partying all night.'

'I see.'

'Yes, and it is obvious that he is drunk, and, if I'm not mistaken – and I don't believe I am – he's high on something. Not only that, but he says he is going to drive the Zodiac on this morning's swim. There is no way he is in any state to be in charge of a vehicle or people. In his present condition he is a danger to himself and to those he is supposed to be looking after. You need to sort this out.'

'Of course. You're right. Don't worry, I won't let him drive the Zodiac, or swim for that matter. I haven't actually seen him this morning, otherwise I would have already had a word.'

'Do it now. Honestly, this is like a day at work. This is supposed to be a holiday, where I get to relax, not have to deal with drunk cokeheads!'

'I'm really sorry. This will get sorted. I promise you.'

'See that it is,' Nisha replies.

'I swear to you, Alan, if that woman comes anywhere near you again, I'll swing for her! The bloody nerve, making a pass at you like that. What did she think you were going to do, with me in the next room?' Debbie is flinging her towel and spare swimsuit into a dry bag. 'And as for spending any time with her on the boat, well, I just can't . . .' She stops and brushes a tear away.

'Oh, love. Don't upset yourself. I hate to see you like this. Look, we'll have a chat with Sophie and see what can be done. I'm sure we can work around it. Now, let's go and have some breakfast, look forward to the day. We should make the most of our last couple of days here. What do you say?'

Sniffing, Debbie says, 'You're right. I don't see why we should let her spoil our holiday.' What she saw last night confirmed her worst fears – that Claire was attracted to Alan – though she is comforted by the fact that Alan rejected her advances.

They go in search of Sophie and find her in the kitchen, along with Nisha and Oliver. Nisha is standing with her hands on her hips, a defiant look on her face. It is obvious there is some sort of quarrel taking place.

'Sophie, I'm fine. Really. You're making far too big a deal about this. I'm perfectly okay to drive the Zodiac,' Oliver says.

'And I say you're not.' She drags him by the arm, snarling into his ear. 'Just what are you on? I can smell the booze on you, but it isn't just that you're pissed, is it?'

'Okay, so I did a little blow. Just to fire up the system. It's no big deal. Christ, Sophie, you're being a real pain. I can handle myself. You've got to learn to chill.'

'Excuse me for interrupting your tête-à-tête, but have we got this sorted yet?' Nisha says. 'I don't see that there's anything to discuss. Oliver stays in the villa today. There is absolutely no way I am going to be anywhere near him' – she jabs him in the chest with her finger – 'while he's in this state. And, I shall be letting the others know that he isn't safe to be around.'

Oliver looks down at Nisha's finger, then at Sophie, and raises his hands in a gesture of defeat. 'Okay, okay. Have it your own way. You all go off and leave me here. See how you get along without me,' he says, stomping off to his room.

Sophie is relieved that Oliver has left the scene, but now she is faced with the dilemma of how to manage a group of swimmers of varying abilities on her own.

Debbie and Alan are hovering.

Clearly feeling awkward, Alan speaks. 'Morning, Sophie. Can we have a word?'

Sensing from his tone that Alan is going to add to her woes, but forcing a smile, Sophie says, 'Sure. What's up?'

'Um, well. It's a bit delicate. Last night when we were coming back from the restaurant. We were all, well, quite tipsy, and Claire was … very tipsy.'

'Yes, I remember,' Sophie says, getting an inkling of where this is going.

'Yes, very tipsy,' repeats Alan. 'And she, she—'

Debbie, who is getting impatient and angry, says. 'She tried to have sex with Alan. She basically assaulted him!

He had to fight her off. I don't know what would have happened if I hadn't found them. And there's no way I want to be anywhere near her for the rest of the holiday.'

'Ah, oh dear,' Sophie says as she thinks about the implications of this news. 'Are you going to stay here then for today's swim?'

'Me? No! I'm not the one at fault here, neither is Alan. No, if anyone is going to stay away, it's her. And you need to tell her so. If she had any decency – not that I expect she does – she'd be offering to do so anyway.'

Sophie's brain is scrambling to think of a solution to this latest problem. It's obvious that Debbie needs placating, but what if Claire insists on swimming?

Alison strolls in with an empty cereal bowl, oblivious to the discord in the room. 'Morning. Just been having my breakfast by the pool. It's a lovely day.' There's no response. 'Everything okay?'

'You'd better ask your friend,' Debbie says, turning away and filling the kettle.

Sophie looks at Alison's questioning face. 'It appears there was an incident last night. Debbie and Alan are demanding that Claire doesn't come out with us today.'

'An incident? What kind of incident?'

'I think it would be best if you asked Claire yourself,' Sophie says. 'And, you'd be doing me a big favour if you could ask her to stay here today. I think it would be better coming from you.' She hopes Alison can persuade Claire.

When Alison goes back to their room, Claire is lying on the bed with a wet cloth on her forehead.

'Claire, what happened last night? Sophie has just asked that you don't come on the swim today. Something to do with Alan and Debbie.'

Claire sits up. Now she is going to have to confess what happened. She feels so ashamed. 'I wondered where this would go. Can't say I'm surprised. Oh God, this is so embarrassing. I made a right tit of myself last night.'

'Please don't tell me you made a pass at Alan?'

'Yep. And I was none too subtle about it, if I remember correctly, though it's all a bit fuzzy. When you lot left, we stayed on for another hour or so. Alan helped me back, and I, well … I tried to kiss him. Of course, he wasn't interested, but I wouldn't take no for an answer.'

'Oh dear, and I suppose he went and told Debbie straight away?'

'Worse than that. She found us.'

Alison catches her breath. 'Flipping heck. She must have been really upset.'

'You could say that,' Claire says, turning her face to reveal the scratches.

'Debbie did that?'

'Yes, she did. I'm pretty sure she got a handful of my hair too, judging by how sore my scalp feels this morning.' A smile plays upon her lips. 'I wouldn't have thought she had it in her. Just goes to show.' She wonders how the hell she can make this right. Poor Debbie, she had every right to be angry.

'Bloody hell, Claire. What were you thinking?'

'Obviously, I wasn't.'

'And today? What are you going to do?'

'Well, I feel totally crap, so it's a relief not to have to go swimming, to be honest. I'll stay here. At the moment all I want to do is to have a cuppa and some painkillers, then go back to sleep.'

'Do you want me to stay and keep you company?'

'No, no. You go and enjoy the day. This is my mess. I'm sorry for making things awkward for you.'

'I'll get you a cup of tea and bring it to you, so you don't have to face anyone just yet.'

'Alison.'

'Yes?'

'Thanks. Yesterday, you know, listening and everything. All this. You're a good friend.'

Alison smiles. 'I'll get you that tea.'

Sophie is busy in the kitchen making breakfast, her mind going over recent events and wondering how she is going to manage the day. Ben wanders in, with his habitual, easy-going smile in place. 'Morning. What's going on? You could cut the atmosphere with a knife out there.' He lifts his chin towards the patio where the others are sitting.

'Where do I start? Apparently, Claire made a pass at Alan last night. Debbie is fuming, understandably. Worse is that Oliver rocks up this morning, drunk and high as a kite.'

'Jeez!'

'As if that wasn't bad enough, the first person to see him was Nisha. She knew instantly he was off his face, and flat out refused to entertain the idea of him driving the Zodiac.'

'Where's he now?'

'In our room, sulking. I don't know what I'm going to do about today. We're going all the way up to Carboneras, and it's a six-kilometre swim. At least, it's supposed to be. Without Oliver I don't see how I can organise the swimmers. I suppose there's one less now it looks as though Claire won't be with us, but even so.' She turns her attention back to the eggs on the stove. 'It's a right fucking mess. Oliver is such a prat. I am so sick of him!'

'I would have thought the solution is clear.'

Sophie looks at him.

'Me.'

Chapter Seventeen

'Shit! This bloody thing!' Ben exclaims, exasperated with the outboard motor. Despite Oliver telling him it was temperamental, he hadn't realised things were quite this bad. As a consequence, Ben cannot let the motor idle and has to keep moving, otherwise it dies. He is accompanying Debbie and having trouble not constantly getting ahead of her. Added to the issues with the Zodiac is the fact that Debbie has been paired with Nisha, a much better swimmer. Even now he can see the gap between the two of them is widening to such a degree that Nisha is left exposed and without anyone overseeing her. He screws his eyes up in the dazzling sun and sees she is going off course. Picking up the radio, he contacts Josh.

'Josh, can you give Sophie a message? Over.'

Static, then Josh's voice. 'What's the message? Over.'

'Tell her to turn around and make her way back to us. My swimmers have got separated and one of them is going off course. Over.'

'Roger that.'

Ben cuts the motor and shouts, 'Debbie! Debbie!' She doesn't hear him so he starts the motor again and drives over to her. As he cannot stop, he has to keep circling while trying to catch her attention.

She frantically treads water while looking up at him. 'What's up?'

'Would you be able to get into the boat for a bit? I want to catch up with Nisha. She's way ahead and can't be sighting properly as she's swimming straight out to sea.'

'Sure, can you help me in?' She doesn't look overly pleased to have to get out of the water.

'Give me a second while I turn off the engine.' Once done, he goes to help Debbie. It takes several attempts; the first few times, she slithers out of his grasp and back into the sea. The sides of the boat are pretty high out of the water, and Ben can see that she doesn't have the upper body strength to lift herself up and over. He has found it difficult enough, so he sympathises with her. By the time she is onboard, Debbie has several bruises on her arms where Ben has grabbed her. He sees her massage the marks and is appalled.

'Oh no. Did I do that? I'm really sorry.'

'Don't worry, I tend to bruise easily. Let's try and avoid having to do that again, hey?' She looks out to sea. 'Where's Nisha?'

'God, no. I can't see her. I should have given her the tow float instead of you.' He scans the horizon, desperate to spot her.

'There!' Debbie says, pointing to the pinprick of bright orange that is Nisha's swimming cap.

'Good spot. Right, let's catch her up.' He goes to

start the outboard motor, but nothing happens. 'For God's sake. Come on, you bastard piece of crap!' On the fourth attempt it bursts into life.

The radio crackles and Josh's voice can be heard. 'Ben, Sophie is heading back. You should see her soon. Over.'

'Roger that.'

Ben turns to Debbie. 'Do you think we should pick up Nisha first?'

'Nisha is going way off course, so yes, let's,' Debbie says.

'Yeah, I think you're right.' As they approach Nisha, they see she is treading water and waving at them. Ben is relieved to see her.

Between them, they manage to haul Nisha on board without too many problems. Ben decides to radio Josh and let him know what is happening. Nothing. All he can hear is static and he realises that he is out of range. Distracted, he tosses the radio onto the floor and it slides to the back of the vessel, into a puddle of bilge water.

'Okay, ladies. We're going to meet up with Sophie and the others before continuing with the swim. Won't be long,' Ben says, trying to sound confident. 'Could we all be on the lookout for the others, please?'

'Probably best if you head to the coast,' Nisha says. 'Oh dear, my sighting is terrible. I was heading to Italy.'

'Easily done,' Debbie says. She is going through her bag and pulling out the contents.

'What are you looking for?'

'My arnica cream, it's good for bruises. Now, where is

it? I know I had it here somewhere.'

An array of balms and ointments are now sprawled about the boat, the EpiPen that Debbie keeps with her among them.

'Found it!' Debbie unscrews the cap and starts to liberally apply the cream.

In the time it has taken to stop and get Nisha aboard, Ben sees that they have drifted with the current, and they are a significant distance away from the shore. He kicks the engine into full throttle and heads to the coast. The bow of the Zodiac rises as he picks up speed, obscuring his forward vision.

Alison is swimming and has her face in the sea. She can hear the metallic, whiny sound of an engine in the water. It's getting louder. Lifting her head, she sees the Zodiac racing in their direction. She is not the only one to have spotted it. Sophie is treading water. She is waving her arm above her and blowing a whistle. The Zodiac continues straight toward them.

Alison looks on in horror. 'Oh no, he hasn't seen us. He isn't going to stop!'

'Oh fuck,' Alan says.

Sophie is still blowing the whistle and now Alan is shouting. The Zodiac is on a direct collision course with the swimmers. As the boat hurtles towards them, Alison knows it is useless to try and outswim it. She is thinking of her boys – both parents dead, orphans. She should never have come on this holiday. She should have listened to her mother. She closes her eyes, waiting for the inevitable.

Alan and Sophie are now screaming at the top of their lungs and waving their arms frantically. Suddenly the boat swerves violently, only just avoiding the group.

Alison is hit by the wake the boat creates as it turns. She opens her eyes, not quite believing she is out of danger. She really thought that was it.

'Oh my God. Oh my God. Is everyone all right?' Ben's hands are shaking as he clutches the steering wheel. Nisha has slumped against the side of the Zodiac, while Debbie is hanging over it, looking for her husband.

In the water, Alison says, 'I think I've wet myself.'

'Is that all?' Alan says. 'I almost shat my Speedos.' Although he laughs, Alison can tell he is badly shaken by what has just happened.

As the person in charge, Sophie manages to maintain a semblance of calm and authority. 'Are you both okay? I think perhaps we should all get in the Zodiac and head to shore for an early lunch.'

Alison couldn't agree more. Her limbs feel like jelly and she doesn't think she could coordinate them enough to continue swimming. 'Fine with me. Alan?' Although whatever he decides, she is getting out of the water.

'Yeah, not really in the mood to swim now.'

'Are you both all right getting to the Zodiac?' Sophie says.

They nod. If anyone wanted to reproach Ben for what happened, one look at him would stop them. He is ashen-faced, his perpetual smile vanished. 'Sophie, I'm so sorry. Are you all okay?' He helps her up. Alan is already there, clasped in Debbie's embrace. She is crying.

In a quiet voice, Sophie reassures Ben. 'Don't worry about it now, we'll talk it over later, hey? The important thing is no one was hurt.'

'I feel terrible, Sophie. I swear, I just didn't see you. Thank God for Debbie. She saw you all.'

Back at Villa Hermosa, Claire is outside on a lounger, sheltering from the sun under an umbrella. She is wearing dark glasses but it does not help her raging headache. She thought a gentle swim in the pool might, but a couple of laps had made her want to throw up so she quickly got out. She is bored. She can't focus on reading and has no company. It is very quiet, only birdsong and the occasional movement of palm leaves when a breeze hits the terrace. Too much time and space to think. She doesn't want to think.

Hearing somebody coming out of the house she looks at her watch. Surely they're not back already?

It is Oliver.

'Back so soon?'

Startled, Oliver jumps. 'Claire. What are you doing here? Shouldn't you be out swimming?'

'I could ask you the same thing.'

'I'm being punished,' he complains.

'Um, me too. I made a right fool of myself last night and had to suffer the wrath of Debbie.'

'Can't imagine Debbie getting angry about anything.

She's so meek and mild.'

'Yeah, well, if you make a pass at her husband, turns out she can be a right nutter.' Her remark is flippant and doesn't reveal how badly she really feels. She's glad she bears the scratches of Debbie's rage – she deserves it.

Oliver howls with laughter. 'Claire, you scarlet woman. What made you do that? Were you drunk or something?'

'Just a bit.' Not wanting to elaborate, she says, 'Anyway, what about you? How come you're here? What did you do?'

Oliver hangs his head. 'The demon drink too, I'm afraid. I wasn't quite sober enough to drive this morning. Partied a little too hard with Josh.'

'So, are you feeling rough then too?'

'Actually, I feel fine. I was just going to rustle up a bacon sandwich. Do you want one?'

Shaking her head violently then wishing she hadn't, Claire says, 'Urgh, no thanks. Though if you're making coffee, I could do with a cup.'

'Coming right up.' He returns with two mugs and a plate balanced on top of one of them. 'There you go.'

Oliver is chomping on his sandwich. He swallows and then says, 'It does seem a bit much, leaving you behind. I mean, of all the people on this trip you're the one most enthusiastic about swimming. Not to mention the fact that you are the best swimmer, by far.'

'I don't know about that. Debbie insisted I not be on the boat today. Said she couldn't stand to be anywhere near me. Can't say I blame her. I think I would have done the same if it were me.'

'Then why didn't she stay behind? It's not like she's that bothered about swimming. Not like you; it's your passion. She's only doing it because of Alan.' Oliver takes another huge bite of his sandwich before continuing. 'And what's going to happen tomorrow? Does she expect you to stay away again? Hardly seems fair, does it?'

Claire hadn't thought about the next day and she suddenly realises it's the last swim. She doesn't want to be excluded again. 'I dunno. I've made things awkward, and I don't know if I can put it right.' She pauses. 'But everyone does stupid things when they're drunk, don't they?' She's trying to convince herself, but it's not working – the shame is too much.

The boat is anchored off Torre del Rayo. Everyone is onboard having lunch. While they are eating, Sophie draws Ben aside. 'How are you doing?'

'I'm fine. I still feel terrible though.'

'Well, I want you to stop feeling guilty. I've been thinking it over and it was terribly unfair of me to let you take responsibility for the swimmers like that. After all, you are supposed to be a client. It was far too much to ask of you, so it's me who should be apologising.'

'Look, I'm more than happy to help out; that's not an issue. You shouldn't feel bad at all. The person at fault is Oliver. This is his gig as much as yours, and he's behaved recklessly – not thinking about his clients, nor you for that matter.'

'Right, let's agree to blame Oliver then, shall we?' Sophie gives a weak smile. 'We should talk about this afternoon's swim. I'd really like it to go ahead as we had to cut this morning's one short. Do you think you could manage it okay? It's a fairly straightforward swim.'

'I had a look at the chart earlier. As far as I could see we just go parallel to Playa del Agarrobico.'

'Yes, that's right, three kilometres or so. As long as I make sure Nisha is more vigilant about her sighting. I'm going to get her to swim with Alison and Alan, and see that they bunch together. I'll keep an eye on all three of them, so you'll just have Debbie to worry about. For increased visibility, I'm going to make everyone wear a tow float. We'll let Debbie go first, give her a good head start. I'll swim with her for a while and when I turn back to swim with the others, you can accompany her in the Zodiac. Does that sound okay?'

Sophie's plan works well, and the swim is a success, although this doesn't stop Ben from being on tenterhooks throughout. At the end of the swim he relinquishes the Zodiac, attaching it to the main boat so he can travel back with the others.

He's lucky there are no recriminations from Alan or Alison. They've been very understanding. Alan even manages to joke that Ben owes him a pair of Speedos and claps him on the back, saying to put it down to experience. 'Ben, never, and I mean never, volunteer. Even if it is to impress a pretty girl,' he says.

They dock in the San José marina. Josh says a timid

goodbye and tells them he will see them tomorrow. He has had a ticking off from Sophie for partying with Oliver and is now under strict instructions not to go drinking for the duration of the holiday. Sophie is well aware that if Oliver was drunk that morning, then Josh's blood alcohol level couldn't have been safe either. She's warned him that her head is on the block should any of the group wish to complain. Not wanting to get his little sister into trouble, he has meekly agreed to tow the party line.

Once back at the villa, the group are lugging equipment and bags through the door when they are met by Claire, a determined look on her face.

'Sophie, could I have a word with you please?' Then looking at all of them, she says, 'In fact, I'd like a word with you all. Shall we say in half an hour, in the living room?'

Chapter Eighteen

'Thank you all for coming. I'll try not to keep you too long, but I think there are a few things that need to be said.' Claire is standing and addressing the group, who are seated around the living room.

'I feel like I'm in some kind of work meeting,' Alan whispers to Debbie.

'Yes, I know what you mean. She's obviously used to lecturing her minions,' Debbie replies, still seething, but curious to find out what Claire has to say for herself.

Claire continues. 'I expect by now you all know the reason why I was excluded from today's swim.'

Nisha pipes up. 'Actually no, I don't. I know it has something to do with Alan and Debbie, but Sophie was very discreet and didn't go into detail.' She looks around at the others. 'Am I the only one who is in the dark?'

Ben looks embarrassed. 'I know. But only because I overheard the conversation between Debbie, Alan and Sophie.' Eager not to incriminate Sophie, he adds, 'No one was gossiping or anything like that.'

Claire clears her throat and looks unsure of how to start. 'The night of the meal coincided with the second anniversary of my dad's death and I wasn't handling it too well. I didn't want to be sad, so stupidly I got very drunk as a way of coping.'

People are looking sympathetic and Debbie can feel a wave of compassion about to pardon Claire, which she is not pleased about. 'That's all very well, Claire, but you're not exactly telling the whole story, are you? Like how you jumped on Alan and tried to tear his clothes off?'

There is a collective intake of breath at this revelation.

'That's not exactly what happened, Debbie, but yes, I did make a pass at Alan and I am very sorry.' Now she looks directly at him. 'Alan, I can't apologise enough. I was totally out of order and I hope you can forgive me. Debbie too. I am *so* sorry. If I could turn back the clock ... You have to believe me when I say I would never normally behave like that. I was too drunk to know what I was doing.'

'Don't give me that!' Debbie feels a mounting surge of anger. 'You've been all over Alan ever since you met him. You've been waiting for your chance and you went for it when I wasn't around. As for trying to get everybody's sympathy by going on about your dad, well, that's really out of order. You've never mentioned him before. I think you're just using that as an excuse.'

'That's enough, Debbie!' Alan says. 'I believe Claire's apology is sincere and I'd like to put the whole episode behind us. Can we just let it go?'

'Why are you taking her side?' Debbie feels her lip

wobble and she bites on it, not wanting to cry.

Attempting to mollify her, Alan replies, 'I'm not. I just don't think this is helping things.'

'Just so long as she stays away from us. I'm not having her on the boat with us tomorrow, that's for sure.'

Oliver interjects, 'I think Alan is right. Everyone's done daft things when they've had a few too many.'

'I expect you would know all about that,' Nisha says, looking cross.

Ignoring her comment, Oliver continues. 'And, I don't think it's fair to "punish"' – he uses air quotes – 'Claire by making her stay here for another day. Let bygones be bygones, shall we? What do you say, Debbie? You won't be swimming in the same group as Claire and you can keep to opposite sides of the boat.'

'Yes, but who will she be swimming with, hey? Who's been her swimming partner this whole time? Alan! How do I know she won't try and rip off his Speedos in the water?'

'Now you're just being ridiculous!' Claire says. 'I'm not some kind of nymphomaniac who can't control herself.'

Debbie harrumphs, crosses her arms and looks up at the ceiling.

Alison listens to the exchange and wonders if she should say something. She recognises the need to stick up for her friend but knows that Claire wouldn't want it disclosed just how upset she had been that evening.

'Debbie, I know you're angry, but you're wrong to imply that Claire is lying about how she feels about her dad. She wouldn't want me to go into detail, but she has had a lot to deal with these past couple of years, and things just got to her yesterday.'

Claire gives Alison a small smile, while Debbie stays silent.

Sophie says, 'Perhaps if we split into two groups, like we did today?' She glances at Ben, who looks down at the ground, his ears pink.

Alison says, 'I don't want to sound mean, but I really don't think putting Ben in charge of a group is a good idea. Look what happened today. Somebody could have been seriously injured.'

'Alison's got a point,' Nisha says. 'It's certainly not Ben's responsibility to put things right.' She glares at Oliver, her expression hostile. 'Plus, this is his holiday, he's paid for it. He should be able to enjoy it.'

Standing up, Oliver squares his shoulders and looks Nisha in the eye. 'You're right, of course you are.' He turns to Sophie. 'I think we should have a chat in private, don't you?'

The pair go to the kitchen and there is a stony silence among those left.

Alison wonders what solution they'll come up with. She knows Claire will want to swim and will push for that. She hopes there is going to be no more arguing.

Eventually, Sophie and Oliver return. 'Okay, we have a

solution that we think will keep everyone happy,' Oliver says, a wide smile on his face.

Sophie speaks. 'Yes, we'll run it by you all and see what you think. So, we propose that tomorrow the planned swim north to Agua Amarga goes ahead as scheduled. Alan and Nisha, being faster swimmers, can follow Josh. I'll ask him to keep alongside you as much as possible instead of going on ahead and waiting for swimmers to reach him. I will be in the water with Ben and Debbie.'

'What about me and Alison?' Claire asks.

Now Oliver speaks. 'You can come with me in the Zodiac and we'll repeat part of the swim we did on the first day, from Punta del Castillo to Morrón de los Genoveses. What do you think?'

'Ooh, that was the really lovely beach,' Alison says with enthusiasm. 'Oh yes, I'd definitely be up for that. What about you, Claire?'

Claire considers the idea. 'That's a really short swim. I was looking forward to doing more, especially as I didn't get to swim today.'

'You should have thought about that when you stuck your tongue down Alan's throat,' Debbie says, her face red and blotchy.

Nisha huffs, 'Oh for God's sake, Debbie. Put a sock in it, will you?'

Debbie clamps her mouth shut.

Alison gets up and stands next to Claire. 'I think we should take this option. It will be really nice, just you and me in the water, that beautiful beach.' Then, as an extra push, 'Plus we get our own swim coach, just the two of us.'

The final comment is persuasive, and Claire says, 'Okay, let's do it. Sounds great actually.'

'At last!' Nisha says. 'Now, can we all just try and get along, please, and enjoy the last part of the holiday.'

Oliver turns to Claire and Alison. 'I'm glad you agreed. We'll have a great time.' Looking at Claire, he lowers his voice. 'It'll be nice to be with some proper swimmers for once.'

The next morning, in order to keep warring factions apart, Oliver has suggested that those who will be taking the main boat and swimming with Sophie have breakfast at a different time. Their journey is a longer one so it makes sense for them to eat earlier anyway. Once they have all left the villa, he goes to Claire and Alison's room and knocks on the door.

'The coast is clear. You can come out of hiding now.'

Claire pops her head out of the door. 'This is all very cloak and dagger, isn't it?'

Rolling his eyes, Oliver agrees. 'Yeah, I know, but probably best to avoid any further confrontation. If you two get yourself something to eat, I'll see you out front in an hour.'

An hour and a half later, Alison and Claire are standing outside, but there's still no sign of Oliver. Just as Alison is going to look for him, he appears. 'Sorry to keep you waiting. I couldn't find the VHF radio we use for the Zodiac. We normally charge it in the same place, but it's nowhere to be found. I wonder where Ben put it?'

'Maybe he left it on the Zodiac?' Alison says. 'He was in a bit of a state by the end of the swim.'

'Um, so I heard. Still, it's a bit off to not bring the radio back.'

'Can we still go if the radio isn't fully charged?' Alison says, her tone anxious.

Brushing off her concern, Oliver says, 'Oh yes, it's not as if we're going far, and with two experienced swimmers like you guys, I can't see what trouble we could get into.'

As the three of them walk down to the marina, Claire feels more relaxed than she has done in days. The sun is intense and the forecast has been for unseasonably high temperatures. By the time they get to the Zodiac, it is very hot.

Oliver wipes his brow. 'Phew! I envy you getting into the water on a day like this. It'll be boiling in the Zodiac, with no shade.'

As they load up the Zodiac, they hear loud male English voices. Their noisy laughter penetrates the harbour. Oliver lifts an eyebrow. 'Lads-only holiday, I expect. Might be a stag do. I bet they're off to hire some jet skis – bloody things, they should ban them.'

'I would have thought you'd be all for them. All that speed and action,' Claire says.

'Not when any idiot is allowed on them. There need to be more regulations and training before people get on one.' Seeing the women's surprised expressions, he continues, 'Yeah, that's right, I can be sensible sometimes,' and they all chuckle.

Alison comes across the radio, lying on the floor at the back of the boat. She picks it up, the bag it is in dripping seawater. 'I've found the radio. Here.'

'Great,' Oliver says, taking it from her, then frowning. 'Oh blast.'

Claire looks over his shoulder. 'Is it out of juice?'

'It's not that. Water has got into the storage bag. Even if it were charged, it wouldn't work. What a pain.'

It takes a couple of attempts to get the outboard started. Claire says, 'Ben did say he'd had trouble with that.' She doesn't comment on the battered nature of the Zodiac.

'Just a bit temperamental, that's all,' Oliver replies. 'There! You've just got to have the right touch.' He grins at them as the outboard kicks into life.

As they head out of the marina, Oliver's prediction proves to be right, and the peace of the morning is shattered by the roaring of two jet skis. They are racing against one another, egging each other on. They thunder up behind the Zodiac, shouting and whooping. One peels away and rides alongside Oliver. The driver waves at the group in the Zodiac, not noticing their disapproval, then shrieks at his friend, 'Come on, you fucking wanker!' and laughs loudly.

Alison tuts. 'British, then. What a great advert for the UK.'

'Yes and using such colourful vocabulary,' Claire says.

The other jet ski draws level on the other side of

Oliver and then screams back to his companion. 'Tosser! Tenner says you're last out of the harbour.' They tear off, their wakes rocking the Zodiac.

'What a couple of dickheads,' Oliver says through gritted teeth, then mindful he is with clients, 'Sorry, ladies.'

'Don't worry about it, Oliver. I quite agree,' Claire says. 'Let's hope that's the last we see of them today.'

Chapter Nineteen

Agua Amarga is not as far north as the previous swim to Carboneras. Nevertheless, the boat journey is nearly an hour long, plenty of time for the group of four swimmers to sit and talk. Sophie is with Josh at the wheel. Debbie is chattering away, blind to the silence of the others and the muted atmosphere. She is happy that her foe has been relegated to another swim, satisfied that Claire will be nowhere near Alan for the last day of the holiday. No one is paying her much attention, but Nisha picks up on something she says. 'What was that, Debbie?'

'I said, isn't it great that Claire isn't here lording it over us? Or bleating on about her dad.'

'I really don't think there's any need for that, Debbie, and I don't remember her "lording it" over us, as you put it,' Nisha says.

Ben shifts in his seat. 'Look, I wasn't going to say anything about this as it's a private matter, but I think you should know just how cut up Claire is about her dad. That evening, the one when we all went out, I overheard her. Their room is next to mine, and all the windows were open so I could hear everything. She was really upset, crying her eyes out. Alison had to persuade her to come out of the bathroom. Now I know it was the anniversary of the death of Claire's dad, but did you know he died of Covid, and she couldn't see him in hospital, that he died alone? That's the bit that has really shaken her, that she didn't get to say goodbye.'

Debbie is quiet for a moment, then says, 'Oh, I didn't know that.' She feels bad now for the nasty comments she's made. How must she have sounded?

Ben continues. 'I know how tough that can be. My grandma was in a nursing home and we couldn't see her for months, just through the window, that's all. Couldn't hug her or hold her hand. She had dementia and couldn't understand why we didn't visit. I really loved my grandma, she was always great fun when I was little. It was terrible seeing her so distressed. Worse, though, was when she died. My mum …' His voice chokes and he stops to compose himself. 'My mum fell apart, said she felt so guilty, that she should have insisted on seeing her, that they should never have put her in a home. It was so awful, and then we couldn't even have a proper funeral. My grandma had loads of friends and family who would have been there. Instead, we had this ceremony that didn't reflect the person she was, nor the life she had led. So I can empathise with how Claire must be feeling. Plus, I think she had to deal with all of it alone. At least my mum had all of us to turn to.'

'That's rough all round. Grief can affect people in so many ways,' Alan says. He turns to Debbie. 'Remember your Uncle Pete, when your aunt died?' Then to the rest of them. 'He wouldn't get out of bed for weeks. The family were all really worried about him.'

Recalling this period in her family's history, Debbie says, 'Yeah, it was bad. Perhaps I may have been a bit harsh with Claire. Sorry, have I been a complete cow? These bloody injections, they're sending me round the bend.'

'Debbie's having IVF treatment and getting hormone injections. It's affecting her personality quite a bit,' Alan says, by way of explanation.

'Um, they can be pretty bad, PMS on overdrive,' Nisha says. 'I think this has been good. You know, to clear the air. It might have been better to have done it yesterday though, then we could have all spent our last swim together. I'm going to miss Alison as my swim partner today.'

Oliver cuts the motor of the Zodiac. The sea is calm and the sound of it is almost inaudible against the hull. The three of them take a moment to enjoy the tranquillity. Claire quivers with the anticipatory excitement of the swim to come. This is her drug of choice; nothing can beat it. She'd have a swim over a cake any day.

'So here we are again at Castillo de San José,' Oliver says, breaking the silence. 'You can choose between swimming straight across the bay here or hugging the coast.'

Claire says, 'Normally, I'd choose the crossing – I

love that feeling of swimming in really deep water – but that would mean a short swim. I know you like looking at the marine life around the rocks, Alison. Do you want to go for that?'

'Yes, I'd prefer that. Much more interesting.'

So it is agreed. Even though it is fairly early in the day, it is very warm and it is with some glee that they splash into the water.

Oliver looks on. 'I wish I could join you. Think I'll have a swim from the beach before lunch. The water looks incredible.'

'This is wonderful!' Alison says. 'What a shame it's our last swim. We won't be back in the sea for months.'

'Best we make the most of it then,' Claire says. 'Come on, no dilly-dallying.' After spending yesterday in the villa, she's eager to swim, particularly as this is the last open-water one she'll do in a while.

Sophie is not having such a relaxing time. Her group are far from competent, and trying to keep them all together is nigh on impossible. Alan is way ahead in front. Nisha's sighting is pretty much non-existent; once she starts swimming, she doesn't seem to bother at all and constantly veers off course, so Sophie has to swim after her and set her right. Up to this point, Alison was the person doing this. Then there's Debbie, who does her best, but her stamina levels are still not up to much. She gets tired quickly and has to stop frequently, thus falling back further and further. As for Ben … easy-going Ben, so anxious to help and not be a bother. He is so far behind and such a bad swimmer that she fears for his safety. Trying to do this without Oliver in the Zodiac bringing up the rear really isn't practical nor sensible. She still feels guilty for talking Ben into this holiday; he really is out of his element. The plan that Josh keeps an eye out for the fastest swimmer isn't really working either. He seems incapable of slowing down sufficiently and only checks the water periodically to make sure all is okay. Added to that is the difficulty of having no radio. Sophie is getting more and more frustrated and more resentful of Oliver. It seems to her that she has been doing the lion's share of the work this week. Unlike Oliver, she decides that this swimming venture will be her first and last. Thank God this is the final swim and a relatively short one. Soon it will all be over.

'How lovely is this?' Alison stretches out on the sand. They had reached Morrón de los Genoveses in no time at all. Oliver dropped anchor, unpacked provisions and a couple of beach umbrellas, then quickly went off for a swim, leaving his clients to their own devices.

While Claire has enjoyed the swim, she's sorry it was so fleeting. Of course, she only has herself to blame. Plus she's missed not swimming with the group, even Debbie, who she's started to get used to. Claire yet again feels the burn of shame. She certainly didn't deserve the way I behaved, she thinks. I really upset her. How could I have been so thoughtless? What an idiot, pouncing on

Alan like that. Even now she can't quite believe she did it. Thank God nothing more came of her advances, that Alan wasn't interested. She may not be Debbie's greatest fan, but she hates the fact that she has done wrong to her in this way.

She looks at the water. It's beautiful. If only she could stay on this beach forever ... but of course that's not an option. Come tomorrow, she'll be heading back home, back to reality. 'Think I'll follow Oliver's lead and go for a swim,' she says, and picks up her cap and goggles, putting them on as she walks to the shoreline. Then she is gone, slipping through the water.

Alison has fallen asleep, lulled by the lapping of the waves. She is rudely awoken by the return of Oliver. Disorientated, she sits up. 'Where's Claire?' she says, alarmed not to see her.

'I passed her a while back. She's fine.'

'Oh yes, of course. She went for a swim.' Her heart is still thumping. Her concern for Claire has been mounting these past few days and for a moment – just a moment – she had feared something she can't articulate for her friend. 'It gave me a bit of a fright, her not being here. I fell asleep. I don't know how long she's been gone.'

Oliver plonks himself down next to the cool box and opens it. 'Oh,' he says, disappointed. 'I was really hoping Sophie had packed a few beers. I could just do with one now.'

'Should you really be drinking anyway?'

'One beer is hardly drinking, is it? It's virtually a soft drink.'

Alison prickles with indignation but holds her tongue. She's grateful that alcohol wasn't included in the picnic lunch. She finds Oliver's laissez-faire attitude unacceptable. He doesn't seem to have grasped the fact that he isn't on holiday, and needs to take his duties more seriously. She should have raised the matter before; hardly worth doing it now, though she might say something to Sophie once they're back in the UK.

She sees Claire coming out of the water, looking a lot happier than earlier. 'Good swim?'

'Excellent! The water is ideal. I'm hungry now, though. Oliver, what delights are in the cool box?'

It's a good spread and they tuck in. Sated, they fall back onto their towels. Alison and Claire sit together in the shade of one of the umbrellas. Oliver lies out in the sun, his arms behind his head and in no time at all, he is gently snoring.

Claire nudges Alison. 'I was thinking that we should ask Oliver to take us around the point and do another swim a bit later. I mean, what we've just done is nice, but it wasn't much of a swim, was it? And with me not swimming yesterday. What do you think? Do you reckon he'd agree?'

'I think it's the least he can do, to be honest,' Alison whispers. 'He's not exactly overworked himself, has he? Yeah, I think we'd be well within our rights to ask for another swim. It doesn't have to be any longer than ninety minutes, and we'd still be back before the others.'

It is agreed, then, that once their food has settled they'll make their request. Satisfied, Claire sits, hugging her knees, looking about her. It really is a beautiful beach and they have it all to themselves. What a gift.

Sophie climbs up the ladder onto the boat. She is the last one aboard. Alan was first back, a full half hour ahead of Ben, with whom Sophie was swimming. She is feeling tired physically and mentally. Ferrying between swimmers has been taxing, and the stress of looking out for them all has taken its toll. Thank fuck for that, she thinks as she leaves the water, relieved the last swim is over and done with. Any joy that she has felt on the trip has completely evaporated. She'd thought teaching diving lessons was difficult, but they are a piece of cake compared to the full-on nature of this work. It never stops. Of course, it doesn't help that Oliver hasn't pulled his weight. Ben has been more helpful, which is ridiculous given he is a client. Sophie's relief is not shared by the swimmers, who are seated in the shade and lamenting the end of the holiday.

'Back to the grindstone soon then, love. Still, at least we have a few days in Granada before we head home,' Alan says.

'Yeah. It's strange, but it feels as if we have been here longer than a week, doesn't it?'

Sophie couldn't agree more, but she is pretty certain it's for entirely different reasons.

'Alan and I were wondering when you were thinking

of doing your next trip,' Debbie says. 'We thought around Easter would be nice, not too far off and it would give us something to look forward to over the winter.'

Aghast at the thought of going through the experience again, Sophie is a little surprised the others would be up for a second holiday. She's glad they have enjoyed themselves, though, and that the whole thing hasn't been a complete disaster. She looks at Ben, who is conspicuously quiet, and sees a diplomatic way out of making a further commitment.

'We'd have to wait for Ben to brush up on his swimming so he gets the full benefit of the trip. I think Oliver and I owe him a freebie for all the effort he's put into helping out.'

Ben looks alarmed at her comment until Sophie catches his eye. She's already told him that she has no intention of organising another swim holiday.

'Yes, I'll have to get a few more swimming lessons under my belt before I attempt another holiday like this. Don't think I'll be up to your standards by Easter though. You might have to make other arrangements,' he says, playing along with Sophie.

Josh appears with a bottle of cava and five glasses. 'I thought it might be nice to toast your last swim,' he says, opening the bottle with an expert hiss of the cork. 'I've also got some of those *milhojas* pastries for dessert.'

Nisha smiles. 'If only Claire were here. She'd love that.' The others laugh in agreement. Debbie goes pink and looks down at her lap.

'I wonder how they're getting on? Probably back

at the villa by now,' Ben says. 'Shame they missed this last swim. Alison told me she was looking forward to seeing the beach at Agua Amarga and treating us all to a cocktail on the last day.' He sighs.

Chapter Twenty

The outboard motor won't start. 'Well, ladies, that extra swim might be off. I think it's finally conked out.'

'Can't you work your magic on it?' Alison says. 'Doesn't it always take a couple of times to get it going?'

Oliver tries again, this time with success. The women cheer. As they do, they hear the buzzing of the jet skis.

'Oh no, not those wallies again,' Claire says.

The jet skis zip past them, keeping close to the coastline. 'Looks like they are going the exact route I was planning to take,' Oliver says. 'What a pain. I don't want to risk having those idiots anywhere near you when you swim, particularly as we have no radio. So just to be on the safe side, I'll take us a couple of kilometres out and go down the coast a bit before you get into the water. What do you think?'

Claire shrugs. 'I don't have a problem with it. Do you, Alison?'

'Not at all. It makes sense to keep as far away from them as possible. They are an accident waiting to happen.'

The outboard is behaving itself now and they move

out to sea, parallel to the shore. The coastline changes from beach to rockface and tiny deserted coves. Claire is impressed. 'Wow, absolutely nobody about. The only way to reach these coves is by boat. You could have your own private little beach. Do you reckon you could stay overnight on one of them, Oliver?'

'I don't see why not, as long as you brought provisions,' Oliver says. 'Could be something we offer on the next trip.'

Claire thinks it sounds idyllic and already wishes the next holiday was here.

'I think we'll be okay to swim from here,' Oliver says. 'I can't see or hear those jet skis. As nothing formal is planned for this, I propose that you swim for say forty to forty-five minutes, then we double back to Morrón de los Genoveses and head home. What do you say?'

Claire and Alison get into the water and kick away from the Zodiac. Oliver keeps moving so that the outboard doesn't stall. Claire is wearing her own tow float containing two bottles of water. She leads the way and Alison can easily sight the float trailing behind her.

Oliver watches them go, a self-satisfied smile on his face. He gives Claire and Alison a cursory look as they swim away. They are good openwater swimmers – they don't need much supervision. In fact, there isn't much for him to do, aside from keeping them in his line of vision and having the outboard ticking over. After half an hour or so he decides they should turn around. He sees that

Claire and Alison are no longer swimming parallel to land but toward him. Puzzled, he moves a little closer, then cuts the outboard, waiting for them to get to him. Claire, rather than staying with Alison, has pulled ahead and is swimming, race-like, at him.

Despite the speed at which she is swimming, Claire is taking some time to get to him. He realises that the Zodiac has got caught in a strong current which is pulling it further out to sea. He doesn't want to start the outboard again only to have to stop it shortly afterward while the swimmers get on, so he waits.

Claire reaches him, fighting for breath. 'Jellyfish! Lots of the buggers! Help me up, will you?' Oliver grabs hold of her arms and sees angry red welts on both of them. He winces, knowing how painful they will be. The sight of them hastens his intent and he is so caught up helping her that he doesn't notice a bloom of jellyfish floating to the surface of the water, starting to surround the Zodiac.

A blood-curdling cry can be heard from the water. Claire makes a monumental effort and pulls herself into the Zodiac. 'Alison!' She whips her head around and sees Alison about a hundred metres away. She is thrashing around in the water, shrieking, completely surrounded by jellyfish.

'I'm going in for her,' she announces and prepares to dive.

'Don't be stupid. Stay put,' Oliver orders. Miraculously, the boat starts first time and he covers the distance to Alison in seconds. 'Hold the steering wheel and keep us steady,' he tells Claire. She obeys without question and Oliver reaches for Alison, his hands immersed in the gelatinous soup of jellyfish. Claire knows he is being stung.

'Alison, we're here. Take my hand.' Alison can hear him but cannot see him. Her eyes are closed shut, swollen with multiple stings. Her goggles are nowhere to be seen.

She is screaming in agony. 'Help me! Help me! I can't see!'

Petrified by what she is witnessing, Claire starts shrieking. She cannot stem the panic bursting out of her. 'No! No! No!' She leans over the side of the Zodiac and as she does so, the outboard stops abruptly.

Oliver has to hold her back to stop her falling in. 'Claire! Shut up. Help me get her.'

With some effort, she manages to stop screaming, and side by side they drag Alison into the Zodiac.

Alison lies whimpering on the floor. She is covered head to toe with jellyfish stings, her distended lips a giant blister in her swollen face. She goes to touch them with bloated fingers. Claire's breathing is coming in ragged bursts and she is frozen with fear as she stares at her friend.

'Don't touch your face,' Oliver says to Alison in a low, soothing voice. 'Claire, I need your help. Start pouring seawater over her legs and see if you can find something to scrape off any tentacles.'

Faltering for a second or two, Claire starts to search for some plastic cups and then goes to dip them into the sea. She has to use the lid of a Tupperware box to clear a space in the infested water. She pours salt water onto Alison's legs, then using the blunt side of a knife she has found with the picnic stuff, she starts to carefully move down her friend's skin, scraping off tentacles where she finds them. Helping her friend calms her.

Meanwhile, Oliver is tending to the upper half of Alison's body. Calmly he tells her each time where he is going to touch her. She looks close to unconsciousness and her skin is clammy. This is something even more sinister. She is wheezing and having difficulty breathing.

'What's happening to her? What's wrong?' Claire asks, her fear increasing.

'I think she's going into anaphylactic shock, a bad reaction to the jellyfish stings. Oh shit, this is not good.'

Claire clasps her hand to her mouth and steps back. As she does so her foot touches something. She looks down and cannot believe what she sees. Debbie's EpiPen pack. Ripping the box open, she takes out a pen. 'Oliver! Here, quick. Use this.' She hands it to him.

'What the …? Where did you get this?' exclaims an incredulous Oliver. His hands shaking, he scans the instructions on the side of the pen. He pulls off the blue safety release and places the orange end against Alison's thigh. Pushing the pen firmly, he waits for the sound of a click and holds it there for ten seconds.

Claire and Oliver wait expectantly for the adrenaline to take effect. It seems like a lifetime, but slowly Alison's breathing returns to normal and she is calmer.

Claire unfolds the accompanying leaflet. 'It says here that in extreme cases, a second dose should be given fifteen minutes after the first. I guess that's why there are two in a pack.'

'I still don't know how or why there was a pack of EpiPens lying on the floor,' Oliver says.

'They must have fallen out of Debbie's bag the last time she was in the Zodiac,' Claire says. 'Thank goodness for her wasp allergy.' And to think she'd been dismissive of Debbie's paranoid insistence that she always had an EpiPen with her. Looking at Alison now, she understands why Debbie is so fearful.

'It's beyond lucky, it's saved Alison's life. But we still have to get her to a hospital, and quickly. Keep dousing her in seawater, and let's open up one of the umbrellas and hold it over her. The last thing she needs is to overheat.'

'On it,' Claire says, jumping to get more water and reaching for an umbrella.

Alison attempts to say something but Claire hushes her. 'Don't try to talk.' She opens the umbrella to shade her, momentarily propping it against the seat while she continues to pour water onto Alison's limbs.

Oliver goes to start the outboard. Nothing. He cranks it again. Still nothing. After half a dozen attempts it still shows no signs of life.

Claire is looking on, anxious. 'Why can't you get it to start?'

'I don't know.' Frustrated, Oliver goes at it again and

again. With every passing minute, the current is taking them further out to sea. After endless attempts, he slumps, defeated. 'It's no good. It's flooded.'

'What are we going to do?' Claire asks.

'We'll have to wait. It usually takes thirty minutes or so.'

'And what if it doesn't start then? We need to get Alison medical treatment as soon as possible.'

Oliver roots around in his dry bag and pulls out a phone. 'No signal, didn't think there would be.' He looks toward the shore. 'We're drifting from land. This is not good.'

Claire glances at Alison and wonders how long she can survive out here. It is deathly quiet, and they are completely alone. 'Here, hold this.' Claire gives him the umbrella. She goes to the cool box and takes out a bottle of water.

'What are you doing?' Oliver asks.

'Swimming to shore and getting help.'

'But we're miles away from anywhere.'

'I reckon it's about four and a half K. I can swim that, no problem.'

'Against this current, it will seem a lot longer. Plus, the jellyfish – what about them? I don't think this is a good idea.'

'What other option do we have? I am not going to sit here and do nothing while my friend is like this. I'll skirt around the jellyfish. I'll do it somehow.' She looks into the sea. 'Anyway, there don't seem to be as many now, and on the other side of the boat I can see a break where there are none.'

Oliver stands up. 'Then I should go. You've swum quite a bit already and you have jellyfish stings too.'

'No!' Claire says, taking charge. She speaks so that Alison cannot hear her. 'Alison is my friend, and she is only here because of me. This is my fault, and I'm going to put it right. When this is all over with, I need to be able to look her boys in the face and tell them I did everything I could. Also, you have the first aid training; you're better placed to look after Alison when I've gone. Now give me my tow float.' She holds out her hand and waits, refusing to be dissuaded. Eventually Oliver gives it to her. She snaps the cord around her waist and holds the float in her hand.

'When I get in, give me the water bottle,' she instructs Oliver. 'And give Alison that second dose in about ten minutes.'

Cautiously, she eases herself into a clear patch of sea and maps out a path in the water that is safe. Oliver hands down the bottle. She gives him a wobbly smile. 'See you back at the ranch.'

Chapter Twenty-One

'Hard to believe we'll all be freezing cold when we get back to England,' Nisha says as they make their way back from the marina. 'I shall miss this lovely weather. Oh look, the ice cream place is open. Why don't we stop and have one? I know it's not cocktails, but it's a nice treat.'

Debbie agrees. 'Good idea. We should make the most of the last few hours of this holiday. And you're right about the weather in England: cold, windy and wet by all accounts. Who knows when we'll next be able to sit outside and eat ice cream again.'

Sophie had been hoping to get back to the villa as quickly as possible. She is tired and all she wants to do is have a shower and pour herself a large drink. But Debbie has a point, and she can't begrudge them wanting to squeeze out the last drop of fun. So she agrees, hoping her lack of enthusiasm isn't apparent.

Ben puts his arm around her shoulders and gives her a little hug. 'Come on, I'll treat you. Anything you want.'

'Can I have an ice cream as big as my head?' she asks.

'Absolutely! I think you deserve it.'

Nisha says, 'Ben's right. You've worked very hard this holiday and it hasn't gone unnoticed.' The implication that Oliver has been a real lazybones is implied but wisely not spoken.

Still with his arm around her, Ben says, 'I've really enjoyed spending time with you, Sophie. It's been good to reconnect. I was hoping that when we got back to England, we could carry on seeing each other, not lose contact. You could come up to London and visit if you like.'

The weight of Ben's arm on her shoulders feels good, and Sophie likes the idea of seeing him on a more frequent basis. 'I'd like that a lot. We should set a date, rather than let it drift. Once we get back to our regular lives it will be easy to let it slide.'

'Oh, don't worry about that. I have no intention of letting that happen. Now, let's get you that ice cream.'

The others are already inside, inspecting the array of flavours on offer. Debbie is swamped with indecision. 'Ooh, so many to choose from.'

'I know what I'm having,' Nisha says. 'A big scoop of the pistachio, and the Belgian chocolate.'

Ben and Sophie join them and they spend several minutes deciding. Orders made and paid for, they go outside to sit on the terrace. Debbie gives her ice cream to Alan to hold while she searches for something in her bag. There is whispering among the group and Sophie wonders what is going on.

Alan gives a little cough. 'Sophie, we wanted to thank you for all you've done this holiday. I know we had our little upsets.'

'That's putting it mildly,' Nisha says.

'Yes, but be that as it may,' Alan continues, 'this being your first trip and all, there were bound to be a few wrinkles to be ironed out, and it has all worked out in the end. And I, for one, have had a great time.'

Debbie has a small gift-wrapped box in her hand, which she pushes across the table. 'We had a whip-round and got you a present to show our appreciation.'

'Everyone contributed,' Nisha says, keen for Sophie to know this. 'We didn't know what to get Oliver, so we have a nice bottle of cava at the villa for him.'

Sophie is touched and feels guilty that moments ago she had wanted to ditch them all. She takes the package and rips at the paper. Opening the box, it contains a small silver pendant in the shape of a starfish.

'I hope you like it. Alison saw it the other day in one of the little shops nearby. It's made by a local artist so completely original. We wanted you to have something special to remember your first swimming trip,' Debbie says. 'And, as well, I wanted to say I'm sorry if I made things difficult for you. It can't have been easy trying to sort everything out. I promise to be more relaxed on the next trip.'

'This is so nice of you all, but the best thing is knowing that you've all enjoyed yourselves. Oliver will be particularly pleased to hear that you're keen to do another holiday.' She takes the necklace out of the box and puts it around her neck. 'How does it look?'

'Beautiful,' Ben says, gazing at her.

Alan says, 'Shall we head back then? I hear you're cooking tonight, Ben. What's it to be?'

'Lasagne, followed by apple crumble and, sorry, more ice cream.'

Nisha pats him on the arm. 'My dear, you never have to apologise for serving ice cream.'

Pushing open the heavy door to the villa, Sophie finds it in darkness. The shutters are still closed and the place is devoid of people. 'That's odd,' she says. 'I would have thought Oliver and the others would have been back by now. The plan was for him to be here around two, so he could help get the place straightened up. They were only going to do that short swim, after all.'

'Probably decided to stop off somewhere in town, like we did,' ventures Nisha.

Debbie adds, 'Or they decided to hang out on the beach for a few hours. It was a favourite of Alison's.'

'Um, maybe,' Sophie says and thinks it's typical of Oliver, avoiding any extra work.

'I'm going to start on the lasagne,' Ben says.

Nisha looks up at the time. 'So soon? It's only three o'clock.'

'I like to get everything prepared ahead, and then I can assemble it all just before I put it in the oven.'

'Do you need a hand?'

'Actually, that would be good. You can be my sous-chef.'

'Yes, chef!' Nisha says, as she salutes him. 'And as

we'll be working so hard, I think we deserve a glass of cava to help us along.'

'Just make sure you don't drink the posh one we got Oliver,' Alan warns.

'Don't worry, there's plenty of the other stuff to guzzle.' Ben laughs. 'Come on, Nisha, lots of chopping and dicing to be done.'

'I'm off for a shower. I feel as if I'm caked in salt.' Sophie scratches at her scalp.

Alan suggests that he and Debbie go and sit by the pool. 'I'll get us a glass of cava before the two chefs in there drink it all.'

After her shower, Sophie goes to the pool area, where Alan and Debbie have given up nipping in and out of the kitchen for wine; instead, an ice bucket with a bottle is by their side.

'Cava?' offers Alan, waving an empty champagne flute.

'Yes, please, that would be lovely. Still no Oliver?' She picks up her phone to make a call. 'I'll remind him that he has things to do here. If I know him, he's found a nice little bar and the three of them will have lost track of time.' She listens as the phone call is immediately diverted to voicemail. 'Odd. He must have switched off his phone.'

'Or it's out of range,' Alan says.

'But they can't still be at the beach, or even making their way back in the Zodiac. It's gone four.' A prickle of fear hits Sophie. 'I'll check with Josh. Maybe they're with him.'

But a short conversation with her brother does nothing to quell her uneasiness. He hasn't seen or heard from Oliver.

'I don't like this. They should have been back ages ago. It's not like Oliver to turn his phone off, or not to check in with me. He's crap about a lot of things, but that isn't one of them. I think I'll go into town and see if the Zodiac is moored.'

'We'll come with you,' Alan says. 'I'll just let Ben and Nisha know.' He pops his head around the kitchen door. 'Oliver and the others still aren't back. Sophie is a bit worried so we're going to town to have a look for them, okay?'

Nisha's eyes are watering from the onions she's chopping. 'All right, we'll carry on here. They've probably just stopped at a bar.'

'I expect that's what it is. Still, better safe than sorry. See you later.'

At the marina none of them can see any trace of the Zodiac.

'Should we call the authorities?' Debbie asks.

Sophie's eyebrows are knotted together. 'To be honest, I'm not sure who I would call; plus my Spanish isn't up to much.'

'Look. There's Josh,' Alan says, seeing him strolling towards them with a bag of groceries.

'Hi there, sis. What are you doing here?'

'Looking for Oliver. He and the others are still not

back from their swim. I can't get hold of him and I'm getting worried. Oh God, Josh. Where the hell are they?' Sophie feels herself starting to panic. 'What are we going to do?'

Josh takes charge. 'Well first, I'll call the local police, then I think we'd better take the boat out and go and look for them. At least we've got a starting point to go on.'

Debbie says, 'I'll call Nisha, just to check that they're not at the villa and to let them know what's going on.'

'Good idea,' Sophie says.

There's no good news from the villa, but Nisha has promised to call them immediately if Oliver returns.

Josh ends his call with the police. 'They said, given the circumstances, the situation is not considered an emergency yet but we should contact them again if we don't find them soon. I think we need to get out there. Any idea where we should head to, sis?'

'God only knows. I thought he was going to head south, but maybe he changed his mind. Oliver can be a law unto himself at times,' Sophie says. She feels a mixture of dread and especially anger. Oliver has a knack for always managing to come up smelling of roses, so her primary thought is how she'll really lay into him when he does turn up. 'He'll probably wonder what all the fuss is about.'

'What do you want us to do?' Alan says. 'Should we stay here or come with you?'

She hesitates, unsure. 'Stay here, I think. If Oliver shows up you can let him know what's going on and contact us. Here' – she passes him another VHF radio – 'you can use this. We should stay in range.'

The two pairs separate. Josh says to her, 'I hope this will all come to nothing and it's just Oliver being a prat. This is going to be like looking for a needle in a haystack.'

Chapter Twenty-Two

Claire has been in the water for hours. She doesn't know how long; her body is on autopilot. She's trying to ignore the physical discomfort she is in: the smarting of the jellyfish stings, the skin on her back stretched taut from sunburn. These are insignificant compared to the mental torture she is suffering, though. Her mind drifts to another agonising time, just two years ago, when someone else she loves is in pain.

There was no loss of smell or taste, no continuous cough to alert her. She hadn't been sleeping that well, despite an overwhelming tiredness that had dogged her for days. It had been manic at work so she'd just thought that was why she was feeling crap. So busy had she been that she'd not noticed her appetite leave her, nor had time to drop in on her dad, as was her custom a few times a week. They had grown very close ten years before when her mum had died, aged fifty-five, of breast cancer. The family had been devastated. Less than a year later her brother Stuart had been promoted to nurse practitioner and was transferred to a hospital in Sheffield – though it might have been Sydney in terms of the distance it created between them as a family. Claire's father had never forgiven him for deserting them before the first-year anniversary of his wife's death. Over the years the gap between them had widened, which even the arrival of grandchildren had not breached.

Claire usually visited her dad on her way back from work. They would have a cup of tea and she would tell him about the latest drama, making him laugh as she described the various characters. He loved hearing her anecdotes and would regale her with tales of when he too had worked as an accountant. By the time she was able to see him, he was in bed, gasping for breath, too sick to administer his insulin shot.

As she swims, Claire tries to shake the memory of what followed, but it plays in an endless loop: calling 999, gulping for air and reasoning she must be having a panic attack. But it had turned out not to be that. Her father had been bundled onto a stretcher and whisked away, leaving her forgotten. She collapsed onto the same bed he had just vacated, and it was only twenty-four hours later as she resurfaced that she knew what was wrong with her. The knowledge, too, that what had happened to her father was her fault.

Claire stops swimming. She has relived the events countless times, but it is as if they have only just occurred. Even though she would do anything to forget, she cannot tear her mind's eye away.

When she'd called the hospital, she was told that her

father had been intubated and was very poorly. At the time she did not know what the euphemism meant. Two days later, he was dead. Even now it shocks her. She was too sick to say goodbye. When her brother arrived, Claire could barely lift her head from the pillow. The funeral took place without her in attendance, without her father's wishes taken into consideration, because only she had known where he kept his will and her brother had not thought to ask. She was furious with him for that, although now she's starting to think it may be time to build bridges with him. He had his own way of dealing with the loss of their mother. She cannot blame him for running away; isn't that what she has been doing these past two years?

Weeks after the funeral, recovered from Covid and with Stuart back in the bosom of his family, she stood by the mound of earth that was her dad's grave. She howled her sorrow and clawed at the damp soil, weeping. She had not cried since that day, terrified by the enormity of her grief. It was locked away, pushed down. However, in the past few months it had reappeared to haunt her, married to the guilt she felt every single day. It was unbearable and uncontrollable.

During the weeks and months that had passed since he died, Claire had been caught up with the business of death. The bureaucracy of contacting banks and civil servants. The kindness of strangers as she put on her bravest face. She had not been there for her father when it mattered, but she was damn well going to be the most dutiful daughter she could now. Hours spent at the family home, painstakingly going through every item of clothing, washing and pressing them before they were given to her father's favourite charity. Every trip made with business-like efficiency; the thanks from the volunteers at the shop, the benevolent smiles telling her what a good person she was, only Claire knowing the truth. If sorting through Dad's clothes was difficult, the mountains of photographs were even worse. At least she could legitimately keep these without it being considered unhealthy. Each photograph pored over, dated and catalogued into albums which now lined the shelves of her home. Before his house was put up for sale, she had scrubbed, cleaned and painted, wanting to present it in its best light. She still wanted to make her father proud. All of it helping to atone, but not enough, never enough …

The sighting of land – how long ago? She is no longer able to think coherently – gave her hope, and with hope, the strength to carry on. But hope is ebbing away as quickly as the ability to continue. The shore had seemed tantalisingly close, but now? She stops. Barely able to believe it. Her feet are touching the bottom! She attempts to stand but her legs give way. She puts her hands out in front of her and they hit the sand. It is a glorious feeling. She tries to stand again but cannot, so crawls out of the water and collapses, utterly exhausted.

She lies there awhile before sitting up. It feels good to be on terra firma, and momentarily she is jubilant.

Her elation, though, is quelled by her driving thirst. She checks the water bottle again, knowing it is empty but unable to stop herself. As she gathers what strength she can, she tries to get a bearing of which cove she is in.

While gazing at the point, her mind fuzzy as she tries to calculate and plan her route, she hears a noise. What? Could it be …? Glancing over her shoulder she sees the two jet skis from earlier in the day, coming toward the cove. She can't quite believe this second piece of freakish luck. Staggering to her feet, she waves both of her arms above her head, her attempt to shout thwarted by her extreme thirst. It doesn't matter. The two men have seen her and are waving back. Dismounting, they make their way over to her.

'All right, love, you okay?'

'No! You have to help, there's been a terrible accident.'

Both men move forward and Claire puts her hands out to stop them. 'Not me. My friend … my friend. You have to get help to them!'

'Woa! Slow down there. What's this all about? What friend? I don't see anyone else here,' says one of the men, looking around the empty cove.

'They're out at sea, stranded.'

The other man says, 'You were with the people in the Zodiac, right? We saw you coming out of the marina earlier.'

'Yes, that was us. The motor conked out and wouldn't start. My friend is very ill. She needs to get to a hospital. I swam for help.'

'Fuck. Where did you swim from? I can't see any

Zodiac,' the jet-skier says, shading his eyes with his hand and scanning the horizon.'

'It's a few kilometres out to sea. Please, help me.'

'Tell you what, you go back to the marina with Mike and raise the alarm, and I'll go and try find your friends. Can you point me in the right direction?'

Claire does this as quickly as she can. It takes a few minutes to compose herself sufficiently to get her head together and give directions. She's finding it hard to think. 'Do you have any water? I ran out ages ago.'

'Course,' Mike says. 'Dave, don't you have a full bottle? Think she'll need it.' He looks at Claire. 'You look done in, love. How long did it take you to swim here?'

'A few hours. Look, can we go, please? I'm really worried about my friend.'

As she watches Dave leave, she prays that he finds Oliver and Alison and lets them know that help is on its way.

Claire clutches Mike's waist as he speeds back to the marina, everything a blur as they rush along. Slowing down by the entrance, Mike turns around and says, 'We can't go any further. Jet skis aren't allowed in. We have to park up here. Come on, I'll help you off.'

Across the marina, Claire screws up her eyes, trying to peer through the crowds. Where is the *Alba*? She scans the pontoons again. The place is crowded and all the boats look the same. She starts to panic, her brain not functioning properly. Could that be them? She shields her eyes from the sun. Yes! She spots two blond heads against a backdrop of Spaniards. The breath hisses out of her body and she points, momentarily speechless. 'There! Over there! Quick! My friends. You've got to get to them and let them know what's happened. Go. Go! Don't worry about me, just get to them!'

Mike sprints away, avoiding people milling around the various bars. He's a fast runner and Claire can see he'll reach the *Alba* in time. She holds onto the jet ski for support. She's done all she can for now.

Chapter Twenty-Three

Mike is now on the *Alba* with Josh and Sophie, giving them directions. Sophie holds up a pair of binoculars and is scanning the water. She makes out the bright purple umbrella being held aloft in the Zodiac. 'I can see Oliver. He's holding the umbrella over someone … I can't see who.' She turns to Josh, a look of dismay on her face. 'I can only see two of them.' She swallows; terrible scenarios race through her mind. 'There's a jet ski with them, must be Mike's friend. He's waving at us.'

Now that it's been located, it doesn't take Josh long to reach the Zodiac. As they draw level, they are met with a horrific vision. Sophie takes a sharp intake of breath, covering her mouth with her hand. Mike averts his eyes from the scene below, then acknowledges his friend on the jet ski. Oliver looks up from an unconscious Alison. His eyes are red and tears are coursing down his face. His voice cracks. 'I think you're too late.'

At the marina, Debbie calls to check in with Ben and asks him to come and meet them in the hire car. She thinks it would be wise for them all to be together in case they are needed to help. A short while later he pulls up at the agreed point. Nisha is with him; both look anxious. Getting out of the car, Nisha says, 'Now what? We're here, but aside from looking out for Oliver and the others, there's not much we can do.'

'Actually,' Ben says, looking a bit guilty, 'I'm starving and could do with some food. Nothing is ready back at the villa, and to be honest I don't feel much like cooking. There's a pizzeria here. We could get something to eat and still keep an eye out for the others. What do you think?'

'Now that you come to mention it, I'm hungry too,' Nisha says. 'There's no point in us not eating. There's nothing more we can do at the moment.'

During the meal, conversation is muted and they ponder how the holiday, which had promised so much, could come to this. Debbie is mulling over the things she has said and done in the past few days and is not proud of herself. Feeling claustrophobic, she says, 'I'm going for a walk. I could do with some fresh air.'

'Do you want me to come with you?' Alan says.

'No, that's all right. I need to clear my head, be on my own for a bit.'

The restaurant next door is very busy, full of people spilling out onto the pavement, their noisy laughter at odds with her emotions. Not wanting to stray too far, she strolls across to the other side of the marina. Overlooking the small harbour, the castle on the point is now a shadowy outline. In contrast to where she has just come from it is deserted, and all she can hear is the sound of the sea. Feeling a bit vulnerable here on her own, she decides to walk back to where there are more people. As if to justify her fears, she sees a drunk meandering toward her, weaving left and right. She goes to turn away, but something makes her look again. It is a woman and she is wearing a swimming costume.

Claire is exhausted. Just getting off the jet ski takes a monumental effort and she staggers to stand. The rough concrete is painful against her bare feet as she begins to walk along the pavement. She feels dizzy and disorientated, unsure if she is going in the right direction. She swallows, her thirst unbearable and her head pounding. She treads on a piece of broken glass and is immediately distracted by this fresh agony. Crying out in pain, she continues to limp on, aware that in only her swimming costume she must look an odd figure. The chafing of her costume at the top of her legs as she walks is excruciating. Ahead of her, she makes out the form of a woman. She tries to shout, but the sound comes out as a mere croak and cannot be heard. Frustrated, she begins to cry, waving her arms around to attract attention. The woman begins to walk away. 'No!' A silent scream from Claire. Then the woman starts to move in her direction. 'Help! Help me, please,' Claire rasps. The woman gets close enough for Claire to see her face. It is Debbie.

Running towards her, Debbie reaches Claire as she collapses onto the pavement. 'Claire! Thank God you're safe.'

'Alison …' she pants, 'Alison needs help. She … jellyfish …'

'Josh and Sophie are out on the boat looking for them. A couple of jet skiers found the Zodiac and one of the men is showing them where it is.'

The sense of relief upon hearing this is enormous. She is not a religious person, but every atom within her is offering up prayers of thanks. She falls against Debbie. It's going to be all right, she tells herself, hoping against the odds that it will be. The thought that her efforts may have been in vain is too awful to bear, so she shuts her eyes tight, allowing the physical pain to swamp her.

Debbie hugs her. She's never been so glad to see someone and reflects on how just a short time ago she hated this woman with all her being. It seems so ridiculous now in light of what has happened. Claire is not looking good. Even in the dim light, Debbie can make out the livid sunburn on her shoulders. Her lips are cracked and bleeding. She has nothing to cover Claire with, who is now shaking.

Pulling out her phone, Debbie sees that she has a couple of missed calls from Ben. She rings him and he answers immediately.

'Debbie, I've been trying to reach you.'

'I've found Claire. We're at the other side of the marina, near the entrance. Come quickly, and see if you can get hold of a blanket or something, Oh, and water.'

Debbie and Nisha are gathered around Claire, who is still sitting on the ground, Ben has gone in search of something to cover Claire with.

'Claire, my dear. How are you feeling?' Nisha says. 'We've been so worried. Let's take a look at you.' Taking in the sunburn and the chapped lips, she asks, 'Do you have a headache?'

'Like the worst hangover ever,' Claire says. 'I feel really dizzy too.'

'Yes, that will be dehydration, you've probably got a little sunstroke too.' She touches Claire's shoulder which flinches. 'We need to get you back to the villa.'

'I don't think I can walk.' Claire indicates her feet and Nisha examines her soles.

'Um, your feet are pretty cut up and there's a wound which is bleeding quite a bit.'

'I stepped on some glass.'

Nisha examines it more closely. 'Nothing too deep. I don't think there's any need for you to go to hospital. I can treat you, if that's all right?'

'Yeah, fine. All I want is some water and to get into some dry clothes.'

Ben runs up to them, a brightly coloured towel flapping behind him. He is gripping a large bottle of water. 'There you go,' he says, shaking out the towel and wrapping it around Claire.

Claire laughs.

'What's so funny?' Ben asks.

'The Little Mermaid. Really?' Claire says, looking at the towel.

'I thought it was apt.' Ben smiles and unscrews the cap of the bottle. 'Here.' He proffers the water.

'Just little sips to start with,' instructs Nisha. 'We'd better get you to the villa. I need to dress your wound – we don't want that getting infected. You need to rest and rehydrate. Now, Ben, do you think you could carry Claire to the car?'

Ever eager to help, Ben says, 'Sure, not a problem,' and scoots down to gather Claire up in his arms.

They get some funny looks from the customers at one of the restaurants as they approach, until they see Claire's bleeding foot and blistered lips. Prompted by the sight, the Spaniards rally around to help. A chair is produced for Claire to sit in, another for her foot to be placed on. The bartender has a first aid kit, which he gives to Nisha who explains in halting Spanish that she is a nurse. At her request, a bowl and clean towels are produced in an instant.

Nisha is able to clean Claire's feet and apply ointment. She dresses the various cuts with large plasters and places a dressing on the main wound. 'That will do for now. I'll take a look at them again later.'

Ben has gone to fetch the car and arrives at the marina barrier. The bar owner hurries over to let him through, and Ben pulls up by the group. A couple of the men leap up to carry Claire to the waiting car, leaving Ben redundant.

Once back at the villa, Nisha is eager to re-examine

her earlier handiwork, but Claire brushes her aside. 'First things first, Nisha. I need to get this fucking costume off before it kills me!'

Chapter Twenty-Four

Sophie jumps down into the Zodiac and leans close to Alison's face, her two fingers checking for a pulse. 'She's alive! Her breathing is very shallow though. What happened, Oliver?'

He looks at her, his expression vacant. 'She was getting better, then she passed out. I don't know why … I used the other EpiPen.'

Fearful now, Sophie shakes his shoulder in an attempt to get him to focus on her. 'Oliver, listen to me. Tell me why you had to give Alison adrenaline.'

'She swam into a bloom of jellyfish. I swear there were hundreds of them.'

Now that she looks at Alison again, Sophie can see her body is covered with the red welts of jellyfish stings. It wasn't immediately apparent – there are so many of them, it is almost impossible to see untouched skin. Sophie says to the others, 'We need to get her out of here now. Help me move her.'

Mike and Josh jump down. Oliver is shaking violently now, dropping the umbrella he has been holding. It falls into the sea. Alison is moved onto the main boat's rear platform. Sophie sees that Oliver is making no move to leave the Zodiac. He is rooted still, apart from the quivering of his body. She calls to him. 'Oliver, Oliver. Look at me.' He does as she asks. 'I want you to hand me the rope from the Zodiac. I need to attach it, so we can tow it.' Automaton-like, he complies. 'Okay, that's done. Now your turn, Oliver. Do you think you can manage on your own, or do you want me to help you?'

'I'll be fine. I can do it,' he says. Once onboard, he sees Alison lying on the deck. He staggers slightly and Sophie rushes up to him, but he brushes off her assistance. She watches him as he kneels beside Alison and takes her hand.

Josh is already at the wheel and radioing for the emergency services. Mike opted to travel back with his friend, too squeamish to stay anywhere near Alison. Although the journey only takes a matter of minutes, it feels a lot longer. The ambulance can be seen at the jetty and Josh heaves a sigh of relief. As soon as the boat comes alongside, the paramedics are aboard, assessing and treating Alison. There is an exchange in rapid Spanish and Josh turns to Oliver.

'They want to know when you gave Alison the adrenaline. How long has she been unconscious?'

Oliver doesn't immediately reply, his expression dazed as he tries to figure out the timings. 'I … I don't know for sure. Maybe an hour since I used the first one? She's been unconscious for about fifteen minutes, maybe? I don't know.'

Josh relays this to the paramedics, who turn to each

other, shaking their heads.

'What did they say?' Oliver says. His eyes are wide as they dart between the paramedics and Josh.

'They said they can't give her any more adrenaline if you've given her two shots already.'

Sophie grabs Josh's arm. 'But they can still treat her, right?'

'I suppose it'll be down to the doctors in the hospital now,' he replies, shrugging.

The group stands by, looking on as the paramedics bring aboard a stretcher and carefully move Alison onto it. They all help lift her off the boat and into the ambulance.

'I'm going with her,' Oliver shouts. Josh tells the paramedics that Oliver probably needs medical attention too. They look at him, nod and he gets into the ambulance. The doors are shut and they race off, sirens and lights blazing.

Those left behind wilt, drained by the events. No one realises that Claire is not there.

Chapter Twenty-Five

Oliver looks like a small child lying in a hospital bed and when Sophie sees him, she feels a flood of affection and rushes to his side to comfort him. The doctors have given him antihistamine and a mild sedative for shock. Medically he is fine and will be able to leave shortly, unlike Alison, who is in pretty bad shape. She was rushed immediately to intensive care as the paramedics communicated her status and the circumstances of the incident. The group is waiting for more information on her condition, but for the moment the doctors aren't saying much. It is a tense time and all thoughts are for Alison.

Oliver is staring into space and has not noticed Sophie coming into his hospital room. She is alone; Josh is being discreet and waiting outside in the corridor. To Sophie's surprise, when he does see her, Oliver begins to cry. Silent, copious tears. Reaching out, she takes him into her arms and he weeps into her chest.

'Sophie, Sophie. I'm sorry. Please say you forgive me. I've made such a mess of things. Alison … I really thought she was dead.'

Hushing him, she pulls away to look him in the eyes. 'There's nothing to forgive. It's not your fault that all those jellyfish appeared. It was just a terrible accident. No one could have predicted something like that happening. If it hadn't been for your quick action, Alison would have died. That's what you should remember.'

'I suppose you're right,' Oliver says, wiping the tears away with the back of his hand. 'Thank God for Claire though. She's the real hero here.'

'What do you mean?'

'Going into the water and swimming for help. When the outboard wouldn't start, I was all for staying put, didn't think it was safe enough to go back into the sea. But she insisted. Incredible. Swimming all that way and getting help like that.'

Shocked, Sophie asks, 'So Claire left the Zodiac to find help?' It is now dawning on her that nobody had thought to ask about Claire's whereabouts. How could they have forgotten about her?

'Yes, how else would she have raised the alarm?' Oliver seems puzzled by Sophie's questions.

'What time did Claire go into the water?'

'I don't know, I can't really remember.'

'Think, Oliver. It's important!'

'I guess around five o'clock? I can't be sure. Why does it matter?'

'Because Claire didn't raise the alarm. I was concerned that you weren't back so asked Josh to take the boat out to search for you, but he couldn't find you. We went back to the marina and a guy who'd been out with his friend on jet skis said they had seen you and knew where you were. There was no mention of Claire.'

'If that's the case, where is she now? It's nearly nine o'clock.'

'I don't know.' She puts her hand to her head, momentarily engulfed by this new crisis. 'I'll be back in a bit. I'm just going to have a word with Josh.'

Josh jumps from his seat when he sees a distressed Sophie leave Oliver's room. Grabbing her by the arm in an attempt to calm her, he says, 'What's wrong? Is it Oliver? Is he okay? She looks at him, her eyes round with fear.

The doctor walks down the corridor toward them. He is extremely tall and has a full red beard. Josh's assumption that the man cannot be Spanish is proved correct when the doctor opens his mouth and speaks with a broad Scottish accent. 'Good evening, I'm Doctor Fraser. You're friends of Alison Harris?'

They nod and Sophie asks, 'How is she, doctor? Is she going to be okay?'

'She's in intensive care. Her condition is serious. However, her vitals have stabilised which is a good sign. We are treating her intravenously with steroids and antihistamines, and she is responding well to those. She's also suffering from dehydration so she's on a saline drip. I gather her companion' – he looks down at his notes – 'Oliver Sanderford, was with her at the time and administered adrenaline.'

Sophie responds, 'Yes, but he really didn't have any choice. They were miles from anywhere and the boat's motor wasn't working. He couldn't wait around.'

'Oh,' Doctor Fraser says, peering at her from behind thick glasses. 'It was definitely the right course of action. We'd be talking now of a fatal incident if he hadn't acted as he did.'

'So she'll be all right, then? I mean once all the treatment takes effect?' Josh pushes for a definitive answer.

'Alison is very sick and will need monitoring closely. The next twenty-four hours are crucial. However, she is strong and in good health and that helps. She suffered an enormous amount of envenomation over a large area of her body. I've seen my fair share of anaphylaxis, but I have never seen a patient subjected to this number of jellyfish stings. The treatment will continue during the next few days, then we'll reassess. After that, we'll prescribe a course of oral antihistamines. She will probably need to attend a clinic once she's back in the UK, for further testing to see whether this will give her a lasting allergy. But let's get her through the next day or two before we think of all that.'

Sophie and Josh are shocked to hear such a grim prognosis and are silent. They had thought that once she got to hospital, Alison would be fine, that the worst was over. Obviously, this is not the case.

'And my boyfriend? I mean Oliver. Will he be able to leave tonight?'

'Oh yes. He's shaken more than anything. I believe

they're preparing him for discharge now. If you want to wait, you can take him home.'

They murmur their thanks and the doctor strides away. As they watch him retreat, Sophie says, 'It doesn't sound good, does it? Poor Alison. Shit, it could have been any one of us. It makes you think, doesn't it? Claire is going to be devastated when she hears this.'

At the mention of Claire's name, she remembers the other emergency. Oh my God, she thinks, will this nightmare ever end? 'I'll call Alan and update him about Alison.'

Josh excuses himself to use the bathroom and when he returns, Sophie is talking on the phone. 'Well at least that's some good news.' She acknowledges Josh then continues her conversation. 'Let her know that Alison is stable and that there's no point in visiting her tonight. Best she gets some rest after her ordeal. See you in a bit.'

'What's the latest from Alan then?' Josh asks.

'Claire is with them at the villa. Apparently, they found her wandering around the marina in just her swimming costume. She was in a bit of a bad way.'

'How did she get there?'

'The jet ski guy, Mike. He must have brought her. Maybe he found her in the water? I don't know. He didn't say anything and we were all so focused on finding Alison and Oliver, no one thought to ask.'

Chapter Twenty-Six

Screwing up her face, Claire carefully lifts the straps of her costume and rolls it down her body. She is in the bathroom she and Alison share. Nisha is waiting in the bedroom. Ever since they got back to the villa, Nisha has been following her around, keeping an eye on her. In front of the mirror, Claire turns around so she can inspect her back. There is a white criss-cross where her costume was, in stark contrast to the angry pink of the rest of her back. Her skin is already beginning to stiffen and she knows by morning she will be feeling very sore. For the moment, though, it is the terrible headache that she'd like to deal with. She lifts a glass of water to her lips and drinks, her thirst abating. She's hungry and wonders whether Nisha will allow her to eat soon.

'Claire, are you finished in there, my dear?' Nisha asks through the bathroom door.

'Just a minute.' Claire grabs a towel, and winding it around her, goes into the bedroom.

Nisha is standing with a thermometer in her hand. 'I'm going to take your temperature; is that all right?'

'Sure,' Claire says. She sits on the bed with the thermometer in her mouth.

'Hmm, it's a bit high. Let's run you a cool bath.'

'Can't I just take a shower?' Claire whines, getting a bit fed up.

'No, a bath would be better. There's a full-size tub in the main bathroom. I'll go and run it. Back in a jiffy.' She scurries away while Claire sits waiting for her and sipping water.

On her return, Nisha holds out her hand as if waiting for a small child. 'Come on, Claire.' Claire takes it and goes with her. She's too tired to argue.

Lying back in a bath of cool water, Claire feels her eyelids droop. She is awakened by Nisha, who is sitting in the corner.

'No falling asleep. At least not yet.'

'How long do I have to stay here?'

'Another twenty minutes, then I'll check your temperature again. If it's gone down, you can go back to your bedroom. I've put the air-conditioning on so it's nice and cool in there.'

Claire half-listens as Nisha keeps on talking in an attempt to stop her from falling asleep.

Sitting on the sofa in the living room, Debbie and Ben are waiting for the others to return. Alan is in their bedroom, speaking to Sophie. It's been a trying day for everyone and Debbie is struggling to cope. All she wants to do is to curl up in bed with Alan and try to forget everything.

Ben seems lost in his own thoughts while Debbie is chatting. She is aware that she is wittering but can't stop herself from doing so. She feels sick to her stomach over what has happened. Tea! Yes, she'll make some tea – give her something to do. She asks Ben if he wants some, but he doesn't respond.

'Ben. Ben, did you hear me?'

'What? Sorry, Debbie, I was miles away.'

'I said, I'm going to make a cup of tea. Do you want one?'

'Sure, why not.'

Debbie goes out to the kitchen and potters about with the kettle and the crockery. She is still talking. Shut up! she commands herself, aware that Ben isn't participating in this one-way conversation. She goes back into the room with two mugs and a packet of biscuits she's found.

'Thought we might as well treat ourselves,' she says. As she goes to put the mugs down on the table, one of them catches on the corner and crashes to the floor. It shatters and the scalding contents go everywhere. 'Oh no! What have I done? What a mess. How could I have been so stupid?'

Ben seems taken aback by her overreaction. 'Debbie, it's only a mug and some spilled tea. Compared to what's gone on today, it's pretty insignificant, don't you think?'

'You're right. Sorry, I'm such an idiot.' She can't help herself – she bursts into tears.

Ben stands there, arms at his side, clearly at a loss to know what to do. He spots a box of tissues and takes a few, thrusting them at her. 'Please don't cry.' But she can't stop. She attempts to explain why she is so upset, but she knows she is babbling incoherently.

Alan walks in to see his wife bawling her eyes out and a confused Ben standing next to her. 'What's going on?'

'Alan, thank God! I mean, ah, good you're back,' Ben says. 'Debbie is a bit … er, a bit overwhelmed by the events of the day, I think.' He steps aside as Alan moves across the room to comfort her. She latches onto him as though her life depended on it.

'There, there, love,' Alan says, his arm around Debbie. 'Sophie is on her way back from the hospital. They've discharged Oliver.'

'And Alison?' Ben asks.

Alan shakes his head. 'Not good, not good at all. She's in intensive care. They weren't allowed to see her. The doctor says she's responding well to treatment, but the next few hours will be crucial.'

'Bloody hell! Should we let Claire know?' Ben says.

'Think we should leave off telling her just yet. It's been hard enough stopping her from going to the hospital as it is. Let Nisha treat her and see that she takes it easy. Sophie didn't know Claire was here. The guy on the jet ski who helped them find Alison and Oliver didn't mention her. A bit odd.'

Alan and Debbie have gone to bed. Ben says he is going to wait for the others to come back. When they return, his face lights up at the sight of Sophie.

Sophie is just about done in and she can't cope with Ben's puppy-like attention at the moment. Plus she's fretting about Oliver, who was unusually quiet on the journey back and no matter which tactic she tried, wouldn't be drawn into conversation.

Of all of them, only Josh appears to be unaffected and is his normal self. 'Right, sis, if you don't need me for anything else, I'll be off.' Giving Oliver a friendly bump on the arm, he says, 'You take care, mate. Rest up.' He kisses Sophie on the cheek. 'I'll see you all tomorrow, bright and early.' Sophie isn't sure what he means by that – it's not like Josh to be 'bright and early' for anything – but she says nothing.

'I'm going to take a shower,' Oliver says and plods out.

Ben attempts to hug Sophie. 'It's good to see you.'

'Not now, Ben.' She shrugs off his arm, then seeing his gloomy expression, says, 'I'm exhausted, I need to get to bed. See you in the morning, hey?'

'Yeah. Yeah, of course. Sleep well.'

Claire opens her eyes. The headache is gone. Good. She stretches – big mistake. The skin on her shoulders and back complains as it is pulled taut. Reaching for her phone, she sees it's only 7 a.m. The memory of yesterday rushes back and she thinks of Alison, in hospital, alone. She had wanted to go there last night. However, the others had persuaded her to stay put, reasoning that she would only be in the way and probably not be allowed to see Alison anyway. The sensible thing would be to get a night's rest and go the next day.

She wonders whether she should call Alison's eldest son to let him know what has happened, but thinks an eighteen-year-old is unlikely to be awake at 6 a.m. on a Saturday morning. Let him sleep. What she really wants to do is go to the hospital and see things for herself so she can give him the latest update.

She swings her legs out of bed and tentatively places her feet on the floor. Gathering her strength for the expected pain, she flinches as she stands and puts the full weight of her body on her bandaged feet. 'Jesus Christ!' she says out loud, then moves first one foot, then the other. Still pretty bad. She hobbles over to a chest of drawers and pulls out a pair of trousers and a long-sleeved T-shirt. She's aware that her reddened skin will draw attention, plus she doesn't want to expose it to any more sun, so covering up seems sensible. What to do about her feet though? How is she to go walking around a hospital like this?

Then she remembers a trick that some hiking friends had told her about. She drags out a pair of trainers and some padded sports socks, then goes rummaging around in Alison's case, pulling out a packet of sanitary towels with 'wings' – she's always found the term slightly ridiculous. Taking the insoles of her trainers out, she places a sanitary towel on top of each one and wraps the wings around the underside. Now it won't move, and will provide extra cushioning. Hikers do this to absorb sweat and help to prevent blisters. For Claire, it means she has something to mop up blood, should any of her wounds bleed. She puts on the trainers and does a test walk up and down the bedroom. It's a big improvement and she reckons as long as she takes it easy, she'll be fine.

Her stomach rumbles and she remembers she hasn't eaten properly since yesterday lunchtime. Going out to the kitchen she is surprised to find Josh. A young Spanish woman with a mop and bucket is with him.

Josh sees her and smiles broadly. 'Claire! The hero of the hour.'

'Hardly,' Claire replies, arching an eyebrow.

'Hey, what you did, jumping into a sea full of jellyfish, then swimming all that way on your own to raise the alarm, I would have been bricking it. You've got my respect.'

Claire is surprised by what Josh has said. She hasn't mentioned the details of her swim to anyone. 'How do you know all that?'

'It wasn't from our jet ski pal, that's for sure. The way he told it, it was as if he and his mate had been the only ones involved and they'd saved the day. I thought something was a bit off with his story at the time. No, Oliver told us what you did.'

'Oh. But to be fair to those guys, if they hadn't come along when they did, Alison would have had to wait a lot longer to get help. In the end, what I did was very little.'

'Rubbish! Without you, who knows how long it would have been before Alison and Oliver were found. No, Claire. Credit where credit's due. You did an amazing thing.'

Claire looks down at her feet and shuffles awkwardly, not knowing how to respond.

Josh asks, 'How are you feeling? I hear you have your own personal nurse.'

'Oh don't. She's super strict, wouldn't let me eat more than a yoghurt last night. Said I shouldn't be overloading my system.'

'Well, she's not here now, so help yourself. There are loads of eggs, and bread. Tell you what, I'll make you some scrambled eggs on toast. It's about the only thing I can cook.'

'Sounds like heaven. I could eat a horse, and I'm dying for a cuppa. Wasn't allowed one of those yesterday either.'

It takes Josh no time at all to make breakfast and Claire is soon cramming eggs and toast into her mouth. 'Sorry,' she says, wiping some butter from the side of her mouth. 'I'm not being very ladylike, am I?'

Laughing, Josh takes her empty plate. 'More toast? Tea?'

'You read my mind!' Josh chuckles and busies himself with toast and tea-making.

'Actually, Josh, I have a favour to ask.'

'Fire away. What can I do for you?'

'Could you call me a taxi? I'm desperate to see Alison. I'm afraid my "nurse" will try and stop me going if she sees me.'

'Course I can. You want it as soon as possible, I take it?' Josh makes a call. 'It'll be here in ten minutes, which probably means closer to twenty.'

'Thanks, that's great.' Hearing a clatter from the hall, she asks, 'I presume that young woman is the cleaner?'

'Yeah, the villa is supposed to be vacated by midday, but I think in all the drama people might not have remembered.'

'Oh God, really? You're right. I had totally forgotten about that. Look, there's no way I can visit the hospital and pack, plus I won't be going back to the UK until Alison is able to come with me.'

Josh scratches his head. 'I'm afraid you won't be able to stay here. The villa's owner and his family are coming back and want the place for Monday. I'll get Maria to clean your room last. That should give you until the afternoon, later if I can persuade her to do it after siesta.'

'Could you? Oh, that would be really helpful. Then I suppose I'll have to try and sort out some accommodation near the hospital. I'd better get a few things together and wait outside for that taxi. If I don't see you again, it's been nice knowing you, Josh.'

'Likewise,' he says, giving her a cheeky smile.

Nisha is the first of the rest of the group to emerge from her room. She's been disturbed by the clattering about of Maria the cleaner. Josh is outside, scooping up fallen leaves and dead insects which have landed in the pool. Nisha smiles at the cleaner, says 'Hola' and helps herself to cereal. Seeing dirty dishes in the sink she wonders who else is up. The door opens: it's Sophie.

'Morning, Sophie. Did you sleep well?'

'Like a log, although I feel a bit guilty for doing so when Alison is so ill. I have to say, I'm shocked that she's in intensive care. I know she looked awful, and jellyfish stings are painful, but I didn't think they could be life-threatening.'

'What you have to remember is just how many stings Alison received and that her body reacted to them by going into anaphylactic shock, and that is very serious indeed. Why do you think Debbie is so vigilant about carrying her EpiPen with her?'

'Yes, I understand that now,' Sophie says. 'I don't even want to imagine what would have happened if they hadn't found the EpiPen.'

'Indeed, and more importantly that Oliver recognised what was happening to Alison. Otherwise, we probably would have been looking at a fatality, given that they were stranded at sea.'

Sophie shudders at the thought. 'I don't think we should mention any of this to Claire.'

'That's if she hasn't worked it out for herself already. I feel a bit bad about not telling her that Alison is in ICU, but I didn't want her to go racing off to the hospital last night when she wasn't well either.'

'Yes, poor Claire, I feel sorry for her now I know more about her situation. She'd told me the holiday was a much-welcomed break from all the stress at work. Of course, we now know there was a lot more to it than that. This has probably made everything even worse than before.'

Nisha sighs. 'Yes, no doubt about that. It's not been

the relaxing holiday I had been hoping for either. To be honest, I'll be relieved to go home.'

'I'm sorry things haven't gone as we'd hoped for. I suppose now …' Sophie stops, she's not sure whether she should confide any more to Nisha than she already has.

Nisha changes the subject. 'I've made a pot of tea and one of coffee, something for everyone. Right, I'll take Claire a cup of tea and see how her night was.'

Sophie pours a cup of coffee and puts some bread in the toaster. She's already decided this morning's breakfast can be a DIY affair; she's had enough of waiting on people. While she's buttering toast, Ben comes in and says a tentative 'Hello'. She knows she was short with him yesterday and feels bad about it.

'I'm sorry about last night. You know, for snapping at you like that. My only excuse is that I was really tired and had been so worried about Alison; then Oliver was acting all weird on the car ride back.'

'That's all right. I understand. Yesterday can't have been easy, I found it stressful enough and I wasn't in the thick of it like you. Forget about it.'

'Has anyone seen Claire?' Nisha has reappeared, the cup of tea still in her hand.

'No, I haven't seen her,' Ben says.

'I presumed she was still asleep,' Sophie says, sitting down at the table with her toast.

'That's what I thought, but her bed's empty. I hope she hasn't taken it upon herself to go to the hospital. It was all I could do to stop her yesterday.'

'Sorry to tell you, but that's exactly where she's gone.' This from Josh, who has just come in and heard the tail end of the conversation.

'What? She's in no fit state to go prancing off before I've checked her out.' Nisha is clearly indignant her medical orders for Claire to take it easy have been ignored. 'I don't know, there's no helping some people. I'm going to pack.' She storms off.

They all exchange a smirk and Josh says, 'Oh dear, I don't think Nurse Nisha is used to people disobeying her. I'd better not mention that it was me who called Claire a taxi. Don't fancy getting on the wrong side of her! Anyway, I'm glad you're both up because I wanted to remind you that you have to vacate the villa by midday. The place needs to be tidied up, and the cleaner is already here.'

Sophie nearly chokes on her coffee. 'What? You have got to be joking, right?'

'I'm not telling you anything you didn't already know. Being out by midday was all part of the deal.'

'Yeah, but given what happened yesterday? Come on, Josh. Can't you be a bit more flexible?'

'No can do, sis. Sorry.'

Ben interrupts. 'Josh, mate, there must be something you can do. We're all exhausted and nobody had time to pack yesterday with all that went on. Claire isn't even here to sort out her stuff. And what about Alison's belongings? It's not as if she can pack, is it?'

'As I said, *mate*, there's nothing I can do. The owner and his family will be here on Monday. Once the summer season is over, they come back here to live.'

'Oh for fuck's sake, Josh!' Sophie gets up from the table, scraping her chair back. 'I suppose I'd better wake Oliver and the others and let them know. Thanks a bunch.'

Chapter Twenty-Seven

'You don't understand, I need to see Alison Harris now. It's important.' Claire is doing battle with the receptionist at the front desk of the hospital. In her rush to get here, she hasn't given a thought to visiting hours, nor the fact that she isn't family. Adding to her frustration, the receptionist doesn't speak much English and Claire's constant referencing to the translator on her phone is doing nothing to smooth the process.

The receptionist picks up a phone, and holding up her hand to silence Claire, she speaks rapidly into the receiver. The conversation is brief. Replacing the handset, she says to Claire, '*Un momento, por favor*,' then turns to deal with the next person in line.

Left there for several minutes, Claire begins to wonder if she should ask the receptionist what she is supposed to be waiting for. She is busy trying to find the translation for this when she hears a deep voice with a Scottish accent say, 'Are you here for Alison Harris?' Turning, she sees a bear of a man in a doctor's white coat.

'Oh, thank God, you're English.'

'Scottish, actually. I'm Doctor Fraser.'

Immediately embarrassed by her faux pas, Claire apologises. 'Yes, of course. What I mean is that you speak English. Yes, I'm a very good friend of Alison's. I'd really like to see her if that's possible. I've been trying to talk with the receptionist, but I'm afraid my Spanish isn't up to much and she kept talking about "Ooo see" and I couldn't find the translation for that on my phone. Can you tell me what that means?'

She is surprised to see him let out a gentle laugh, then he explains, 'What she means is UCI. The Spanish pronounce acronyms as one word rather than saying the individual letters. It can be confusing if you don't know. What she was trying to tell you is that Alison is in intensive care.'

Claire staggers as she hears this, and the doctor has to catch her to stop her from falling. No one had told her that Alison was in intensive care. 'Oh my God, no. I knew she was going to be in a bad way, but not this.' Clutching at his arm, she looks into his eyes and asks, 'She is going to be all right though? She's not going to die? Please don't tell me that.'

'She is getting all the treatment she needs and she's responding well. I must stress that her condition is very serious, but we are pleased with her progress so far. The next few hours are crucial, but we have every reason to believe Alison will come through this.' Then seeing Claire's worried expression, he adds, 'Perhaps you would like to see her? She's sedated, but it might help you, and her, if you talk to her for a bit. Put your mind at rest.'

‘I can see her in intensive care?’

‘Yes, it’s normal practice. As I said, even if a patient is unconscious, we believe they will still be aware of visitors and that it helps with recovery. You won’t be allowed to stay for long, I’m afraid, but you can visit every day if you wish.’

‘I’d like that very much, doctor.’

‘I’m headed to intensive care now. Would you like me to show you the way? Oh, and you can call me Mark.’

‘That would be great, Mark. Thank you.’

He precedes to march off ahead and Claire struggles to keep up with him. Her feet are not up to racing through hospital corridors. Finally, she has to speak. ‘I’m sorry, Mark. Do you think you could slow down a bit?’

‘Sorry. Force of habit. Don’t realise I’m doing it most of the time. You’re not the first to complain.’

Claire smiles and they continue at a more sedate pace. After what feels like miles of hallways and doors, they reach intensive care. It is a small ward with six beds, of which only three are occupied. Claire gulps as she sees her friend hooked up to various drips and monitors.

Mark says, ‘It can be distressing to see someone you care about attached to all these machines, I know. Try not to be too alarmed. The good news is that the oedema on and around her face has subsided. She still has some swelling in her airway which was giving her breathing difficulties, so we are keeping an eye on this in case we do end up having to intubate her. We’re hoping the antihistamines she’s on will avoid this, though. The next step will be to bring her out of sedation.’

Now that she is able to get a better look, Claire can see the improvement in Alison's face. 'The swelling around her eyes is a lot better. When we got her into the boat, she couldn't see because they were swollen shut. She was petrified. It was so frightening.' Her voice trembles at the memory.

'Why don't you go and sit with her for a while? Before you leave, there are forms that need to be completed: date of birth, next of kin, that sort of thing. All very standard, I can assure you. I'll be at the desk at the end of the hall, catching up on my paperwork.'

'Fine, I can probably give you all the information you need. Alison is my best friend.' She adds the latter comment more for herself than the doctor. Mark leaves and Claire pulls a chair next to Alison's bed and sits down. She takes Alison's hand, careful of the cannula. At first, she is silent, thinking about what to say.

'Hello, luvvie. How are you doing? I did promise you a holiday you wouldn't forget, didn't I? Not quite what I had in mind though – sorry about that. I've been chatting to your doctor, Mark, and he says you're doing well, that you are strong. He doesn't know the half of it, just what strength you have. Luckily for me he's Scottish, so he's been able to update me in English. I was having a hard time trying to get through to the receptionist with my ropey Spanish. Should have paid more attention to Señor Lopez in high school. He used to tell me that I'd be sorry for not working harder in class. How right he was. Another regret, so many of them … that's going to change, though. Once I get back home, I'm going to sort myself out. Get some grief counselling for starters. Then, I think I'd better knock the old booze on the head, don't you? None of this would have happened if I hadn't got drunk and tried to snog Alan. What was I thinking, hey? Bloody idiot. You were really nice about that. You could have really had a go at me, but you backed me up, as always. You're such a good friend. I don't deserve you, but I will try to be more worthy of you, I promise. You just have to get …'

Claire can't go on as she contemplates the very worst outcome and her voice chokes. She wants to throw herself at Alison and cry her heart out, beg her to live, but she restrains herself.

'You need to get better so we can both fly home. Tell your boys of our adventure. They won't believe it, all that drama. Me going to the rescue, like something out of *Baywatch*. And of course Oliver. I know we both thought he was a bit of a prat, but when push came to shove, he really did what had to be done. I was losing it, to be honest, when I saw what a terrible state you were in, so frightened … but Oliver was so calm.' She stops, aware that she is rambling. Instead, she just sits, holding Alison's hand. She's there awhile when she hears Doctor Fraser come in.

'I think we should let Alison rest now, Claire,' he says quietly.

Claire bends down to Alison and kisses her on the forehead. 'I'll be back tomorrow. You get some rest. I'm going to call your mum and let her know what has happened. I'll tell her not to worry, though you know she will. Oh, and I'll let work know too.' She knows the PIN for Alison's phone, so going into her contacts won't be a problem.

She follows the doctor to his desk and they both sit. He takes out some forms. 'This shouldn't take too long.' They spend some time going through them, recording Alison's details. Claire is surprised at just how much she knows about her. She's never really thought about what good friends they are until this holiday. She's aware that during the past couple of years she has been wrapped up in her own grief and has paid little heed to what has been going on in her friend's life. Another thing to rectify once this is over. She promises herself she'll never take their friendship for granted again.

Mark interrupts her musings. 'Now, you've given Alison's mother as her next of kin. Would you like to inform her as to where Alison is and what has happened to her, or do you want the hospital to?' he asks, his pen poised above the form.

'No, no. I'll do it. Her mother can be … she asks a lot of questions and demands answers. She used to be a head teacher and I think she sometimes forgets that she isn't in charge of everything and everyone. She can come across as a little' – she searches for the word – 'brusque.'

Mark chuckles. 'I think I know the type. Thank you for that. Being one of the few English speakers in intensive care, that task would have fallen to me, so you've saved me a job. I owe you one.' His eyes twinkle as he says this, and Claire feels that Alison is in safe hands with this good-natured man.

'Right, well, that's it with the paperwork. You are free to go.'

She hesitates before getting up and asks, 'I was wondering if there was anyone who could order me a taxi, or give me the number of a company that speaks English?'

'Where do you want to go?'

'Back into San José. I need to pack up our things. We're supposed to vacate the villa we're staying in today.'

Looking at his watch, he says, 'My shift ends in around half an hour. I'm headed that way. I can give you a lift if you like?'

'Really? Oh, that would be fantastic, thank you so much.'

'Nay problem. Find your way to the canteen and I'll meet you there. Maybe get yourself a coffee? If you don't mind me saying so, you look like you could do with it.'

'Yeah, now that you come to mention it, I'd love a coffee.' Just the thought of a caffeine hit makes her feel better.

'Oh, before you go. You mentioned you have to leave your villa today. Do you have a place to stay sorted out yet? How long do you intend staying in Spain?'

Claire sits back down in her seat. 'Do you know, I'd totally forgotten about that side of things. God. No, nowhere to go. I guess I'll have a look online. And as to how long I'll be here, well, that depends on when Alison is discharged and ready to go back to the UK. I won't be leaving her here on her own.'

'Hmm,' Mark says, stroking his beard. 'I do know of a one-bed apartment not far from the hospital. I stayed there for a while. I can give the owner a call and explain your situation, see if they'd be willing to rent to you for a bit?'

'Absolutely, that would be amazing. Yes, please do.'

'Consider it done. Now, I'd better get to work.'

Claire thanks him again and excuses herself. She manages to find her way out of the labyrinth of corridors to the canteen and squeezes into a corner, glad to be resting her feet. Her physical discomfort is considerable; the skin on her body is tight from sunburn and just about every muscle aches. However, it feels good to be able to do something practical for Alison, such as packing her things and contacting her family.

Mark returns after she has finished her coffee, brandishing a piece of paper and a satisfied smile. He smacks the paper onto the table. 'All sorted. You have a place to stay and for as long as you need it. This is the phone number for Amaya, the owner of the apartment. She does a lot of holiday lets for Brits, so her English is pretty good. You can give her a call to sort out the finer details.'

His helpfulness and kindness to a stranger touches Claire to the point of tears. 'Mark, that's … I can't thank you enough.'

'It's nothing. I've had plenty of people help me out in the past when I needed it. I'm just returning the favour to the universe. Now, I need my bed. Are you ready to leave?'

Chapter Twenty-Eight

Nisha is in her room when she hears raised voices. Going to investigate, she discovers Josh with Sophie and the others in the living room. Maria the cleaner is hovering in the background, looking nervous.

'And *I* say you need to pull your finger out and get this sorted, Josh,' Alan says. 'Given what we've all been through, I would have thought a little bit of leeway is the least we deserve. Kicking us out like this when we're all in shock, it's just not on. None of us is in a fit state to pack and get out of here in the time frame you're demanding.' Josh glares back at him.

Ben adds, 'That's what I said, but he was having none of it.'

'Just butt out of this, Ben. This has got nothing to do with you,' Josh fires back.

'Er, I think it has, actually. I'm affected too, you know. And I seem to remember when I asked about it at the beginning of the week, you told me there was no problem hanging at the villa on the last day, we could leave as and when we needed to.'

'Yes, I remember you saying that,' Debbie says.

'Did I? Well, things change. The circumstances are different now and the owner will be here tomorrow.'

'More like you cocked up and you're expecting us to cover your arse!' Alan is really angry.

Oliver has been standing on the sidelines but steps in now, his tone conciliatory. 'Look, guys, why don't we all try and calm down. This is an oversight. I'm sure Josh meant to tell you about the change in plans. No harm done, hey?'

'You would say that, Mr Irresponsible!' Nisha has been listening to the exchange at the door.

'Hey Nisha, I don't think you should be having a go at Oliver,' Sophie says.

'And why not? He hasn't taken his duties seriously at all. Drinking, partying … taking drugs, for goodness' sake! Look what happened. It's just luck that nobody has been killed on this holiday.'

Oliver defends himself. 'I think you're being a bit overdramatic, Nisha.'

'Am I? Where is Alison now? Just answer me that. She's not going to be skipping out of hospital anytime soon, is she?'

'You're out of line, Nisha,' Sophie says, her face red with rage. 'That was not Oliver's fault, and you know it. It was a terrible accident. No one could have predicted that happening.'

'Perhaps if he had not gone off on an unplanned swim? Or ensured that the boat he was using was in full working order?'

'She's got a point there,' Ben says. 'If the Zodiac had

been working properly, Alison could have got to shore hours earlier, and Claire wouldn't have gone through what she did.'

Sophie looks at Ben. 'Thanks for pointing that out.'

Ben says nothing more and hangs his head.

Debbie has been quiet throughout and looks distinctly uncomfortable, but now she says 'I don't think blaming each other is serving much purpose. I, for one, know I had a part to play in all of this. If I hadn't reacted the way I did, Claire and Alison would have been swimming with us, and none of this would have happened. Arguing about it doesn't solve our immediate problem, does it?'

Alan agrees. 'You're right, love. Okay, let's just get on with packing, shall we? Whose flight leaves first? Debbie and I aren't in a rush, we're driving on to Granada and staying there for a few days.'

'My flight isn't until 10 p.m.,' says a sullen Ben, 'but I can get to the airport early and hang around there. I suppose I'll have to.'

'My flight is' – Nisha looks down at her phone – '*was* an hour ago. Oh no! I've missed my flight. Bloody hell.'

Josh laughs. 'What? The woman who's having a go at everyone for making mistakes has what – made a mistake?'

'Josh, that isn't helping,' Sophie says.

'Yes, shut up! Oh God, now I'll have to phone Devan and explain what has happened and I'll need to get another flight. He'll give me grief about this.' She sighs loudly.

Debbie says to Alan, 'We'd better get packing

then too.'

'You're right. Come on, love,' Alan says, calmer now.

Sophie touches Oliver's arm. 'We should pack up too if Josh is to take our things back to the *Alba*.'

'Yes, you're right. Thanks for sticking up for me.' He gives her a wan smile. 'I'll clear out the fridge, then I'll sort out my case.'

Ben catches up with Sophie in the hall. 'Look, what I said in there—'

'I haven't got time for this, Ben.' She looks at him coldly and walks away.

Claire waves at Mark's departing car and lets herself into the villa. She can hear people in their rooms as the doors are all open. From the sound of it, everyone is packing. She shouts out, 'Hello, I'm back.'

Nisha scuttles out, a frosty look on her face. 'Ah, there you are! Not very good at following advice, are you?'

'Yeah, sorry about that.' Claire wears what she hopes is a guilty expression. 'I couldn't sit around here not knowing what was happening to Alison. I had to see her. Surely you can understand?'

Nisha's expression softens. 'Yes, I suppose it's only natural. But how did you manage to walk about on your feet?' She looks down at Claire's trainers and takes in her clothing. 'At least you had the good sense to cover up.'

'An old hikers' trick for the feet, and just gritting my teeth. Actually, the pain isn't too bad. I'm tough.'

'That you are,' Nisha concedes. 'Now tell me, did they let you see Alison?'

Claire tells her where Alison is and how helpful Mark has been. 'I was shocked she was in intensive care. You don't seem surprised though.'

'I have a confession to make. I already knew where Alison was. Sophie told us last night.'

Now it's Claire's turn to be angry. 'And you didn't think to tell me? Why the hell not?'

'Because I knew you'd go racing off and you were in no fit state to do so. Think about it: you wouldn't have been able to see her anyway and what purpose does it serve if you have to be hospitalised as well? If you want to support Alison, you need to be around for her.'

Claire doesn't say anything. She knows Nisha's right, but doesn't appreciate being treated like a child, nor the fact that everyone but her knew that Alison was in ICU.

Nisha continues. 'You're a sensible woman; you know I'm right, hey?'

'Yes, I know,' Claire says, feeling like a belligerent teenager.

'Now tell me, did they let you see Alison?' Claire nods. 'And how did she seem?'

'She's sedated and hooked up to all these monitors. It's terrible to see her like that, but at least the swelling around her eyes has gone down. It was so bad she couldn't see. You could tell she was terrified by that. When she comes to, she'll be able to look around her, even if the rest of her is feeling terrible. That should be a comfort.'

‘Is her prognosis good? What did the doctor say?’

‘To be honest, he was a bit cagey. Kept saying she was poorly. When doctors say that, you know it’s serious. They don’t like to use the *D* word, do they? I kept pushing for an answer, but he wouldn’t be pinned down. What do you think? Should I prepare her mother for the worst? I don’t know what to do. I don’t even want to think about the worst-case scenario, but’ – she stops speaking and swallows – ‘it would be dreadful for her mum and the boys if Alison went away on holiday and never came back. Unimaginable.’

‘Well, there’s never any way to soften that blow, I’m afraid. I’d hold off saying anything that’s going to worry her unnecessarily. Obviously, I don’t know the full details, but from what I’ve heard, the fact she was given adrenaline so soon after the anaphylaxis manifested itself should mean she will make a full recovery. Sometimes, I think doctors like to err on the side of caution when dealing with relatives or friends of patients. You definitely need to let the family know that Alison is in hospital though. If I were you, I’d focus on the positive aspects, such as the swelling going down on her face, that the doctors are very nice and know what they are doing, that sort of thing. If her mum or sons keep asking questions, you’ll just have to tell them you don’t know any more, which is the truth.’

‘Yes, I think that’s what I’ll do. Thanks for that, Nisha.’

‘When will you be able to see Alison again? Have they told you?’

'The doctor says I can go every day, so I'll be there first thing and then have a chat with the nurses about how often I can pop in. I'm renting a flat nearby so I can be on hand. I still have to speak to the owner about when I can pick up the keys, sort out payment, et cetera. I'm going to give her a call now before I pack.'

'I suppose I'll have to look for a hotel for a couple of nights. On top of everything, I managed to miss my flight and can't get another one until Monday afternoon. Devan was not best pleased, I can tell you.'

'Hmm, I have an idea,' Claire says. 'Let me speak to this Amaya, the owner of the flat. I'll ask her if you can stay with me. Seems silly to have to go to all the hassle of booking a hotel. Plus, it would be nice to have some company.'

'Oh, that would be a load off my mind, thank you. Perhaps I can come with you to the hospital, see if I can get an inside track on things. What do you think?'

'I think that's a great idea, thank you.'

While Claire is in her room making the phone call, Debbie and Alan come into the living room, pulling cases behind them.

'We're all packed and ready to go,' Alan says. 'Do you need a lift anywhere, Nisha? We can wait for you if you'd like?'

'That's very kind of you, but I don't know where I'm going yet. Claire has managed to rent a flat near the hospital, it might be possible to stay with her. She's just checking now.'

'Oh, she's back then,' Debbie says. 'How's Alison?'

'Still in intensive care. We'll have more news in the next day or so.'

'I was hoping we'd have something more positive to hear by now,' Alan says.

The three of them stand in silence and are contemplating this information when Claire comes in. 'Good news, Nisha, I've just—' she stops abruptly when she sees Alan and Debbie, not sure how to act. 'Oh, hello you two.'

Debbie steps forward. 'How are you? We're so sorry about Alison.'

'Thank you. And thank you for being so kind last night when you found me. It was really good of you, especially in light of …' She isn't sure how to end the sentence, so doesn't try.

'It's forgotten,' Debbie says. 'In the scheme of things, it's nothing and to be honest I think my reaction was a bit over the top. I'm sorry about that.'

'Well, thank goodness for that!' Nisha says. 'I'm very glad everyone is being an adult about this. After all, once we're back in England we'll still want to go to the swimming club and get along.'

'Yes,' Claire says. 'I just hope all of us will still be going.' Her voice cracks a little and Debbie hugs her.

'I'm sure Alison will be okay, Claire. Please keep in touch and let us know if there's anything we can do. You'll call us, right?'

Claire is too emotional to speak so just nods her head.

Alan touches her on the arm and says, 'You look after yourself. You've been through a lot as well.' Then wanting to lighten the mood, 'And that shade of red on your skin doesn't suit you at all, you know.'

'Oh, piss off.' Alan's comment has done the trick and she laughs.

He gives her a gentle hug. 'Remember what Debbie said: if there's anything we can do, give us a call. We're in Spain until Wednesday.'

'Thanks. Thank you both,' Claire says, sniffing.

'Come on, let's go,' Debbie says, 'or you'll get me started.'

'Have you said goodbye to Sophie and Oliver?' Nisha enquires.

'Yes,' Alan says, 'and Ben. I've arranged to go for a beer with him when he's next on the South Coast. Right then, let's be off. See you all again back in Blighty.'

Claire turns to Nisha. 'As I was saying, Amaya is absolutely fine with you staying at the flat for a few nights. There's a sofa bed in the lounge that you can use. And she's going to meet us there at five o'clock with the keys. Apparently, there's a restaurant next door so we could have lunch while we wait.'

'Sounds as if Claire is back,' Oliver says. 'Do you think I should go and speak to her? See how she is and if she has any news of Alison?'

Sophie is kneeling on the floor, folding clothes and trying to squeeze them into what little space is left in her suitcase. 'Give her some time, she probably has a lot to sort out. I imagine she has to phone Alison's family and let them know what's happened. I don't envy her that. Besides, you are nowhere near packed. You've been staring into space for the past ten minutes.'

'I've got a lot of stuff going round and round in my head. I'm finding it hard to concentrate.'

'Well try, hey? We haven't got much time if we want a lift with Josh. The cleaner has already done the kitchen and all the bathrooms. I think she wants to be finished before lunchtime.'

'She'll be lucky,' Oliver says.

'Are you worried about Alison then? Is that what's on your mind?'

'Obviously, yes. I'm sick to the stomach about what happened to her. Claire too. I take two people out for a swim and both of them end up injured, one of them now in intensive care. I feel like … well, I didn't take this holiday seriously enough, did I? I thought it would just be like taking a bunch of mates away with me. I didn't think about the responsibilities that went with being in charge, thought that because they were adults they could look after themselves. Got that wrong big time. And it's not only Alison and Claire I've let down. It's you, too.' He looks at Sophie, his eyes glistening. 'I left you to do all the heavy lifting and expected Ben to take up any slack. He's a good bloke. Better for you than me. You know I wouldn't blame you if you wanted to … I've seen the way he looks at you. The way he is around you. He's smitten. I can't blame him; you're great and I haven't appreciated what we've had together. I'm sorry, Sophie, really I am.' He looks down, busying himself with his packing.

Sophie is at a loss for words. She has spent most of the trip being angry and resentful towards Oliver, and she cannot deny she has feelings for Ben. However, seeing Oliver like this moves her and she is reminded of a different side of him, the one she fell for. 'Now is not the time to talk about our relationship. We need to get back to England first and then we'll think about our future. And, for the record, nothing has happened between Ben and me.'

'I wasn't accusing you of—'

'And I wasn't saying you were. I just wanted you to know for sure. As for Alison and Claire, the jellyfish bloom was not down to you – it was a terrible freak occurrence. And Claire chose to leave the Zodiac and swim to shore. If she'd stayed put, then she would have been fine. As you said, they are adults. She made her own decision to do what she did; you weren't responsible for that. Yes, as a business partner, you've been pretty rubbish. But what happened out there ... I want you to stop beating yourself up about it. Okay?'

Chapter Twenty-Nine

Claire tiptoes around the tiny kitchen in the flat she has rented. Nisha is snoring on the sofa bed on the other side of the breakfast bar. Trying not to wake her, Claire switches on the kettle and makes a face as it fires up. It is early, and try as she might, she has been unable to stay in bed, twitchy for news of Alison. She had lay there for as long as she could before admitting defeat and getting up. A spoon on the countertop crashes to the floor as Claire reaches for the coffee. Nisha turns over, one eye blearily looking over the top of the sheet.

'Sorry, I couldn't sleep,' Claire apologises.

Stretching and yawning, Nisha says, 'Don't worry, the children are early risers, I'm used to it. What time is it anyway?'

'Half past six. Do you want any breakfast? Amaya left some basics in a welcome box. There's cereal if you fancy it?'

Waving the offer away, Nisha says, 'Too early for me, although I wouldn't mind a coffee if you're making some.'

'Coming right up,' Claire says, getting another mug

from the cupboard. 'What are your plans for today?'

Nisha thinks for a moment. 'Nothing really. I would like to go to the hospital as soon as possible though. Did your doctor friend say when you could visit?'

'He's not exactly a friend, but yes, he said I could go along at midday and check in on Alison. Normally doctors' rounds are earlier, but it being a Sunday they are a bit later and there won't be any new information until they've seen Alison and discussed how to proceed.'

'I see,' Nisha says. 'Well, in that case, after my coffee I'll have a shower then I think I'll go for a walk around the neighbourhood. Do you want to join me? Oh, silly me, of course you won't. How are your feet feeling today?'

'A lot better, thanks, but I'd be grateful if you could take a look at them, maybe change the dressing on that cut?'

After breakfast, Nisha examines Claire's feet. They are looking better and the wound from the broken glass is healing nicely. She goes off for her walk with assurances from Claire that she will be fine on her own, that she has a good book she wants to read. However, once Nisha has gone, Claire cannot settle and ends up reading the same page time after time before eventually giving up. She looks at her watch; it's only 8.30 a.m., far too early to call the hospital. She needs something to do, something for Alison, but she can't think what. Yesterday afternoon she called Alison's mother to let her know that they wouldn't be landing in England that evening and explained the reason why. At first, Alison's mum had been anxious and panicky, but Claire had managed to calm her down with assurances she didn't really believe herself. She plans to message Alison's work, but it's too early for that now; she doesn't want to ruin the head teacher's Sunday morning with the news she'd have to find a cover teacher. Let her at least enjoy breakfast and the newspapers before that bombshell.

Nisha returns and they spend the rest of the morning sporadically conversing, with Claire looking at her watch every ten minutes. At 11.30 a.m., she jumps up and says, 'It's no good. I can't sit around here any longer. I'd rather be waiting in a hospital corridor than this. Can we go? It'll take me ages to hobble there anyway.'

The journey does take them some time. Frustrated at how slowly she has to walk, Claire is soothed by Nisha's patience and mild manner. Arriving at the empty intensive care reception desk, Nisha tells Claire to take a seat.

'There's no point in you standing. Take the weight off your feet while we wait for someone to appear.'

Her feet are a bit sore and Claire welcomes the chance to sit, so she does as Nisha suggests. They wait for a while with no one in sight. Claire is getting impatient now. Even Nisha is shifting from one foot to another.

Standing up, Claire says, 'I've had enough of this. Come on, I know where Alison is. Let's just go and see her.' Without waiting for Nisha, she shuffles in the direction of Alison's room, Nisha trailing behind her. When they arrive, the door is firmly closed, but through the glass panel they can see a crowd of medical staff surrounding the bed. Alison is obscured from view. A nurse comes out, her expression serious. She sees the two loitering and gives them a stern look and barks something at them in Spanish. Nisha attempts to speak to her, but the nurse is clearly in no mood.

Claire, frightened by what is going on, says in a loud voice, 'Please, what is happening? Does anyone speak English?'

The door opens and Mark stands in the gap. 'Claire, I thought I heard your voice. Didn't I tell you to come later?'

'I know, it's just I've been worried and ...'

He looks at Nisha. 'Can you take Claire to the seats at the end of the hall and stay there? I'll be with you shortly.' Not waiting for a reply, he closes the door. The two women do as they are told. All manner of thoughts are racing through Claire's mind. She wants to cry but holds back the tears. Eventually, Mark appears. He is wearing a grim expression. Claire clenches her fists on her lap, preparing for the worst.

'Is she ... is she dead?' Claire can hardly believe the word has passed her lips.

Shaking his head, Mark says, 'No, no. I'm sorry if we scared you. The nurses were turning her and reapplying antibiotic cream. Alison has a number of open sores which have to be dressed and changed. We're keeping her in a medically induced coma at the moment, due to the number of stings she received. They cover quite a large part of her body and will be painful, similar to burns. Luckily, those around the eyes have done no lasting damage and, as you know, the swelling has receded dramatically since she was admitted. We have had to intubate her because the swelling in her throat, though not too severe, was beginning to cause her breathing difficulties.'

Nisha speaks now. 'If you've intubated her that would indicate she has got worse since she arrived.'

'The adrenaline she received helped initially, but then we noticed that the swelling in her throat was returning. It wasn't immediately apparent how this might develop. So, to err on the side of caution we intubated while it was still possible, rather than wait and have to perform a tracheotomy.'

'That makes sense,' Nisha says.

'What does this mean? Is she getting better? I don't understand,' Claire says, panic in her voice. 'I thought once she was in hospital everything would be fine.' As she utters this, she feels a sense of déjà vu. When her father had been taken away in an ambulance, she had watched it leave, safe in the knowledge that he was in the best possible hands. Only that hadn't been enough. She starts to shake and breathe rapidly.

'Are you okay?' Mark says.

'I don't feel very well … I can't breathe.' Claire clutches at his arm.

'Come on, let's sit you down.' He guides her to a nearby chair. 'Now, I want you to breathe in through your nose slowly and deeply, nice and gently. Good. Now breathe out slowly and deeply through your mouth. Yes, that's right. Do it again, and this time count to five as you breathe in, and five as you breathe out. You can hold my hand if you want.'

Terrified, Claire does just that and it helps – as does the breathing technique. After a few minutes she begins to feel better.

'Have you felt like this before?' Mark asks.

'Yes, a few times. Not like this, though. I thought I was having a heart attack. What's wrong with me?'

'I'm pleased to tell you it's not a heart attack. What you have just experienced is a panic attack. Have you been under any kind of stress recently, aside of course from what has happened to Alison?'

Claire looks sideways at Nisha, who says, 'I'll go and get you some water. Back in a bit.'

'Yes, I have been under a lot of stress, for the past couple of years really. I've tried to ignore it, you know, just get on with things. I thought this holiday would help.' She laughs. 'That didn't go to plan, did it?'

'Can you pinpoint any event in your life that might have triggered this?'

'Yes, I can. I know exactly what it was. My dad … nothing has been the same since he died. From Covid, it was …'

'Oh, that must have been terrible. Have you had any support? Husband? Your mother perhaps?'

'Mum died ten years ago, from breast cancer. It was just Dad and me. Well, I have a brother, but he's … we're not close. No husband either, I'm afraid. Just me. God, I do sound sorry for myself, don't I?'

'Not at all. Grief is hard enough to deal with, but

with no family support it's all the more difficult. But you do know there are organisations that can help?'

'I was sent some leaflets by the hospital, but I was so ill – I had Covid too. Plus there were a lot of other things that needed attending to. I just never got around to even reading them. In the end I suppose I thought nothing could help.'

'I think you need to seek support. There's no shame in admitting it. Promise me, once you get back to England, you'll at least have a read of those leaflets, maybe give them a call? Most of these types of organisations have helplines you can ring if you don't fancy doing anything face-to-face.'

'I will, I promise. I'll get in contact with them. I'd been thinking about doing so anyway.'

'Excellent. In the meantime, I think it would be a good idea to have one of my colleagues examine you, just to be on the safe side. How does that sound?'

She is surprised at how relieved she feels, as if for all this time she was waiting for someone to recognise how dreadful she was feeling.

Chapter Thirty

Sophie and Oliver are on the *Alba*, moored in the marina. Josh is out and about, so they have the boat to themselves. Their flights to the UK are on Tuesday and work at the Aquarium for both of them starts late on Thursday. Sophie thinks that Oliver should take a few days off. However, in an uncharacteristic display of conscientiousness, he says he doesn't want to let anyone down and will be turning up for his shift as planned. They haven't, as yet, further discussed the subject of their relationship, nor Ben. He said his goodbyes to them the previous afternoon and sulkily slunk off to the airport. Sophie doesn't know what to make of this different side to his nature. Before he went, he wanted to have a conversation with her about the two of them, but she felt it wasn't the time to do so. Besides, she is not sure how she feels about the idea of 'them'.

'I'm going to make a sandwich. Do you want one?' Oliver offers.

'Yeah, that would be nice. I fancy a beer. What about you?'

'Think I'll pass, I've got a bit of a headache. I expect

it's the stress of the past few days. I didn't sleep that well last night either. I'll take a couple of painkillers and I'll be fine.'

Ben isn't the only one who seems to have had a personality transplant, thinks Sophie. It's not like Oliver to be so quiet. Even in the worst of situations, his exuberant nature usually shines through. 'Perhaps after you've eaten you should have a lie down?' she suggests, although even as she says it she thinks it unlikely he will heed her advice.

'I think I will. I do feel tired. A little siesta might do the trick. Sorry to be such a wet blanket. I'm not much fun to be around at the moment, am I?' He looks at her, his expression glum.

'You don't have to be up all the time, you know. It's okay to feel sad or worried. It's not a crime.' Her phone rings. 'It's Nisha. She told me she'd keep me up to date with what's happening with Alison.'

She answers her phone and while she is speaking, she looks at Oliver. She contemplates that for the first time in his life, he is having to face up to the consequences of his actions. And, despite her assurances, he feels incredibly guilty about what has happened and shoulders a lot of the blame.

'Right, okay. Thanks for letting me know, Nisha. Send Claire our love. Bye.'

'Well?'

'Pretty grim, I'm afraid. Alison is still in intensive care, and now they've intubated her – she was having trouble breathing.'

'Oh my God!' Oliver falls onto a chair, raking his hands through his hair. 'She's going to die and it will all be my fault!'

Sophie kneels at his feet and takes his hands in hers. 'Oliver, listen to me. Alison is not going to die, okay? This is not your fault. How many times do I have to tell you? This was an accident. A terrible freak accident. Nisha didn't sound worried. She said it was a sensible precaution. She's a nurse, right? She would know.'

'Do you really think so?' Oliver pulls a hand away from Sophie's to wipe away his tears.

'Yes, I do. Now, why don't you go and lie down? I'll bring you those painkillers. You'll feel better after you've had a rest.'

'All right,' he says meekly.

Sophie is out on deck, drinking a glass of wine. She feels she needs it after hearing about Alison. Despite what she'd said to Oliver, she can't help but be worried. She sees Josh coming towards the boat and gives him a wave.

'You look as if you're drowning your sorrows there,' he says as he joins her.

'Yeah, something like that.' She goes on to tell him about Alison and how Oliver has fallen apart.

'Where is he now?'

'Below. He wasn't feeling well so he went to have a lie down. Fuck, how did this nightmare happen? This was supposed to be a nice, fun way of making money. The first of many trips and then eventually we'd be able to do it full-time. We'll be lucky to get away with keeping our jobs if word gets out. I reckon Nisha's husband will have something to say about all of this once she's home and tells him everything. I wouldn't be at all surprised if he drops us in it with the Aquarium.'

'Shit. That's too bad. But you might be worrying over nothing, you know.' He looks at her half-empty glass. 'Top-up?'

'Might as well. Bring the bottle while you're at it.' At the moment there seems nothing else she can do but get drunk.

Chapter Thirty-One

Claire looks at the retreating taxi carrying Nisha to the airport. Nisha has been a tower of strength, and Claire doesn't know how she would have held things together without her.

She lets herself back into the apartment and flops onto the sofa. Now what? she asks herself. It's too early in the morning to visit Alison. She has her laptop with her, but the internet connection is unreliable so working remotely isn't an option. She wonders how long she will be staying in Spain. Her boss had been sympathetic, but no one's patience will last forever. To say she is frustrated by events is an understatement. Normally she is in total control at all times but it has been overwhelming dealing with everything that has happened during the past week. Trying to cope with her emotional outpourings has been an added difficulty.

A few hours later, the apartment has undergone something of a transformation. Rooting around under the sink she found a plethora of cleaning fluids and equipment, some of which were totally alien to her. She busied herself with sweeping, mopping and scrubbing everything in sight, whether it needed it or not. Finished, she looks around with a certain amount of satisfaction, then seeing the time, decides she can now go to the hospital. If she is lucky, she'll be able to catch Mark on his break. She finds herself smiling at this possibility.

At the hospital, it's still too early to see Alison, so she makes her way to the canteen and is rewarded by the sight of Mark, a coffee in front of him, gazing absent-mindedly out of the window.

'Hello there, Mark. Do you mind if I join you?'

He gives her a smile. 'I was just thinking about you.'

'Really? All good I hope.'

'I have some positive news for you about Alison. She's made some good progress and it's looking like we'll be able to take her off the ventilator today.'

Claire exhales. 'Thank God. I was really worried that she wasn't getting any better, thinking the worst …' Her chin touches her chest as she tries to hide her tears. Mark reaches across and takes one of her hands. 'I'm sorry,' she says. 'It's … the relief.'

'No need to apologise. It's not just Alison who has been having a hard time. This must be very difficult for you. But I can tell you one thing: despite everything, Alison is very lucky. Lucky to have such a good friend to be there for her.'

'Oh, I don't know about that,' Claire says, feeling embarrassed. 'She would do the same for me, has done. So, when do you think I can see her?'

'Come with me now and I'll have a chat with my colleagues. You can find out as soon as I do. Then, all being well, you'll be able to spend a little time with her.'

Sitting in the family room of intensive care, her leg jiggling up and down, Claire nibbles at her thumbnail. Mark seems to have been gone an awfully long time. Is that a good or a bad sign? The door opens and Mark fills its frame. He says nothing and she cannot read his expression. No longer able to contain herself, Claire says, 'How is she?'

Mark's face splits into an enormous smile. 'I'm pleased to tell you Alison was taken off the ventilator a few hours ago. Sorry, I would have told you earlier had I known. And she is conscious and able to speak a little, though she's still a bit groggy. We've been detaching all her monitors and will shortly be moving her to a regular ward. Would you like to see her?'

'Just try and stop me!'

Claire follows Mark to Alison's room. He shows her in and says, 'I'll leave you to it.'

Thanking him as he leaves, Claire pulls a chair close to the bed and takes Alison's hand. She is on the edge of tears, but she keeps them in check. She doesn't want the first thing Alison sees to be her crying. She sits there for a few minutes until a sleepy Alison opens her eyes.

She smiles and a tear slides down her face. 'Claire,' she says, her voice hoarse. 'You're here.'

'Where else would I be?' Claire squeezes Alison's

hand. 'Oh, you don't know how good it is to see you again. The doctor says you're going to be fine. You had me worried there for a bit though.'

'What happened? I remember the jellyfish.' Her voice falters. 'I can't forget that. I've never been so terrified in my life.' She starts to breathe rapidly as she recalls the events. 'They were just everywhere. I couldn't ... I couldn't get away from them.'

'Try not to think about it. You must stay calm. You're safe now. You went into anaphylactic shock and lost consciousness. Luckily, dappy Debbie had left her EpiPen pack in the Zodiac. It must have been the day Ben was driving and had that near miss with you in the water. With all the commotion no one noticed that it had somehow got left behind in the boat, but thank God it did. Oliver used both pens on you. The doctors said that without two you would have died. The anaphylaxis was that bad.'

'Whatever you do, don't tell my mum any of that. What day is it?' she croaks.

'Monday.'

'So, we've missed our flight?'

Claire laughs. 'Is that all you're worried about? Yes, we've missed our flight. New ones can easily be booked, that's not a problem. And, just so you know, I've packed up all your stuff and I'm renting a flat nearby until you are discharged. I've sent a message to your boss, explaining what has happened and given her my contact details. Oh, and I've already spoken to your mum – sorry, she knows the whole story – but she's fine; well, she was once I calmed her down a bit. She'll keep Jamie with her until you're home. She told me you are not to worry about him; she was very specific about that.'

'Sounds like you have everything under control.'

'I do, so the only thing you have to be concerned about is getting better. Do you hear me? Now, I'll leave you to get some rest. The doctor says they're going to move you to a regular ward, so I'll be back to see you there tomorrow. Oh, I almost forgot. Sophie and Oliver visited yesterday, but of course you wouldn't have known that. Poor Oliver has been beside himself with worry. He'll be so pleased to hear you're going to be all right. They're leaving for England first thing tomorrow, so they won't be able to visit again. Right then, I'll be off. See you later.' Claire kisses her on the forehead,

On her way out, Mark is hovering. He has a file in his hand and is clicking the top of a pen on and off. 'I'm glad I caught you. I wanted to have a quick word.'

'Is something wrong with Alison? She seemed fine just now. Has there been a development I need to know about?'

'No, nothing like that.' Mark is quick to reassure her. 'I was just wondering, well, if you fancy going for a bite to eat tomorrow? I know a nice little place in town; nothing fancy, mind, but the food is good and the staff are friendly. As you're here on your own, I thought you might like a bit of company and now that you know Alison is on the mend …'

Claire is momentarily at a loss as to how to respond. It's been a long time since she's been out with a man for dinner that hadn't been arranged via a dating website. Is this a date? No, he just feels sorry for me, she reasons. That's all.

'That would be very nice. Thank you.'

'Great!' Mark exhales. 'Shall we say nine tomorrow evening then? I can pick you up, if you'd like.'

'That would be lovely. I'll see you then, Mark.' As she walks away, she realises she is smiling like an idiot.

Chapter Thirty-Two

The restaurant is small and quiet. It is lit with candles and only a few tables are occupied. The intimate atmosphere is such a sharp contrast to the hospital that Claire suddenly feels a wave of panic wash over her. What the hell is she doing here? And with Alison's doctor? She takes a breath; she's being ridiculous. It's a meal, that's all. No pressure.

They wait by the door before being met by the owner, who is beaming and talking to Mark in Spanish. It is clear Mark is a regular customer. They are ushered to a discreet corner and given menus. Mark chuckles as the owner leaves them.

'What?' Claire says.

'Carlos is very pleased to see me here with a "lady friend", as he puts it. Says it's not healthy to eat all my meals alone.'

'Oh,' Claire says, trying not to feel pleased that Mark doesn't come here with a string of dates. She burrows her head into the menu so as to hide her smile. 'So you eat here a lot?'

'Quite a bit, especially if I've had a busy day. Can't

be bothered cooking for one. When I first got divorced I came here all the time, for the company more than anything.'

'Yeah, I know what you mean. Have you been divorced long?'

Mark strokes his chin in contemplation. 'Three, no, four years now. What about you? Ever been married?'

'Yep. Things didn't work out though. Five years for me.'

'Are you still on speaking terms with your ex?'

'Yes. We're not best friends or anything, but we keep in contact now and again. In fact, he rang me not long ago to say he was going to be a father. What about you, do you see your ex-wife?'

Mark shakes his head. 'God no. Let's just say it was a fairly acrimonious split. We don't have any contact with each other. Her family hates me and I had to move away once we'd divorced – all very messy.' He looks down at his menu and Claire realises it's time to change the subject.

'So what's good? Anything you'd recommend?'

The awkwardness averted, they move onto lighter topics, and Claire begins to unwind and enjoy herself. It isn't until the end of the meal that she realises she's only drunk one glass of wine. That's a first, she thinks. Mark motions for the bill.

'Please. Let me,' Claire says.

'Oh, I couldn't,' Mark protests. 'After all, it was me who invited you. You can get the next one.'

Claire is pleased there is going to be a next time. She

does feel a little guilty, though, that she is having such a nice time while Alison is so ill, and squashes the feeling of satisfaction inside of her.

'Absolutely,' she says. 'It's only fair.'

Back at the apartment after Mark has dropped her off, Claire reflects on the evening. It has been nice to spend time with someone and for it all to be so easy. No stretches of silence in the conversation. Not having to listen to a man brag about his conquests or how much money he makes. Just normal, human interaction with a person she can laugh with and have things in common. She realises this is how she got along with Alan. Unfortunately she had read more into their friendship, and look how that had turned out. She certainly won't be making the same mistake again.

She thinks about the next day. She has an appointment at the hospital for a check-up. She's not looking forward to it, and if it wasn't for the fact that Mark had organised everything, she'd probably chicken out. She puts it to the back of her mind and gets ready for bed.

The next day, Claire is at the hospital. She's had her check-up and is now visiting Alison.

'So? How did it go?' Alison says. She's sitting up today and looking a lot better.

'How did what go?' Claire is all innocence.

'You know very well what. Your appointment here.

You told me you were going to see someone about the panic attack you had.'

'Oh, yes,' she says, fiddling with the bag containing magazines she'd brought for Alison. 'Apparently, my blood pressure is pretty high. The doctor asked me all sorts of questions about my diet and lifestyle. She told me I drink too much and I could do with losing a bit of weight. I have to have a blood test – they're going to check for type two diabetes. She said it's common to develop in a person at "my age". She also said I'm more than likely suffering from stress and depression brought about by my dad's death and the added pressure of my promotion at work. She's given me a prescription for anti-anxiety pills, but I'm to go and see my own GP in England about the depression. She was very strict. I felt like a naughty kid.'

'I'm just glad you've finally seen someone,' Alison says. 'I've been worried about you for ages.'

'You're right. Stupid of me to try and ignore this, although I had already planned to see someone once I got back to England. Everything that's happened has really put things into perspective. And I want to be fully fit and able to help you. You do know *you* are going to need to look after yourself? Take some time off work, let your mum help out more – like she always wants to. I'm not the only one who can be stubborn and independent, you know!'

'Yeah. Point taken. Now hand over those magazines.'

'I can't make any of these results out,' Claire says, screwing her eyes up at the piece of paper she's holding.

Mark puts his hand out across the canteen table. 'Here, give it to me.' He spends a couple of minutes scrutinising it. 'Hmm.'

'What? Is it all okay?' Mark doesn't say anything. 'Come on, you're making me nervous. What does it say?'

'It says you don't have type two diabetes, but you're borderline. You need to keep an eye on this. Make some lifestyle changes, limit your sugar intake.' He eyes the doughnut Claire has in front of her. 'Do you think you can do that?'

Claire can feel herself blushing. She pushes the half-eaten cake away from her. 'Absolutely! Once I set my mind to something I'm very determined.'

'Glad to hear it.' Mark smiles. 'I was wondering if you were free for a walk on Saturday? There are some nice hiking trails locally – nothing too taxing – and the weather is perfect at this time of year.'

Claire hesitates. She has been spending a lot of time with Mark. Is it wise, given she'll be leaving Spain soon? But, she reasons, it's not like there's anything romantic about this. She's not even sure she likes him in that way, despite the fact they get on so well. 'Sure. That would be great. I could do with some exercise – and I don't feel like getting in the water just yet – but my feet are still a bit sore so it will have to be a fairly short walk.'

It's Sunday morning and Claire has managed to find a stack of English newspapers to take with her for her visit to Alison. She'd only managed to see her briefly the day before and wants to spend more time with her.

'Morning!' Claire all but bounces over to Alison, who is sitting in a chair. 'How are you feeling today?' She kisses her on the cheek.

'I'm feeling good, but not as good as you, from the looks of it. I take it your walk with Mark went well?'

Claire grins. 'Yes, it was a lovely day. There were some beautiful views of the sea from the path we took. And we ended up going for dinner.' She doesn't want to mention the goodnight kiss she and Mark had shared. It's too soon to talk about it; besides, it would be tactless of her to wax lyrical to Alison while she is stuck in hospital, so she stays quiet.

'Well, I have some good news,' Alison says. 'I am being discharged tomorrow!'

'Really? That's wonderful.' Claire jumps up and hugs her friend.

'Yes, the doctor told me on his rounds today. They're really pleased with my progress. Of course, I still have to take things easy, and I don't think I'll be up to flying just yet.'

'Not a problem. We can take as much time as you need. I've squared things with my boss and we have the apartment indefinitely. Oh, Alison, I'm so happy for you!' She hugs her friend again.

The following day, Claire and Alison are waiting by her hospital bed. Alison is dressed and ready to leave. 'What's taking so long? I thought I'd be out of here by now.'

'I expect there's admin to be done. You know how these things are,' Claire says. The door opens and Mark walks in.

'Morning, ladies. How are we today?'

'Fine,' Alison says, eyeing the papers in his hand. 'Are those for me to sign?'

Mark is looking at Claire and they are smiling at each other.

Alison coughs discreetly.

'Ah, sorry. These? Yes. Just need your signature on a couple of things.'

Paperwork completed, Claire says to Alison, 'Ready?'

'As I'll ever be. Come on. Let's get out of here!'

Chapter Thirty-Three

West Sussex, October 2023

Claire stands outside the Boat House Café in Chichester Marina. An icy wind buffets her and she pulls her coat hood closer. Peering around, she wonders from which direction he will come. His offer of help with today's deed surprised and delighted her.

'Claire!' A shout from behind. Before she can fully register his arrival, he has engulfed her in a bear hug.

Startled, then laughing, she says, 'Ben. Long time no see.'

'I know. Spain seems like a hundred years ago, doesn't it? Especially when it's so cold here, bloody freezing actually and it's only October. I hope this isn't an indication of how this winter is going to be. Have you got your thermals? It'll be even colder where we're headed.'

'Don't you worry about me. I've got my old lady bloomers on.'

'Where's Alison?' He looks towards the café. 'Inside?'

'Just parking the car. Here she is.'

Alison is treated to the same welcome as Claire. Ben says, 'That's half the swim group here. All we need now are the others and we could all go for a dip.'

'Ha ha, very funny,' Claire says. 'Reckon we'd only last a couple of minutes in the sea – goodness only knows what the temperature is. Plus, Debbie is about six months pregnant, so I don't think she'd be up for it.'

'That's amazing. So, the IVF worked then. I'm so pleased. They must be delighted,' Ben says.

'That's not the half of it. She's asked me to be one of the godparents, says I'd be a strong female role model for her daughter! I still haven't decided whether to accept, though I suppose it would be rude not to.'

'Blimey. That's a bit of a turnaround on her part, but I'm glad she's made her peace with you. You should go for it. Debbie's right, you are someone to look up to; think about all you've been through. I can just see you as Auntie Claire too.' He sniggers. 'Shall we get going or do you want to have a coffee before we go?'

'No, I'd like to do this now, please. When we come back, Alison and I are going to eat here. Please join us. Lunch is on me, by way of saying thank you.'

'I'd love to. But really, don't think you have to pay for me. Any excuse to get out on the water, and it's nice to have company. Dad is a bit of a fair-weather sailor these days.' He turns to Alison. 'I must say, you are looking very well. Are you fully recovered?'

'Pretty good. The medical team in Spain was great, my doctor especially, but Claire will know more about that than me.' She grins at Claire. 'And the follow-up treatment here has been excellent.'

'Something I need to know?' queries Ben.

‘No, nothing. Alison is being mischievous, that’s all,’ Claire says, not wanting any further talk of Mark.

Alison’s breezy assertion of good health and well-being glosses over what she has been through in the past year and is still dealing with. After her stay in hospital, she continued her treatment with oral antihistamines. Added to that, once back in Britain she had to attend a special clinic dealing with allergies, with lots of testing and retesting. Although she had recovered from the physical injuries, the same could not be said for her mental health. She had frequent flashbacks of the jellyfish attack and still suffers from nightmares.

‘What about you? How is life treating you?’ Ben asks Claire.

‘Not too bad at all, actually. I only work three days a week now. I find I’m more productive these days, so that keeps my boss happy. I also volunteer a couple of days a week for Cruse – it’s a bereavement charity. I do some work on the helpline. It’s transformed my life, being able to talk with people who have been through the same sort of experiences, and it’s been really good to help others.’ She’s also met up with her brother and they’ve been getting along better. They’ve been able to share their mutual grief and she’s surprised at how important this has been for her.

‘Sounds like you’ve got yourself together. That’s marvellous.’

‘Well, I wouldn’t exactly say that. I still have my bad days, but now I have some coping mechanisms that help. It’s a work in progress.’

'Even so, good for you.'

'Are you in contact with Sophie?' Alison asks Ben, her breath cloudy in the cold air. 'Aside from when I first came back from Spain to let her know how I was, I haven't kept in contact. You know how it is.'

'Yeah, we see quite a lot of each other now she's moved to London. She's doing a PGCE in physical education. She hopes to teach in a high school once she's qualified.'

'She's going to be a PE teacher?' Alison sounds taken aback. 'Wow, although I wouldn't have thought that would be something she'd go for. I mean, she wasn't exactly overenthusiastic about giving those diving lessons at the Aquarium, was she?'

'I think it was a case of wanting to do something more concrete, with a career path, that persuaded her in the end. Plus, her contract at the centre wasn't renewed at the end of the year; neither was Oliver's. Sophie is certain that Nisha's husband had a hand in that, especially when she found out that he plays golf with the CEO of the Aquarium.'

Claire says nothing. She and Nisha have become good friends and meet up regularly. From their conversations she knows that's exactly what happened – best to stay quiet and plead ignorance. 'I knew that Oliver had left because I still go to the swim club and he disappeared from the classes. No one could tell me what happened to him. I just assumed the reason I hadn't seen Sophie was because the diving lessons were held on a different night. Like Alison, I'm afraid life took over and I never got around to emailing her or anything. I did wonder, given what happened, whether she'd want to keep in contact. Do you know what Oliver is doing now?'

'He got a job with one of the big swimming holiday companies.'

'Really?' Alison says. 'He gave up on the idea of running his own business then?'

Claire says, 'Are you really surprised, given how our holiday went? I wonder how he's dealing with all the rules of working with a proper company.'

'He came up to London to see Sophie and we all had a drink together. He told me he was shocked by how many health and safety regulations there are, and by the extent of the training he had to do. It made him realise just how unprepared they were for our holiday. He's really knuckled down though, I think what happened to Alison had a big effect on him, and even though I'm not his greatest fan, I admire the fact that he seems to have changed his ways. He's already done a few trips in Europe with the company and says he loves it.'

'That's good to hear,' Alison says. 'If anything positive came out of what I went through, I'm glad. Are Sophie and Oliver still a couple then?'

Ben shakes his head. 'No, they broke up when Sophie made the decision to move to London and study there. And before you ask, we didn't get together either, although I would have really liked that. No, Sophie wants to concentrate on getting her postgraduate teaching degree. She says she's had enough of relationships for now. But I am hoping she'll change her mind at some point.'

'Well, don't waste your life pining for someone who isn't going to commit, that's all I'd advise,' Claire says. 'You're a really good bloke. There's someone out there for you.'

'Claire's all about giving advice nowadays,' teases Alison.

'Just giving him the benefit of my years of experience. Right, I'm frozen! Can we get going before I completely lose the feeling in my feet?'

'Follow me,' Ben says. 'I'm afraid she's not as nice as the *Alba*, but there's a heater so we can warm up.' He leads them through the maze of berths until they finally come to a halt by a small boat called *Linda*. 'My mum's name,' explains Ben. He jumps down onto the deck and helps them aboard.

He guides them out of the marina and into Chichester Harbour. All three are crowded together in the cabin of the boat, and the heater gradually thaws them. Claire is hugging a rucksack close to her chest.

'I'm going to go a couple of miles out of the harbour,' Ben says. 'We don't want to do this near any other boats; plus it will be quieter, so we won't be disturbed.'

They are out at sea, the harbour behind them. Ben turns off the engine. 'Is this okay for you, Claire?'

She motions with her head. Already there is a lump in her throat and she doesn't trust herself to speak. Unzipping her rucksack, she takes out an urn, her dad's ashes. She's kept them all this time but only now feels that she can finally do this.

Alison opens the door from the cabin, leading to the stern. 'Do you want me to come with you?'

'No. I want to do this alone. I'll be okay.' She touches Alison's arm.

She makes her way to the back of the boat, clutching the urn, her knuckles white. The water is still and grey. The horizon melds into it so it is difficult to tell where the sky ends and the sea begins. A lone seagull squawking is the only sound to be heard and Claire is momentarily taken back to a childhood memory of a family seaside holiday, her dad buying her an ice cream only for her to have it ripped away by a greedy bird. She couldn't have been more than six or seven at the time. She had burst into tears, whether from shock or the loss of her treat, she cannot remember. Her dad had dried her eyes and bought her another ice cream, making it all better. He always made it better, and the knowledge that he is not here to do that any more still fills her with anguish. At least now she recognises this and it is a little easier to bear. She removes the lid of the urn, her cold hands making it difficult, and gently tips the contents into the sea. The ashes float on its surface. The seagull lands on the water nearby and pauses as if escorting her dad to his final resting place. She had planned to give a little homily, but the words catch in her throat and all she can manage is, 'Bye, Dad. See you later.'

A sob wrenches from her, and rather than stifle it, she embraces it. She feels the presence of Alison and

Ben on either side, their arms entwined around her – she is not alone. All three of them shed tears, each remembering the people they have loved and lost. They stand like that for some time, until the chill air forces Claire to move.

Sniffing and reaching for a tissue, she blows her nose noisily. The sound reverberates in the stillness and breaks the solemnity of the moment. She laughs in spite of herself. Suddenly feeling lighter, she says, 'Time to move on, I think.'

Chapter Thirty-Four

Suffolk, June 2024

'What are you giggling about?' Alison asks Claire. They are driving from the South Coast towards Suffolk.

'Oh, this message from Mark. He made good time from Stansted and is already settled in at the hotel – he's so organised. Anyway, he said he reserved a table for tonight before he checked in because he knew it would be the first thing I'd be worried about when we got there – food!'

'Seems to know you quite well then.' Alison smirks. 'Although I have to say, these days you're a lot less piggy than you used to be.'

'Oi! Enough of that.' The two women laugh.

As she shifts down a gear in the slow-moving traffic, Alison says, 'Looks like the journey is going to take longer than we'd planned. Just as well we left when we did.'

'Yes, the A12 is always a challenge. I remember from when I visited my in-laws in Colchester, back in the day. Still, never mind. If you like we can have a break at the next services and I'll take over the driving.' Claire looks out of the window, then glances down at her phone again and smiles.

The traffic turns out not to be as bad as feared and they arrive at the hotel mid-afternoon. Claire texted ahead and Mark is at the entrance when they get there. She runs up to him and is given a big bear hug and a loud kiss.

'Ah, it's good to see you. You're looking very bonny,' Mark says.

'Clean living, lots of exercise and being in love!' She looks up at him and hugs him back.

From the car Alison says, 'Come on, you two lovebirds. You'll make a girl jealous.' She laughs; it's good to see her friend so happy. She gets out and hugs Mark. 'Good flight?'

'Aye, no delays and straight through customs, no bother. You look good, Alison. Claire tells me your treatment is going well.'

'Yes, it's been a gradual process, but the flashbacks and nightmares are less frequent nowadays. The swimming has helped a lot. I never thought I'd be able to do any openwater stuff again after what happened, but with Claire's help, I've managed. I think we've been to every river and reservoir in Sussex in the past few months.'

'I heard about your wetsuit-buying trip, sounded a hoot.'

'You try putting on a wetsuit in an overheated shop. It's little wonder I fell over and tore down the curtain to the changing cubicle.'

Laughing, Claire says, 'Oh my God, you had to be there. Luckily the staff were very understanding. They even brought out a fan and wafted it in her direction.'

'Only because they wanted to make a sale. You had me trying on the most expensive suits.'

'Well, it was my treat, and I only wanted the best for you,' she says, putting her arm around her friend.

Once inside the hotel, Alison heads to reception, but Claire steers her towards the bar. 'I'm really thirsty. Let's get a cold drink before we head up to our room.'

She thinks it's a bit odd, but follows Claire anyway. They walk in and there is chorus of 'Surprise!' from a group of people sitting at a table. Alison does a double take when she sees who they are. Ben jumps up and kisses her on the cheek, then Sophie and Oliver come over to hug her.

'Come and sit down,' Alan says, and moves closer to Debbie, who has a chubby baby sitting on her lap.

'Who's this then?' Alison says as the baby wraps its hand over her extended finger.

'This is Claire's god-daughter, Violet.'

'She's gorgeous! You must be so happy,' Alison says.

Debbie smiles. 'We are. We're very happy.'

'I can't believe you are all here,' Alison says, looking at everyone.

'Well, we couldn't let you do your first Great Swim with only Claire for company, could we?' says a voice at her side.

'Nisha! Oh my gosh, I can't believe it!' Alison stands to hug her.

Sophie says, 'When Claire got in contact with us to tell us what you were doing, we had to make an appearance. To show our support.'

'Yes, and we thought what better way to do that than to join you?' Oliver says.

'You mean you're doing the swim too? What wave are you in? The ten K?'

'No, Alison, we're swimming together,' Oliver says. 'You, Claire, Alan, Sophie and me. We're all doing the five K.'

'You guys. Oh, I'm so touched. This is going to be such a special weekend,' Alison says.

'That it is,' Mark says. He whispers to Claire. 'I have some news for you.'

In their room, Mark ushers Claire to the end of the bed and sits next to her.

'So, what's this news then?' she asks, impatient to know.

'I didn't tell you, but during the past year, I've been applying to hospitals in the South East. It's been on my mind for a while now to come back to the UK. I've nothing really to keep me in Spain any more – I don't think an ex-wife counts. Last month I had an interview, and I made a sneaky trip over here. I didn't want to tell you, get your hopes up and all. I'd had a few rejections and was beginning to think I wasn't going to find a position. But I have.'

'Where? Is it in London?' Claire calculates that this would be a huge improvement on the back and forth to Spain that has constituted their relationship thus far.

'Bit closer to home,' Mark says, smiling.

'Where? God, if you don't tell me soon …'

'As of September, you are looking at the new head of intensive care at Worthing Hospital.'

'Worthing!' Claire is shell-shocked.

'You're pleased? I know we never talked about it directly, but I thought there was an understanding between us, that we wanted to move forward as a couple. I'm not wrong, am I?'

Claire flings her arms around his neck. 'You couldn't be more right, you lovely man!'

'Phew! You had me worried for a bit there. Of course, there are a few things to sort out. The Spanish side is simple enough – I've already handed in my notice and told my landlord I'm going. All I have to do now is find some digs near the hospital and I'm sorted. In fact, I've got some leads for that already.'

'No need for that. I mean, if we really want to make a go of this, we should try living together, don't you think?'

'Are you sure? I don't want to push you into something you're not ready for.'

'I'm ready, Mark. I'm ready.'

'Snazzy wetsuit,' Sophie says to Claire. They are in the changing area at the Great Swim site. It is thick with women, and the atmosphere is a mixture of nervous anticipation and excitement as the participants chatter away.

'Yes, it's new. This will only be its second outing in the water.'

'Wanted to look your best for us all?' Sophie says, making fun.

'Actually, my old one got too big and I had to go down a couple of sizes.'

'I thought you were looking slimmer. Been on a diet then?'

'Not as such. I don't really drink these days and I'm a lot happier in myself so don't reach for a cake to cheer me up the way I used to.'

'Well, it really shows. You look great,' Sophie says.

'You okay?' Claire asks Alison, who is struggling to pull her suit up past her knees.

'Getting there. If I didn't have to, I'd really rather not swim in this. By the time I get it on I almost feel too exhausted to swim.'

'I know what you mean,' sympathises Claire, 'but just think about the extra buoyancy it gives you, especially as we're not swimming in salt water. And it will keep you warm. A couple of hours in this water and you'll notice the effects.'

'Yeah, not like the Med,' Sophie says. 'Do you think you'll ever be able to face up to swimming in the sea again, Alison?'

'I'd like to think so, but I'm not going to push it. For now, I'm just going to try and enjoy what I can and not stress about it; well, try not to.'

'She's done so well just getting back in the water,' Claire says. 'Been really brave. Do you need a hand, Alison?'

'Think I'm just about there.' She tugs at the wetsuit, pulls it up to her chest and slips her arms into the sleeves. 'Just got to put on my timing chip and I'll be all set. Where are we meeting Alan and Oliver?'

'I said we'd see them in the acclimatisation zone,' Sophie says.

Alan and Oliver are already in the designated area for acclimatising to the water temperature when the others get there.

Alan is laughing at Oliver's expression as he wades in. 'What's up? Bit chilly for you, is it?'

'Bloody freezing! Remember, I've just been to Oman for work. The water there is a tad warmer.'

'You're not being a bit of a wuss, are you, Oliver?' Claire says as she joins them.

'I'm not as tough as old boots like you,' Oliver says, his face contorted.

'I shall take that as the compliment I know you meant it to be.' Claire slips into the cold water without any problems.

The red-capped friends bob around in the water until their wave is called out.

'That's us,' Alison says.

'Are you all right?' Claire asks. She knows just how big a deal this is.

'Bit nervous, if I'm honest.'

'You'll be fine. I won't leave your side. I promise.' Claire grabs her hand and gives it a little squeeze. Alison squeezes back, a grateful smile on her face.

The five of them walk onto the gantry. Nisha, Ben and Debbie – with little Violet strapped to her chest – are on the other side of the barrier and spot them. They let out a whoop and all wave like mad.

'Let's do this then,' Alan says, taking a deep breath. A loud hooter sounds and hundreds of swimmers lurch forward as one. Lagging behind the eager rush, the friends hold hands and enter the water as one group.

True to her word, Claire sticks by Alison's side for the entirety of the swim. Try as they might, Oliver and Sophie are just too fast to do the same, but they are still within sighting distance. Alan is managing to stay behind them all by alternating between freestyle and breaststroke. An initial panic had grabbed at her chest, but Alison is able to relax into her stroke. Every so often she glimpses Claire as she turns to breathe, and it reassures her. She feels safe, and starts to enjoy herself. The training they have both put in before the swim pays off and it is not a struggle for them to do the five kilometres in a good time. They reach the finish and get out of the water together.

'What are Oliver and Sophie waiting for?' Alison asks. 'Don't they know that their time isn't logged until they walk over the timing mat?'

'They know,' Claire says. 'They're waiting for you. We went in together, we leave together. We decided that's what we were going to do. We're here for you, not for our timings.'

They reach the pair, and just as before, they all hold hands and walk out together.

'Now we'll all have the same time,' Oliver says. 'Go Team Alison!' and they all high-five.

The sun warms them as they have lunch at one of the picnic tables dotted about, and they are grateful for it. For the swimmers, the time in the water has chilled them. Those who had taken part in the swim are all wearing the Great Swim T-shirts they were given in their finishing packs, although Oliver's is a little small and is stretched across his broad shoulders, much to the amusement of the others. Claire looks down at the medal she is wearing, also included in the pack. 'You know, it's not like it's an Olympic medal, but I feel very proud of this,' she says to Mark.

'Well, you should. I couldn't swim five kilometres to save my life.'

'Yes, we're going to have to do something about your swimming abilities.' Claire giggles. It's been a long-standing joke between them about Mark's unique style of stroke, which he is quite happy to display but just makes Claire want to fall about laughing.

Nisha says, 'Come on, you lot, I need a photo of the swimmers, all wearing your medals.' She chivvies them out of their seats and spends a minute or two adjusting their poses. 'I want to get this framed for Alison, so let's make this look good.' Finally, she is satisfied. The big smiles of the group are captured for posterity.

Alison steps away from Claire and faces them. 'I want to say something to Claire, well, to you all. Today has meant so much to me. If you had told me last year that I'd be able to do this, I would never have believed you. And I wouldn't have been able to if it weren't for one person, my best friend. For staying with me in Spain after the accident, taking me to my counselling sessions, getting me out of bed on the days I didn't think I could face the world. Being there for me, and doing it while she was coping with her own demons. I'm so proud of how she has turned her life around, and I'm proud to have her as a friend.' She lifts her medal from her neck and places it around Claire's. 'You are my hero.'

Claire lets out a gasp and hugs Alison.

'I'd like to say something too,' Oliver says. 'We came here for Alison, to celebrate what she's achieved. It's amazing. What Alison has said about Claire is true. I saw first-hand what a good friend she is, what guts she's got.' He takes off his medal.

'No, you can't,' Claire says as she sees what he is about to do.

'Yes, I can.' He places his medal around her neck. 'You're my hero,' he says, kissing her on the cheek.

Her heart beats rapidly as she tries to take in what is happening. She can't believe that Oliver has given her his medal. She looks down and tears splash onto it. Someone else is in front of her. It is Sophie. 'You deserve this.' She places her medal around Claire's neck.

Alan is next. He is holding his medal and goes up to Claire. 'The best godmother for our daughter. A true role model.' He hugs her and over his shoulder she can see Debbie, tears streaming down her face, giving her a thumbs up.

She looks down at her chest, now laden with medals. 'I'm overwhelmed. Thank you so much.' She smiles at Mark, who is beaming.

Lost for words, she punches the air. Triumphant.

Acknowledgements

Since my teens I had a vague idea that I would write a novel one day. That process was kick-started by daily writing tasks and weekly tutorials given by Marian Keyes on Instagram. I would like to thank this lovely woman for being so kind and generous with her time and for the encouragement she offered all of us writers.

I had wonderful beta-readers: Leah Hocking, Anu and Barbara Pollock, whom I got to know through an online Curtis Brown course. They all gave me valuable feedback and steered me onto the right course more than once!

To my dear friends, Catalina Cox and Kathryn Walsh, whose enthusiasm and zeal spurred me to continue with this project from the outset. My fantastic mother-in-law, Dixie, whose particular help has allowed me to see this through to the end. Also, to Elena Kennedy, who foretold that writing was in my stars, I am grateful for the celestial approval!

My editor Nicky Taylor has been a true mentor and my novel would not be what it is without her. I loved working with her and look forward to us collaborating together for many, many books to come.

To my proof reader, Lin White, who spotted things that no one else did, I very much appreciate your efficiency and professionalism.

Last, and by no means least, my husband and champion, Dirk. I could not have done this without his guidance, support and love. He has been with me all the way. He has my everlasting gratitude for his devotion to me and my writing.

About the Author

Susan is a former English language teacher, teacher trainer and English language examiner. She lives in the southern coast of Spain with her husband, Dirk, and their dog, Ruby.

Take the Plunge is her first novel. It will be part of a trilogy.

Keep up to date with what's she doing:
www.susancarew.com or
Instagram account: **susan_carew_author**

Milton Keynes UK
Ingram Content Group UK Ltd.
UKHW040112120224
437650UK00002B/17

9 788412 664317